*dis*UNITY

Selected novels
by Anatoly Kudryavitsky

Glagoslav Publications

*dis*UNITY
Selected novels by Anatoly Kudryavitsky

Glagoslav Publications Ltd
88-90 Hatton Garden
EC1N 8PN London
United Kingdom

www.glagoslav.com

ISBN: 978-1-78267-106-0

CONTENTS

SHADOWPLAY ON A SUNLESS DAY

Translated from the Russian by Carol Ermakova

Caelum, non animum mutant, qui trans mare currunt.
They change their skies but not their souls,
those who soar across the sea.

Horace, Epistles, Book I, epistle XI

PART ONE

I.

Anything written is obvious.
First to the writer, and then to the readers.

What is obvious now is the transparent birch trees and the fresh green gold of the foliage melting in the warm May wind. This process gives rise to a philosopher's stone: the Sun, that fiery mass, or rather, that amalgamation of gases which punctually and even persistently illuminates our many and varied paths.

The morning path leads to milk and bread. Ah, those wonderful non-French French baguettes! And the grocery van, cutely parked there, with its piggy snout and its despondent elephant's trunk of doleful little steps trailing down to the ground. This is the gathering point for all the paths which run between Projected Prospect and the newly-felled forest cutting. Incidentally, the cutting has had its own name for more than a week now: Academician Afonsky Street. But there is no street as such yet, only three clearings in the middle of the forest which encircles Moscow. Did this acclaimed academician once live somewhere in these woods? He had a cottage here, at least, for it was on the veranda of that cottage that the prominent artist Nesterov sketched his satire of the academician dancing naked around a table littered with manuscript pages scattering down like autumn leaves. That portrait caused such a furore... It depicts the academician sticking his tongue out and pressing his palms to his ears, which are drawn in the form of huge elephant ears.

The picture is known as Eureka (oil on canvas, 180×120cm, private collection in Baltimore, USA).

How good it is to walk unburdened! It's good to walk burdened with bread and milk, too, though not quite so good. But at least breakfast is underway now, with lilac in bud just under the wide open windows, and the roar of a waterfall as the rubbish cascades down the chute. How do they collect the rubbish from here? How can any vehicle drive up to this clearing? After all, there's no tarmac… Well, they get here somehow.

But for now there are only the stray passersby, sleepy morning bushes and chirpy morning birds. Morning — morning in the forest! Clad in two little yellow bonnets, coltsfoot smiles out from behind a mouldy stump. Someone's shadow is glimpsed behind the y-shaped aspen. A dog's? Well, certainly not a wolf's!

No, not a wolf's. But it wasn't human, either, though it rustled and slunk away like a human. Grey fur, moulting, with pricked ears flattened slightly as it ran. It was probably just some animal or other; maybe it lives here. The only memory it left was the swaying branches and a chill in the spine, as if a gust of wind had whistled by. Or maybe it was nothing more than an apparition. Only its transparency is remembered, and a few opaque details — horn-rimmed glasses and a tie against a background of grey wool. It was a red tie, with little black squares.

2.

"The things you run into in a former soviet forest!" Arefiev was saying to the accompaniment of milk flowing into his stomach and an avalanche of bread.

A shrivelled, silver-haired old lady with marble grey eyes was nodding her head as she meticulously chewed her mortadella. She had just dug all the eyes of fat out of it with a long knife and her nods were for the mortadella, too; every morsel of food — or chymus, to give this substance its proper name — which landed in her stomach provoked a rumbling "y-yes!" as her body approved the arrival of nutrition. The fat eyes were saved for dessert.

"Maybe it was a monkey?" Arefiev suggested.

The old woman was nodding. She had just consumed a fatty sponge cake and was pondering whether she should complete the repast with some smoked fish. After all, sweet and savoury go so well together!

The repast over, it is time for him to go. He leaves, and the house is now hers. She walks through to the other room, the room with the curtained windows where her eyes rest in the darkness, her ears in the silence and her lungs in the dust. She quietly settles herself in the corner, occupying the junction of three planes, and then sets to work. It is as though a transparent thread, fine and youthful, comes spinning out from the very centre of her small, convex, saffron tummy, right from her belly button, recently relieved. How it would gleam in the sunshine, how it would waft in the wind! But here it is motionless. A spider's web?

3.

> *Reality augments itself with us and becomes "surreality",*
> *for we humans are surreal beings.*

People are taught to supplement themselves to reality in school, during grammar classes. This exercise can go by many names, such as "complete the gaps":

"We read about the persecution of scholars in the Middle Ages but then opened the biography of academician Lysenko and…"*

"This stream is narrow but deep and although there are no fish in it, there is something of scientific value and so we carefully…"

---

* T. D. Lysenko, Soviet pseudo-scientist favoured by Stalin, and blamed for the deaths of many Soviet geneticists.

"Without losing his head, the hunter fired a shot at the bear and … but then, unaware of the danger, he walked calmly along the edge of the forest."

"Masha went into the manufactured goods shop where … but at home she gazed for a long time at the cover of "Burda World of Fashion" magazine."

"This year at school we memorised 120 poems by Pushkin, Lermontov and Nekrasov and we found them all really…"

"Larissa went up to the map of the Soviet Union and … but then remembered something funny and laughed."

"Ilyusha took a folio of Pushkin's poems from the shelf and … but then, with his seat raised, he began watching cartoons."

"Soviet writers portray typical scenes of nature and everyday life thereby invoking in us…"

In the latter case the children take their pencils and scrawl: "a sense of deep aversion". They show this to each other, giggle, then rub it out, but they are wrong. In fact they should have written "familiarity with the grotesque" or better still "a sense of the surreal nature of existence".

4.

He walked more slowly on his way home from work. The Sun marked the entrance to the forest with squares and triangles for him. But the forest was melting into the blurred moist haze and slipping away. With each step he took, the forest retreated a step. This went on for some time. Then the forest took a deep breath with its bird-filled canopy and let him in. He followed the fine thread of the path, but then suddenly became aware of someone else walking next to him, following the same fine thread. He shuddered and stopped. The stranger raised his straw hat.

"Excuse me, are you looking for the entrance?" he asked, and his pronunciation seemed somehow overly correct. Curious, foreign, yet oddly correct.

"The entrance?" Arefiev queried, and raised his hand to his mouth in an involuntary, inexplicable gesture.

"*Entrée. Eingang.*" The stranger's reply was utterly incomprehensible.

A butterfly carried the sun's light to the stranger's face. Arefiev shuddered: his face was covered with grey fur, right up to the eyes.

With a deft flick of his wrist the stranger caught the butterfly and it froze on his wrinkled brown palm as though paralysed.

"I didn't even knock her powder off," the stranger congratulated himself. "I'm agile, aren't I? Really agile, wouldn't you say?"

"Yes, you are," Arefiev admitted. "Can I look at the butterfly?"

"How do you like the pattern?" the stranger asked, pointing at the butterfly with his claw-like nail.

Arefiev took a look. The design on the little cherry-coloured wings was unusual: the eyes were not along the edge of the wing but in the middle, forming a spiral.

"The pattern's not right," Arefiev remarked.

The stranger looked at him curiously:

"Doesn't it remind you of anything?"

"It's like a snail," Arefiev shrugged.

"Exactly. A snail," the stranger said sternly. "The acceleration of gravity at the exit is 10G."

"That has something to do with physics, hasn't it?" Arefiev put in uncertainly. He worked in a research institute, and, as everyone knows, a scientist's knowledge only covers one branch of science – the one he is paid for.

The Sun measured out mellow sunset honeycombs on the branches. The gusty wind was strangely cold.

"From applied astronomy, actually," the stranger said. "So you don't know anything about the entrance or the exit, right?"

"It depends what we're talking about."

"About the abstract, my dear, about the downright abstract. As for concrete reality, you will see it on the television this evening. By the way, a question for you: can there be such a thing as an entrance into nowhere and an exit from there?"

Smacking sounds came from somewhere in the distance, as though the bog were readying itself to swallow the Sun. Arefiev remembered he was hungry.

"Well, I'll be on my way then, I think," he said, and without saying goodbye, he wandered off along one branch of the forked path.

"Hey! You aren't allowed down there!" the stranger cried out, and dashed after him.

Arefiev ran, too. For a moment they ran neck and neck, but Arefiev couldn't keep it up. By the time he ran out into the glade, the stranger had already reached the little hill on the far side of the forest.

"The hole is closed," Arefiev heard a mechanical, sexless voice say, and the figure on the hillock vanished. All that remained was a mass of crimson sun, shrivelled spring grass and a heathery wind. Arefiev couldn't spot anyone in the glade, nor anywhere in the vicinity; it was as if the earth had swallowed the stranger. The serene sky shone blue as though it hadn't seen anything.

5.

The blue sky received its blueness as a gift, primordially, and never asked itself why it is blue.

But the blue water collects its blueness gradually, stocking it up from the transparent air, the dark fish and the golden sunshine.

The blue of the sky and the blue of the water are both convincing, just as any success is convincing; but as for dirty puddles, life has more than enough of those so there is no need to splash them over the pages.

Blue sky and blue water — these form an inter-mirror dimension where time sometimes runs forward, sometimes backward, although actually time never runs anywhere; it simply abides freely in weightlessness. Humankind cannot stay between two looking glasses; from time to time we are overwhelmed by cheerless thoughts which chase wrinkles over our countenance and clouds over the forgetful sky. A human is a swimmer under the icy, cloudy skies. That is his element and he is able to screw his eyes up and blot out any light, even the Sun's regal shine. After all, it is more relaxing to swim with your eyes wide shut, especially if you are swimming towards the halls of eternal rest.

"What did he look like?" Arefiev asked himself when he was almost home. "Like anyone else. A Turkish leather jacket, a white shirt, a tie. No, not a red tie, that was the first one. That was a different person. But was this one a person at all? Was it human? And what about the first one? It didn't look like a human, not a bit… But then, who does?"

The block of flats opened up like a book and let him in. A silvery mesh of threads shone through the wall's smooth page. The little old woman was sitting in the bull's eye, gnawing something with her apparently toothless mouth.

"Let there be light!" said Arefiev, and switched on the television.

The mesh of threads turned blue. The old woman purred contentedly.

"Honecker was no longer…" The television was showing the chronicles of the early nineties. "The citizens of the GDR were able to travel to…"

Out poked the predatory grin of a German diesel locomotive.

"That's who's got a really beastly muzzle," Arefiev thought: "Things". He shook some tea leaves into a cup and was about to slosh some boiling water over them when the picture suddenly flickered and something utterly and even improbably familiar appeared on the screen.

Hey, that's our institute! He put the kettle down. What are they showing that for?

When he found out why, the cup fell from his hands and a dry brown tea stain appeared on the carpet. The same stains and puddles were spread over the floor of the institute, except that those were dark red, not brown. The institute had been stormed by armed men who had shot dead two guards and the director, wounded his secretary and then mercilessly clubbed nearly a dozen others who got in their way. On the television the wounded were being led out of the building, then the bodies were carried out, covered in sheets, some white, some blood-spattered.

White as snow, Arefiev sat in his armchair glued to the screen. The old woman worked her jaws, unruffled.

"At three o'clock today, in the institute…" the television was saying.

Arefiev remembered that he had left early that day, at a quarter to three. Fifteen minutes had separated him from…

6.

Bullets were singing in thin air… People were only just starting to get used to contract killings in Russia. It was later that bankers, bandits, politicians and passerby, the ones who had seen something and the ones who hadn't, were culled on a daily basis, and it is still going on; there's no end to it. And there's no point in asking why, because there's always a weapon and a target; as many targets as you can think of. Not to mention that it's a well-paid job, and one doesn't even have to perfect his shooting skills, as he can always take a few pot-shots — just to be sure.

Those killed were buried with much weeping and wailing. And the weeping and wailing rose up under the clouds and then throughout all the years to come it would swoop down onto our good old Earth more often than you could imagine. Listen — it is still there, biding its time!

Then it occurred to him: the man from the forest knew! "As for concrete reality, you will see it on the television this evening…" When was that said? At three o'clock? Slightly later? Yes, that's right. How could he have known? Or had he played an active part in those events? Arefiev felt uneasy. He realised that something hidden, something terrible was going on, and that some unknown entity had given him a particular role in it all.

As always, he soothed himself with music. The cherished chest with its gleaming golden ribs opened up and produced Schubert's quartets. Arefiev donned gigantic headphones, which were more akin to some antiquated apparatus for deadening noise than to headphones, and immersed himself in "Death and the Maiden." An odd name, he pondered, thinking about his own life. He'd had enough death in his life, but as for maidens… And he began to remember all the girls for whom he'd felt anything, even a little, starting from when he was sixteen. He didn't have a good word for any of them now. Not one of them had appreciated him. They had all been so self-absorbed. And apart from certain fluctuating emotions, he was mainly self-absorbed, too. Life is a feast of egoism, he thought. The chest with its LPs exuded unsung peace, and Schubert was intimating some other life which flowed with beauty and harmony.

7.

*Sounds are formed by colours. This secret is known only
to the most skilful sound painters. Black is stillness,
and white is the whole orchestra. A day sometimes reveals
itself as a green andante played by a violin,
and sometimes as a brown solo of a flute.*

That harmony was infiltrated by something persistent and not entirely harmonious; Schubert had clearly written nothing of the kind.

Arefiev half raised his headphones. The telephone's raucous ring came pouring in. He grabbed the receiver.

The hush of offices seeped into the room, offices with unpleasant portraits and clocks with golden pendulums, and with never-ending cellars burrowing into the innards of the earth.

Can we keep someone out of our lives if he, or they, really
want to burrow into them? Alas, we cannot.

"You don't like the portraits on our walls, do you?" enquired a pleasant, gravelly, inanimate voice. "Let's say the choice were yours. Who would you suggest?"

"Malyuta Skuratov,"* Arefiev blurted out with not a moment's hesitation.

"I suppose you think that's awfully ironic, but in fact he could easily hang here. Well, who would you put forward as a positive role model? In your opinion, whose portraits should hang in government offices?"

Whose indeed? Arefiev pondered. Peter the Great? Suvorov and Kutuzov**? You couldn't put writers here — imagine for a moment that Solzhenitsyn were watching from the walls and you could read in his stern eyes exactly what he thought about this establishment...

"Aha, keeping quiet, are we?" the voice laughed gloatingly. "Well then, come on over and we can discuss it."

"Is it compulsory?" Arefiev said after a pause.

"No, quite voluntary," said the receiver soothingly. "We are part of history after all, and as Lincoln said: "we cannot escape history"."

"You are quoting Lincoln?" Arefiev was taken aback.

"We like to study our enemies," said the voice. "And our

---

* Ivan the Terrible's henchman.

** Two great Russian generals of the Napoleon era.

friends, too. Believe me, we know a lot about you. So come on over — let's say, tomorrow, at around ten-ish. No-one's working in your institute now anyhow. They are all listening to music. This kind of music…"

And music came down the telephone. It was the Allegretto from Beethoven's seventh symphony, which some think of as funeral music. There are some who think any music except the hit parade is funeral music, thought Arefiev as he listened to the music over the phone and wondered whether it was Toscanini conducting or Furtwängler. At around bar sixty-four a click was heard and the line went dead.

8.

The following morning Arefiev walked straight out of his house and into the sunshine. Screwing up his eyes against the dazzle, he headed into the forest and opened his eyes, only to discover that he wasn't in the forest at all. In fact, he had no idea where he was. He found himself in the midst of a painted landscape: the grass was coloured in with felt-tip pen, the crooked apple trees were festooned with unrealistically bright fruit, and a painted green sun hung in the sky. Arefiev could have sworn he had not gone more than 50 paces from his house.

A little white track stood out in the middle of the drawing and Arefiev set out along it. It led to a white cottage with a thatched roof. The roof was coloured in orange for some reason. Arefiev had just begun to wonder whether there was a door when one materialised, complete with a doorknocker in the form of a lion's face. Arefiev grasped the knocker. The bronze lion yawned and said: "Aha, so an entrance has come to light."

Arefiev froze on the spot and stood there for a long time because the picture, too, froze on the paper — Someone-Who-Wanted-To-Look was approaching. But Arefiev didn't see who it was as he suddenly felt very weak and sat down, right in front of the door. He put his head on his knees and fell asleep. The last thing he saw was a real dog chasing a rabbit as it scurried across the picture-perfect lawn. The dog apprehended the rabbit and was frog-marching it into the kennel.

"Well?"

"He's asleep, Comrade Captain."

"Where?"

"In the cell. He's leaning against the wall, asleep. Maybe he's dreaming."

"Maybe he is, but he's not telling us."

"We didn't ask."

"We asked all right. With instruments."

"Of course, it is possible he doesn't know anything."

"Anything's possible, but it's not clear how he could be in the thick of it all and not notice anything."

"He probably doesn't want to notice."

"Mmm…"

It was not, as you might expect, people who were talking, but uniforms.

What was inside those uniforms is quite another matter. But it doesn't matter anyway, of course, since whoever was idling in those uniforms was nothing more than a uniform-filler.

9.

Arefiev dreamt that he got married and that his wife was a corpulent, inwardly noisy woman in a gaudy, variegated dress who wanted to make a famous professor out of him and who forced him to meet various evergreen people which meant he had no time for himself when he could listen to his records. To cap it all, when they argued, she made her point by producing a little red pass with a golden coat of arms from some secret place and showing it to him. Of course, everyone knows that a pass like that from the police or the secret service is the pride and joy of every Russian soul, Arefiev thought. Actually, it would be nice to wake up, even in the cellars of the Lubyanka.[*] And with that second thought he did indeed wake up. But not where he had feared, nor in the picture garden; he woke up in his own bachelor's bed at home. For some reason the clock said it was already evening.

He should at least have lunch. He had bought in some sausages, but there was nothing to go with them. He liked to eat off multicoloured plates since his food looked really rather wretched on a white plate. Scientific researchers aren't well paid, he thought as he gnawed a tomato, especially since the inflation of the early nineties when they'd added so many zeroes to each note and money just slipped through your fingers. He wondered what the figure on his next wage packet would be and whether it wouldn't just remain exactly that — a figure on paper. And I have Mother to feed, too. Just as well she doesn't need much.

Just then a suspicious sound came from the corner, followed by a wild squeal. A mouse had got caught in the spider's web and Arefiev would not have liked to be in its place.

He had supper before going to bed. He served up silence. Under his knife the silence fell away into pieces of china sound, sliced air, and a rustle beyond the window. The leaves were evidently begging to be included in the salad, but the window pane kept them out. Offended, they formed a green conspiracy and spread themselves out as a mosaic on the glass to prevent Day from getting in the next morning. Their fingers were slipping over the cold, greenish surface, their flat bodies bristled with cold, but they didn't just curl up and give in. What was it they had drawn on the glass? That life is a punishment, and we don't even know for what?

---

[*] The KGB headquarters and affiliated secret prison on Lubyanka Square in Moscow.

10.

The Institute of Useful Mutations where Arefiev worked was established in the mid seventies. This is how it came about: Early one morning, the phone rang in the apartment of academician Churbasov, who had the pleasure of being personal physician to Leonid Illyich Brezhnev. It was so early that the academician was still somewhere in the cherished depths of sleep. But the telephone didn't let up.

"Yeah…" The enormous academician, waking in a cold sweat, finally raised the receiver to his small, myopic little head: he was vaguely reminiscent of a diplodocus which had somehow acquired glasses.

"We have to create him, my dear fellow," came the obscure rumble.

"Create who, Leonid Illyich?"

"You know, the young builder of Communism."

Having over-eaten the night before, Brezhnev had woken up at five in the morning and couldn't get off to sleep again. Vexed, he fumbled through some papers on his bedside table and picked up the first one which came to hand. By sheer chance it turned out to be the

"Code of the Young Builder of Communism."

Brezhnev yanked the light switch and a lamp in the shape of a five-pointed star came on. It was pink, oddly enough. At first he read half-heartedly, but soon became absorbed.

"But how can we create him, Leonid Illyich?" said the academician, somewhat at a loss.

"Well, Michurin created a new kind of apple, didn't he? So we'll hatch a new kind of person."

"But it's not that simple, Leonid Illyich. A person isn't an apple or a pear. We'll need genetics."

"Well then, gather some geneticists. Genetics isn't banned here now."

"Ah, but where are our geneticists…" sighed Churbasov. "We can't bring them back."

"Then collect some new ones," his conversant breezed cheerily. "Make use of foreign experience."

The academician heaved another sigh.

"Oh and by the way," Brezhnev went on, "Keep all of this… well, you know… under wraps. Otherwise the West will try, too…"

"Understood, Leonid Illyich," replied the academician, trying to imagine how the West, in a mad dash to compete with Moscow, would create an exemplary builder of Communism.

That same day Churbasov summoned two people. The first was an old survivor, the geneticist Wolfson. He was head scientist at the dilapidated and utterly unimportant zootechnical laboratory.

When the academician brought him up to date, wiry little Wolfson gave a sly snigger and the orioles of wrinkles which hid his deep-set green eyes began sparkling like miniature tanned suns.

"That's what's known as eugenics, my dear fellow, the betterment of human nature. There's a whiff of Hitler there — he was interested in it, too, you know."

Churbasov was as big as a mountain. He drew himself up slightly and threw the old man one of his displeased looks, the kind that the members of the nation's medical establishment were so afraid of. But he realised at once that he wouldn't get through to this old devil that way. Nothing would make him crack — you wouldn't be scared of anything after what he'd been through. But just as he was thinking this, Churbasov had a bright idea:

"My dear Lupus Wolfovich, you are a man of science," he said, bowing his diplodocusian neck and looking into those stubborn, owlish eye sockets. "I have explained the task. How you complete it is entirely up to you. You will be granted total freedom of research. Oh and by the way, you will merely be head of science. We'll appoint someone else as director."

This had occurred to Churbasov just a moment ago and he immediately congratulated himself on his wise decision.

"Aha, I see, a young party member with more suitable national identity," grinned Wolfson. "By the way, I am not Lupus Wolfovich but Menahem Yegudovich… OK, let's say we've agreed about the director. Just as long as he doesn't get his hands on the fundamental research — people like that would put everything on sale."

"I'll sort that out with him," the academician agreed, thinking to himself that some people have the bad habit of dotting every letter just to make sure they dot their i's.

II.

Our homeland is eternal sleep, and we expect it to bestow attention and even consolation upon us. But no matter whether we are awake or asleep, all we see around us are icy rocks. Multitudes of icy rocks.

Arefiev was celebrating his trousers' birthday. He deliberately kept forgetting his own birthday so as not to count his each passing year. He didn't really have any friends, and the cobwebby old lady was not up for celebrations; she counted any catch as a cause for celebration. Arefiev had only one pair of trousers and he had bought them exactly one year ago, by chance, cheaply and brand new. A brand new pair of grey Italian cords was definitely worth celebrating!

His trousers were proudly hanging on the corner of the wardrobe door, with the legs bent at the knee giving the impression they had struck up some casual pose. Arefiev was sitting in nothing but his undies drinking cherry liqueur and, like all good folk who can control themselves and train their brains, he was not getting in the least tipsy. Such an unscientific term, "brains", Arefiev thought remembering his university studies. The memory of bygone days prompted him to take a look at himself in the mirror hanging on the inside of the wardrobe door. The door creaked huffily and showed him a pale, flabby old youth of around forty. Nothing had changed yet his age was somehow reflected. He gave a sour grimace and his reflection grimaced, too, as it floated away into the wardrobe, for the door was closing, quietly but firmly. Well, at least I still look human, thought Arefiev. Rattled, he didn't notice that the Sun had covered itself with a cloud for a moment, stuck out its tongue and pulled a monkey face at him. His trousers slipped quietly to the floor and lay in a little heap like a high-spirited school leaver deflated once the steam had gone out of him. Hurrying to the WC, looking somewhere inside himself instead of where he was going, the proud owner of the Italian cords stepped right on the birthday trousers' crotch.

12.

It was the former chief secretary of the municipal Komsomol, Sikofantov, who became director of the Institute of Useful Mutations, with the personal, slobbery-kissed blessing of Leonid Illyich himself. Sikofantov had the lowest forehead in the history of humankind as a biological species. His hair grew in thickets just above his eyebrows and it was hard to guess where he kept his brains. He had a large, protruding goitre and evil tongues wagged: maybe that's where…? The secretary-cum-director was prone to sweating, so before greeting anyone he would give his large Komsomol hand a pre-emptive wipe. The poor man had bulging eyes and bulged with gas, too.

He immediately set aside part of the building and rented it out to a jewellers shop, and a bureau de change was quartered in the far corner.

"I'll pay your wages with the money from their rent," Sikofantov informed his employees when he got back from holidaying in the Canary Islands. "The Director of the Institute of Microbiology doesn't pay any wages because he doesn't let out the property, you see. Although he did buy himself an Alpha-Romeo in Milan, at the same place where I got mine at the beginning of the year..."

At this point a certain hushed silence fell over his employees, for no-one had encouraged him to blab yet he had spilled the beans. But there was this bottle of mineral water standing on the table in front of him, and the label said "Vera". At last a knowledgeable person had shown up: "vera" is the Italian for "true". But it is not the same as the true faith which makes the Russian nation so strong.

Two employees reacted to this revelation with more outrage than was appropriate, and it was explained to them, very quickly and in no uncertain terms, that they could not do anything to the director but that the director could in fact do quite a lot to them. After fuming for a while, they quietly got their own back by inventing a fond nickname for Sikofantov: his full name was German Romanovich Sikofantov, so they called him Romeovich.

13.

Later it became apparent why the late Sikofantov had feared nothing when he disclosed his Alpha-Romeo in front of everyone. When he had left his employment as the Komsomol Chief, Romeovich began working very closely, but very secretly, with a certain organisation, which in fact was more of a society than an organisation. It was called "Central," not in the sense of basketball, but because it had a hand in the division of any spoils. Someone even dubbed this group "kremlinski" on the basis that nothing is more central than the Kremlin. The Kremlin itself took offence at such impudent claims: the journalist who used this epithet in his criminal report was even arrested, albeit not for long, just long enough for him to get his kidneys pulverised by the police. Everyone joked afterwards that he was punished "for divulging state secrets."

It seems that when they confirmed Sikofantov's appointment, those up there in the highest echelons (if, of course, they are the highest, which is relative) didn't know what kind of person they were putting at the helm. It only came to light later when there was no longer any director and a great deal fewer employees.

"Who will be the next director?" the survivors were discussing the matter in muted tones when Arefiev finally showed up at work. He went into his small lab almost at once and, closing the door which gleamed with medically white paint, he shut himself off from everyone. A plaque hung on his door: "Severe Research Scientist Arefiev". Actually, he was the senior scientist but when one of the lab assistants had jokingly changed the name plate, he had decided to leave it as it was. Arefiev was first and foremost a fatalist who didn't like to change anything. And anyhow, "severity", well, it rather impressed him. Before that he had been housed in the former X-ray office where there was a glowing crimson warning: "Don't go in — mortal danger."

As for the door of the director's office, a burnished brass plaque soon appeared on it. It proclaimed the office was occupied by a certain

"A.F. Kannabich".

14.

However there was no Kannabich. In fact, nobody ever set eyes on such a person. The director's office was not locked. Anyone could go in, but an emptiness dwelt in its polished opulence, an emptiness which seemed to breathe and tremble like a frightened bird, blinking its eyelids. Nobody hung around in there for long because you soon had an uneasy feeling of being watched. The staff left memos and reports on the desk and left promptly, aware of someone's eyes following them. The next day they would come back to collect their papers and find them duly authorised, or at least checked through, as was evident from notes in the margins. Notes which were not even in Russian but in some bizarre cuneiform.

One young lab assistant decided to spend a night in the office. He was due to be called up for the army in the autumn so he didn't give a damn about anything anyway. But he wasn't there in the morning. In fact, he wasn't anywhere in the whole institute, though the night watchmen swore no-one had got past them. He couldn't have gone anywhere else, either, as the institute was surrounded by a three metre high concrete wall topped with barbed wire. The only trace of him left in the office was a square-toed black boot made by the Moscow factory "Quickmarch"; the cuneiform in the margins of the documents on the desk looked particularly ominous that morning.

An emptiness settled over the whole country, too.
It had big names, won elections and was discussed
in the papers, but it was still emptiness.

It broadened its reach, took over the courts and hospitals, inadvertently stole into the Kremlin, and danced a victory dance on all TV channels. And the people were sighing: What has become of our glorious hockey players? There are no decent teachers or doctors any more, nothing to read, nothing to watch, nothing to listen to… Ah, but IN THE GOOD OLD DAYS…

And so things got just as bad as they had been in the good old days, only in a different way; everything was tarnished by the white stains of emptiness and the red stains of blood spilt in vain. Why in vain? Because no matter where or when blood is spilt, it is always in vain, in vain and once more in vain. And there is no historical precedence, and no-one ever learns anything from it. For Earth's population is growing and the number of people who are always and in all ways right grows with it. Three, four, ten billion people who are always right… Funny? Frightening, but funny, too, of course.

15.

Some search for themselves within themselves;
some search there for somebody else…

Happiness is never far away, it's always just around the corner, thought Arefiev. Take this cassette which my step-brother lent me, for instance, of the Irish crooner Kieran Goss. One of the songs is called: "Love is waiting just around the corner". But that happiness, that love, is called Death. Brahms was once asked when he was finally going to get married. "I am closer to the grave than to the marriage altar," he replied, and indeed, he soon kept his promise and died. Promises, alas, have to be kept. And that's why it's best never to promise anyone anything but just to go about your business. Like living (an important business, by the way). Or working. Looking for naturally occurring mutagens, natural substances which trigger mutations in organisms. If you have a mother-mutant, why not look into the theory of mutations?

The words "gene", "genetics" and "hereditary" had once been
"firing words".

There are some words for which a person is simply suddenly shot. There are other words for which they might pin a nice little bronze medal on his chest or do some other such pleasant thing. But for these words… Everything is fine, everything is quite in order, it's just that no one should say them. After all, would any respectable soul let such words pass his lips? They shouldn't even enter anyone's head! It's only some vicious followers of Weismann or Morgan* who want to cause a little stir.

We pay a high price for youth: our childhood. But then youth is bartered cut price, exchanged for bitter experience,

---

* Two early geneticists whom the Soviet regime disapproved of. The majority of geneticists in the USSR were persecuted and many ended up in Stalin's Gulag.

disappointment, estrangement, a hopeless longing for warmth and an eternal, ineradicable dampness of the soul. And for some knowledge in the limited space of limitless existence.

It is a well-known fact that mutations appear in the offspring of people who have been irradiated with X-rays, infra-red and ultraviolet, producing so-called freaks of nature. But mutation is not so much deformity as any alteration in what is inherited. Mutations — useful and harmful — will still appear even if people are not tormented with rays, radium or chemicals. Mutation is the whip of evolution. It is always in the coachman's hand and he knows how to use it. In fact, he already has; he used it when he moulded — or rather whipped out — humankind. Mistakes were also made, when the whip struck the wrong place, and the results were disregarded. And so humankind was moulded and whipped into what we are now: homo semi-sapiens.

Then they started lending out the whip. The coachman turned out to be generous and once upon a time the whip handle was sawn up and handed round. Fairytale became reality — the turbines turned by themselves. But then the fairytale turned to dust, and has since been called the dark tale of Chernobyl. And the cry was raised: let us handle whips with care! And the whips were placed in glass cases and guards were stationed next to them. And the coachman, quietly plaiting himself a new whip, smiled a silent smile and stroked his head of cotton wool clouds.

Everyone wondered what else could serve as a whip. The aforementioned academician Afonski described the appearance of mutations in agronomist Rodin after the latter read a leader in the newspaper Pravda entitled "Back to the golden thirties". The agronomist Rodin was fully literate and politically aware, too, but upon reading the article he suddenly became dyslexic, forgot how to read, started walking to work in a budenovka Red Army cap, grew a long cavalryman's forelock in front, and behind — not on the back of his head but considerably lower — a real live tail. Not a horse's tail but a naked, pink, human one. The academician's article on this phenomenon met with a chequered fate: outliving its author, it was sent to the West in the form of a microfilm and published in the respected journal Lancet. The Boston Globe newspaper took up the subject and published a report on the baneful effects of Russian communist ideology on mankind, accompanying the article with a photograph of a microcephalic of unknown, and most likely not Russian, origin. At the same time, two Chinese scholars from Utah State University began studying how articles by Chairman Mao affected macaque rhesus monkeys. No-one knows how it all ended, though legend has it that the macaque changed from rhesus negative to rhesus positive.

16.

He was growing old, and looked upon the new century
with his centuries-old eyes. When Day's noises quietened, he
could hear the primeval creak of creation.

Old man Wolfson gave the laboratories he supervised almost unlimited freedom of research. Arefiev's hopes lay in a polysaccharide known as gamma lactose. Gamma lactose was a bitter-sweet substance noted for producing multiple nipples in the offspring of the laboratory animals, monkeys included, which ingested it. Admittedly, Arefiev was in two minds as to whether the male exemplary of the builder of Communism needed spare milk glands, but they would definitely come in handy for the exemplary builder-ess.

Wolfson chuckled for a long time once he found out what one of the institute's top laboratories was working on, but he did not put a stop to it.

"A brilliant idea," he said to Arefiev. "Doubling everything. In-built reliability. That's precisely where we're heading. Four hands doubling as legs, warm fur so as not to waste money on an overcoat… How do you fancy growing a second reproductive organ, my old fellow?"

Arefiev felt stung, but he needn't have; the institute's board meeting hailed his research as the most promising. The others were studying mutations in tiny drosophila fruit flies, and everyone was heartily sick of those flies with their famous red eyes. As Wolfson said privately, the blueprint of the exemplary builder of Communism would have red eyes from reading all that party literature!

And once again, Arefiev plunged into the emerald leafy pool of the forest after work. The sky over his head thickened with pondweed, and a greenish sun circled by white lotus clouds shone in the glade. The forest was a submarine realm and the leaves swayed unhurriedly in the wind's currents as they sank to the depths of the heat.

Arefiev came up into the glade. An underwater grasshopper struck up its song, then stopped short. A dawdling crow drifted over the branches. The glade seemed familiar. That was the little hill, over there, where the stranger had vanished… And what's that, at the foot of it?! Surely it can't be legs sticking out of the ground?! Arefiev couldn't believe his eyes. He rubbed them. But there was no denying it; a pair of legs was definitely sticking out of the slope, forming a Roman letter V or the sign for "victory".

The legs were poking up with their boots — or rather, one boot – pointing skywards, and they seemed to be living a life of their own. The single boot scratched the other leg behind the knee, then reformed the V for "victory". Arefiev thought that maybe someone had crawled into a hole up to the waist for some reason and was now trying to get out, so he hurried over to the little hill. When he had almost reached it, the legs came together and shot into the hole with unbelievable speed, as though their owner had jumped from a great height. Arefiev was already standing by the spot where the hole should be, but where was it? There was no hole to be seen, just a patch of earth which seemed to have been dug over. A ripped off heel was lying there, and a nail stuck out of it, pointing skywards.

Arefiev picked the heel up. A brand name was embossed on the tip, black on black:

"Quickmarch"

17.

It was Arefiev's lab assistant Milla who felt the disappearance of the young man in square-toed boots most. Rumour had it that her full name was Militia, and Arefiev, curious about who he was taking on in his lab, looked through her documents. This thin, fluffy-haired, coquettish creature was officially called Milena, though she called herself Ludmilla and insisted everyone else did so, too. Girls always smell of makeup but this one smelt twice as strongly and Arefiev, who suffered from incurable allergies, was wary of coming too close.

He watched from a distance. Her little fingers worked quickly and accurately, and that's what counted most for him, so he did not concern himself with what their owner got up to during her breaks when, for instance, the centrifuge was spinning or the samples were steaming in their watery bath. The lab assistant had her own corner which everyone called the Mil-corner, and the walls there were plastered with pin-ups of models. Her favourite was the thin Twiggy with her small bud breasts. Little Milla would pause for ages in front of the round mirror framed with sun-gold wire, either busying herself with her face or studying the results.

Then Arefiev discovered what he later called "the double reflection effect", thanks to which he could look in the glass door of the nearest lab cupboard and see what the Mil-reflection was up to in the far off Mil-corner. Like any self-respecting scientist, Arefiev was precise in all matters and could state that for fifty percent of the time the Mil-reflection studied her own Mil-reflection in the mirror, for another twenty percent she busied herself with a manicure, and a pedicure took up further ten percent. Another ten percent was devoted to studying her pale, boyish bust above her white coat which was lowered to half mast and under which this completely reflecto-person, like any self-respecting graduate of medical college, wore nothing whatsoever. The final ten percent of her time was devoted to some utterly extraordinary activity during which the little white coat was not lowered from above but was raised from below, and a large test tube penetrated the undercoatly innards, after which a strange shuffling got going there. At such moments Arefiev would get up from his white, glass-topped director's desk and fling open the glass door of the lab cupboard so it no longer reflected the Mil-reflection's head, thrown back in ecstasy, lips bitten, but reflected instead his own pale Arefievish physiognomy with dejectedly drooping cheeks and a grimace of disgust.

"So why don't you offer yourself to the girl?" his own undercoatly innards would say to him, and for a minute or two they convinced him, held him captive. But then a certain substance, concealed under the remains of an ashen head of hair, came up with a formula: to live a doll's life you have to be a doll yourself. And Arefiev headed off into the vivarium to watch the monkeys. They did exactly the same sorts of things, and much more besides, and none of them even bothered to cover themselves with a little white coat.

One day the glass reflected the bustle of two white coats, and square-toed black boots flashed in the mirror as they were detached from their owner. Arefiev went out of the lab and a few hours later, when the Mil-reflection floated off somewhere in the direction of the public convenience, he placed a book by a Polish author on the table in the Mil-corner. This book caught his eye as he was looking at his book-shelves. The title read: The Time and Place for Harmony.

The hint, evidently, was taken because now the two reflections no longer stayed in the Mil-corner but would float off into the institute's store room to which the reflection in the square-toed boots had a reflecto-key. The book on harmony came back to Arefiev with a bookmark and an underlined phrase: "harmony is common in art but rare in life, though even in life harmony finds a time and a place for itself."

Ah, the son of a bitch, laughed Arefiev and put the book back in its place. The thought that little Milla could have underlined that phrase herself never so much as entered his head.

18.

"Hmm. Girls," pondered Arefiev in a pause between two experiments. "Feminine principles have the upper hand now. Not to mention the fact that there are male countries, like England and Germany, and female countries like Russia, France and Italy. And they live completely independently. Even the androgynous America is starting to take a look at itself in Venus's mirror."

"But countries are countries, and I'm talking about something else, about femininity," said his inner physical self, licking its lips tonguelessly and liplessly. "Not to mention the fact that there are girls, too, as well as women."

"So I would gladly praise girls as the embodiment of *ewig weibliche!*" soared Arefiev in the ethereal realms of fancy. "Hearken to my hymn:"

Girls are, essentially, super-beings. As if reading minds were not enough, they can see straight through you, too, and can tell at a glance how old you are, whether you are married or not, and how successful you are. Only a letter can confound a girl, provided you don't include a photograph.

Girls know who they want to have children with, and precisely which kind of children they want to have. There are a lot of girls who haven't reached girlhood yet but are striving towards it, and that leads to a great deal of confusion, words, and dreams.

Girls are sublime creatures and they perish when they come into contact with solid matter: their wet hair gets stuck in the hairdryer, or the cassette player tumbles into the bath. Girls live in hope of mastering the material world with its hammers, screws and electric drills, but that world belongs to men. Unwilling to accept this state of affairs, girls arrange things so that the men, with their cars, aeroplanes and bank accounts, belong to them alone. And indeed, for a time, men are theirs.

Women cannot forgive girls, for a girl's dream has not yet come true, whereas a woman's already has.

People don't know what to do with a dream which has come true.

19.

Arefiev was haunted by legs, legs in the shape of a roman letter V. They fascinated him. What had that person been doing there and where had he disappeared to? Maybe he's still sitting in the hole, too weak to climb out? Maybe he, Arefiev, should excavate the hole?

As always, Arefiev was lost in thought as he walked over to the shop in the next street where he went every day during the lunch break. But his musings were flicked aside like a cobweb by none other than a pair of legs poking out of a manhole in the middle of the pavement. It was a deserted alleyway with no-one in sight, yet there was a pair of legs poking out.

Now I'll catch him, thought Arefiev with anticipated glee, and he rushed forward and grabbed a leg by its trousers. Someone underground gave a hollow cough, the legs removed themselves and in their place appeared a red-faced head topped with shaggy straw hair.

"Eh, mucker futher!" The head uttered something quite incomprehensible and Arefiev began apologising profusely.

Another head popped out of the hole. It was younger but just as florid.

"What the hell…?" growled the red chief, then both heads vanished into the manhole.

The manhole wasn't even fenced. Just as well I didn't fall down it, thought Arefiev, distraught; he knew himself only too well. And he delicately placed some dry branches from the neighbouring rubbish heap on either side of the manhole.

The institute's board meetings were chaired by Wolfson, who supported the purely theoretical research of some, the practical tests of others, especially Arefiev's laboratory, and himself experimented with thousands of reagents, trying out highly diverse substances on rabbits and guinea pigs, looking for mutagens. Wolfson almost never reported results of his own, but occasionally left miscellaneous papers on the director's desk.

Not having a director for months at a time suited him well. To his surprise, the ministry which had oversight of the institute knew all about the director. They met with him, talked to him, and expressed surprise that he rarely had contact with his staff. "To put it mildly," Wolfson reflected. On one occasion someone told him, "He's just this moment left".

Wolfson rushed from the office in time to see a figure disappearing at the end of the corridor. It reminded him of someone, Wolfson thought, but then realised it was just that he had a very light step, like an athlete, or an actor.

As he passed Arefiev in the corridor the next day, Wolfson remarked casually, "I saw the director yesterday."

Arefiev was hastening along on his laboratory's business but stopped in his tracks.

"He exists, then?!" Arefiev exclaimed, instantly intrigued.

"His silhouette certainly does. I didn't see a face."

"Why, did he run away?" Arefiev smiled, and the features of his tired, lined face smoothed out. Smiling sorts out most faces, except those that are spiteful masks.

"Who knows? He was certainly in a hurry."

"What use is a director like that?"

"Don't you see, my dear fellow? We couldn't ask for a better director. He doesn't interfere, doesn't push the Party line, doesn't purge the staff or denounce his colleagues. I tell everyone I meet we have an exceptional director."

Arefiev shook his head doubtfully:

"Perhaps he is just a cypher incapable of thinking for himself."

"Ergo, cogito sum," the older scientist restyled Descartes.

Arefiev, who had last heard Latin in his university days, had to ask him to translate.

"A free translation would be, if he exists, it's because someone has a reason for it, and that someone is definitely capable of thinking."

"You mean…," Arefiev began, and pointed upwards.

"Entirely possible," said the old geneticist, who had miraculously survived Stalin's purge of geneticists. "They are everywhere — here, and here," he pointed downwards. "For all I know, they may be listening to us now."

"I am, I am," a dematerialised woman's voice retorted.

20.

They exchanged glances and, without conferring, simultaneously grasped the door handle of the adjacent office.

Kisa, a sumptuous director's secretary since the era of Sikofantov, was on the phone. In a corner of the sofa her friend Milla was filing her nails.

"Receipt of your phoned telegram is acknowledged," Kisa said, hanging up and turning to face them with all the grace of a pregnant cat.

"The investigative team is coming tomorrow, Menahem Yegudovich," she mewed, as usual addressing herself only to senior staff.

"Where from?"

"I heard it's to be a joint team, from the ministry and some other institution."

From the corridor a deafening crash was heard, followed

by the sound of breaking glass. Everyone fell silent and started listening. Somewhere someone groaned.

"What the hell…?" Wolfson muttered, but did not move from where he was.

"Not again!" Kisa squealed, remembering the bullet in her buttocks last time there was a raid.

Arefiev, unburdened by painful memories, looked out into the corridor to see the elderly security man lying on the floor next to the staved in entrance door, groaning and clutching his bald head. Blood was gushing between his fingers. Enormous men who, one after the other, completely blocked the entrance, were stepping over his legs. They wore combat fatigues and black balaclavas which concealed their faces except for a slit for the eyes. Two of these settled themselves in corners and aimed their assault rifles into the depths of the corridor. In short bursts the rest scurried to deploy themselves in the interior of the building.

"Clear!" Somebody roared from the stairs.

Several of the torsos in camouflage appeared at the door of the secretary's office.

"Where's the director?" they yelled in unison.

Kisa flapped a handkerchief, with which, in anticipation, she had been wiping away her tears, at a door upholstered with yellow leather. Two of them burst in.

"Nobody!" they shouted to their people, after which they locked the door behind them. The sound of breaking glass now came from in there.

"May I ask who you are?" Wolfson enquired with total self-possession.

"Us? We're the investigation team," a muffled reply came, filtered through a balaclava helmet.

"And which of you is from the ministry?"

"All of us," the torsos laughed. "From the absolutely most important ministry."

"I wonder which ministry they consider that to be," Wolfson mouthed to Arefiev, who was looking distraught and pale.

Julius Caesar's custom was to select men for his guard who turned red, not white, with fear. It was not that they were any braver, they just reacted faster. He would not have chosen Arefiev.

"Khlamidy Yegudiilovich, we shall have to ask you to come with us," said the stockiest of the torsos, clearly intending to grasp the deputy director's elbow.

"Khlamidy yourself!" Wolfson replied dispassionately and deflected the extended arm. "I'll go without your assistance."

21.

"Where's his laboratory? Show us!" demanded the pair who now emerged from the director's office, and Kisa, lumbering to her feet, led them to the other end of the corridor.

"Who saw Maksyutin last?" one of the balaclavas mumbled.

"Pavlusha?" Milla sighed. "Me, I expect."

Arefiev noted to himself that the episode was clearly getting to her: when she was more herself she invariably frenchified men's names to "Paul" or "Anatole".

"Since the time you reported he has not reappeared?" another torso asked.

"He hasn't," Arefiev responded, instantly recalling the feet in square-toed boots sticking out of the ground.

"And what were you, young lady, up to last time you saw "Pavlusha"?" the torso sneered.

Milla blushed crimson and shot a reproachful look at Arefiev. He shook his head negatively.

"Not telling? Well, if it's difficult to talk about you can show us on my comrade here. He'll pretend to be Pavlusha, maybe not in every detail. Kindly remove that little white coat of yours."

"Hey, what are you doing?!" Arefiev demanded indignantly when one of the torsos pulled up Milla's white coat and cocooned her head in it.

In the sunlight her thin, vulnerable, naked figure seemed like an undressed doll.

"My whole life I've been dreaming of having a Barbie like this to play with," another torso guffawed and started unbuttoning his trousers.

"Hey, you bastard!" Arefiev flared up and was about to take a step in the direction of the sofa when he felt an unexpected pain in the back of his head and the sunlight curled up like a snail, diminished to a point and vanished.

22.

It was reignited as the light from a chandelier, or rather the three large crystal chandeliers in the assembly hall. The blinds were drawn down and all the staff had been herded in. They looked dazed. A young laboratory technician had had his collar bone broken and was holding one arm up with the other. He was close to collapse, looking at the unnatural angle of his shoulder in puzzlement. Someone gave him a pad with sal volatile which he sniffed, recoiled, groaned with pain, and sniffed again.

Masked armed men stood at the doors, intercommunicating in low voices. On the stage a man in fatigues sat writing things down at a table with a golden tablecloth. The director of one of the laboratories had quietly subsided like a sack of potatoes onto a massive oak chair in front of him and was explaining, explaining, explaining… Milla was not in the hall.

Arefiev moved to the next chair so as to be able to see outside through a chink between the blind and the wall. Everywhere was deserted. He heard a murmured conversation:

"Is it the same people as that other time?"

"No, this is the police. That time it was gangsters."

"Forgive me, Vera Polikarpovna, but how can you tell the difference? They're dressed just the same, and wear the same masks."

"Not so many people have been hurt, Alyosha, far fewer. I tell you, this is the police."

A dazzling white sun was beating down; the withered roses in the flowerbed of the institute's courtyard looked in bad shape, but obstructing his view of the flowerbed was something dark with darkened windows. A military, khaki-coloured bus. Arefiev realised he needed to get away from here before it was too late.

He looked at the door again. The armed men were still there, still muttering into their walkie-talkies. That left the stage. He stood up. When he reached the front row, one of the men in fatigues ran up and blocked his further progress. The muzzle of an assault rifle pointed straight at the centre of Arefiev's chest.

"I need to go up on the stage," Arefiev said testily. He had entirely persuaded himself of the necessity and hence was brazenly convincing. "I am a laboratory director."

"Ah, it was you he wanted to see, then," the man with the rifle said and moved aside.

Arefiev went up the red-carpeted steps and never before had walking up on to the stage seemed to take so long. He was expecting to be shot in the back at any moment, but nothing happened. He reached the long row of chairs at the back of the stage and sat down as if waiting his turn. The conversation at the table continued.

Arefiev looked into the hall from the stage. They had been herded together like sheep, he thought. Why? What for? Who knows? No, he needed to escape before he was manhandled into that bus. But how? There were doors to either side at the back of the stage. Arefiev wondered whether to go for the one on the left or the one on the right. The right hand one led to the stairs and from there it was easy to get out through the cellar and the vivarium, but it might be locked. The left one was never locked. It led along a narrow corridor to the director's office.

The left one, Arefiev decided, but it was ten metres away and he was in full view of everyone. There was no way to sneak over to it. He sat there, looking out into the hall, not knowing what he was waiting for. At just the right moment the young lab technician in the hall finally lost consciousness and fell between the chairs.

Somebody shouted, "Quick, get a doctor!" Somebody else said angrily, "Hey, you brutes, someone here is hurt. He needs to be sent to hospital!"

"We'll send him where he needs to go in just a minute," said the man at the table. "And all the rest of you too."

He turned to face the hall and accordingly had his back to Arefiev, who realised it was now or never. He made a dash for the door. Yes, it was open! Here was the door to the director's office. It was open too. The office was in semi-darkness.

"Good day, Igor Mikhailovich," he heard a voice at once familiar and unfamiliar over to one side.

23.

Arefiev started. His nerves were completely frayed. There was a silhouette sitting at the director's table swinging its legs. Once his eyes had grown more accustomed to the gloom, Arefiev recognised him. It was the man from the forest! The hairy fellow.

"Who are you?" he asked.

"Let me introduce myself. I'm Adalbert Franzevich Kanna-bich. The director, so to speak."

"Good God!" was all Arefiev could say.

"What's the matter? I wasn't a bad director, was I?" the man from the forest went on cheerfully. "At least I didn't get in anyone's way. You were all busy with such amusing research here."

"How do you know?" Arefiev was taken aback.

"Of course I know! To tell the truth, it was Wolfson's work which was of most interest to me personally."

"Why?"

"Ah, that's a long story. If I'm not mistaken, you are in a great hurry just now."

"Yes. We've got…"

"I know," Kannabich nodded.

"What about you?"

"Don't worry about me. Do you remember I told you about an entrance? Well, there's one here, too."

"Where does it lead to?"

"Well, that's a long story, too. I believe you still have other business here."

"Can't I come with you?"

"Not now. If I'm not mistaken, there is someone in the next room who needs your help. And then, there's one more matter you must attend to. On your way out, have a look in the left pocket of your jacket."

A commotion was coming from the direction of the assembly hall.

"Go now," Kannabich repeated. "If the worst comes to the worst, come to the little hill on the edge of the forest. But remember: only in an emergency."

24.

Arefiev went into the adjoining room and closed the door padded with yellow leather behind him. Milla was lying on Kisa's secretarial sofa, completely naked, with the sun shining directly onto her closed eyes.

Arefiev patted her on the cheeks. The only reply was a groan.

"Get up, we have to get out," Arefiev said; he was usually more distant with girls.

"Oh, what have they done to me," Milla whispered and lost consciousness again.

Arefiev saw she was lying on the ripped remains of her little white coat, and that a blood stain was spreading out over the tatters.

"Damn!" he exploded.

He picked the girl up and propped her up as best he could on the sofa, then began looking around in search of some sort of garments. He spotted Kisa's pale green top on the chair and threw it over Milla's shoulders. It covered her down to her thighs. We really need something for her lower half, thought Arefiev, but maybe we'll find something along the way.

He peered out into the corridor cautiously. There was no-one in the immediate vicinity, but at the far end of the corridor the staff were being led out through the hall. The door of the next room was ajar. Arefiev remembered it was Wolfson's wash room. If only they could get in there, it connected to the other rooms. But they couldn't risk the corridor, so they had to wait.

He rummaged around in Kisa's desk in search of clothes and unearthed knitting as well as sweeties, knives and forks. In the bottom drawer there was a little bulbous bottle of some transparent liquid.

Now that may come in handy, thought Arefiev, sniffing the liquid. It was spirit.

He splashed some into a glass and added water from another carafe which stood openly on the desk.

"Here, drink this," he ordered the girl, holding the glass up to her lips.

She took a sip and began coughing.

"Drink," Arefiev repeated.

She almost emptied the glass, began coughing again, and then breathed more easily through her half open mouth.

"Ah ha, that's better," said Arefiev when he saw the colour coming back to her cheeks, and he rummaged in the desk once more. He thought he had spotted some sort of cloth there.

He was right. Was it a table cloth? It was golden, like the ones in the assembly hall. Hesitating for a second, Arefiev took some scissors, cut off a piece of fabric and began wrapping it around the girl's hips.

"I'll do it myself," she said at last. Standing up with a groan, she began arranging the piece of cloth.

Arefiev peered out into the corridor. He realised his

colleagues had already gone but someone was still standing by the door with his back to them, talking to someone else.

"Quick, let's go," Arefiev said to the girl.

She tied the ends of the cloth at her waist and made as if to take a step, but then doubled up, groaned and clutched at the base of her belly. Blood dripped onto the floor.

"What's the matter?" It was a rhetorical question; Arefiev needn't have asked. "Well, we have to get the hell out of here."

He picked the girl up and went into the corridor. It was empty, thank God. But now the men would come back and go through the whole institute room by room. The building was probably surrounded. He ducked into the next doorway and came face to face with his reflection in the mirror above the sink. What a sight! Some knight with a rescued damsel in distress I am!

25.

Roads never end even if they seem to have an end.
If you push against the wall, the force of your push sends
you in the opposite direction. This may be the start of your
journey back, which may prove to be the right way for you.
One can write a thesis on the harm caused by barriers —
as well as on their benefits, of course.

Now where? The next room. It was Wolfson's haven but now everything was in a mess, the desk had been overturned, books were scattered all over the floor, and shards of glass from the shattered table lamp lay everywhere.

Great investigative team! Arefiev suddenly remembered and gave an involuntary laugh. The girl looked at him, frightened.

"Nothing," he said. "Come on."

Then he remembered Kannabich's words: on your way out, look in your left pocket. He sat the girl down in an armchair which had been ripped open but spared by a miracle, and thrust his hand in his pocket. What's a piece of paper doing there? he thought, since there should be nothing but a hanky in that pocket.

The piece of paper turned out to be a note from Wolfson. "Take the briefcase in the old distiller tank. I'll explain later. W." The note had been typed on a typewriter.

When had he managed to write that? Arefiev wondered, but then he realised: the note had been prepared in advance so that it could be handed over at any moment.

Where was the old distiller? Arefiev began looking around. One was still working, distilling water, and Arefiev switched it off just in case. The other was already switched off but was obviously in good working order. Was there another? Arefiev went through all Wolfson's rooms but to no avail. Finally, he turned his attention to a heap of old equipment in the corner of the wash room. It was covered with a tarpaulin and underneath he found what he was looking for — a large sailcloth briefcase.

"And now let's get a move on," he said, realising all of a sudden that he couldn't carry both the heavy briefcase and the girl. "Here, hold this," he said roughly and shoved the briefcase against her chest.

She pressed it to herself.

The door out of Wolfson's last room was right opposite the stairs, but there was still the corridor to cross, and they could hear voices there.

26.

"We'll wait," Arefiev whispered and put her down again, on the chair this time.

Men in military fatigues scattered throughout the building. Two of them swung into the corridor. Arefiev watched them through a chink. Which end would they start from? he wondered. If they start at this end, we're done for, but maybe we'll be lucky and they'll search the other end first.

The submachine gunners came closer and closer, then closer still and … walked by. Arefiev bundled Milla up and waited until the two men went into one of the rooms. It was the secretary's office, and it suddenly dawned on Arefiev that they were looking for the girl. There wasn't a second to lose.

He nudged the door with his foot and it opened with a soft groan. Nobody! There was rustling on all sides but the corridor was deserted. Ah ha, here are the stairs. Now down to the cellar as quickly as possible.

They were facing the autoclave room and the laundry. The vivarium was on the right. Where could they hide? He pushed another door, not really remembering what was behind it. Blue light, gas canisters, two huge barrels. Ah! It's the pressure chamber!

Arefiev put Milla down on the tiled floor but she stayed on her feet, holding the heavy briefcase with both hands. Arefiev set about fiddling with the lock on one of the sarcophagi and had it open in a jiffy.

"Lie down," he said to Milla. He helped her get comfortable and stowed the briefcase under her legs.

"Don't lock it," said the girl fearfully. "I'm frightened!"

"Don't worry, it's connected to the next canister. Air's flowing through the opening."

He closed the hatch but opened it again straight away: the girl's pale face could be seen in the glass window panel. He covered her head with Kisa's top, closed the hatch again and took another look through the panel. There was a vague greenish glow. It'll do, Arefiev decided and began tightening the lock. Footsteps rang out on the stairs. He quickly opened the second pressure chamber, lay down, covered his head with his jacket and banged the door shut from inside.

Darkness and silence descended, filling the pressure chamber. He was floating on a stream of silence. It reminded him of the silence of his grandmother's flat and of himself there in that silence, a typical granny's boy, capricious and dependent, forgotten by parents preoccupied with themselves. What have I achieved so far? he asked himself. No family, no children, an interesting job but a strange one, a very strange one. Just look where it's led me…

Just then the pressure chamber juddered. Someone was obviously trying to open the hatch. "Now I'm done for," flashed through Arefiev's head. At that very moment one of the camouflaged figures aimed his pistol at the glass panel.

"Don't shoot," the other stopped him. "There are canisters everywhere. All it takes is a stray ricochet and we'll be blown to pieces."

"But I can't open it," the first retorted.

"There's no-one in there. That's where they keep rags."

Little Milla closed her eyes as tightly as she could and didn't dare breathe, even though there was no longer anyone in the room. They lay in the silence for another five minutes and then Arefiev threw the jacket off his head and tried to open the hatch. He couldn't.

It's got stuck, he realised and a wave of despair swept over him. Well, that's it then. We can't run away now. Why did I go and lock Milla in?

Just then Milla's face appeared at the window panel. She'd got out! Arefiev gesticulated to her that he couldn't open the hatch. She fiddled around with the bolts and soon got them opened.

"You didn't lock me in," she said reproachfully once they were safely sitting on the pressure chamber and greedily sucking in the cellar air.

"Just as well," he declared. "Otherwise we'd have stayed right there."

"Like Romeo and Juliet in adjacent coffins," Milla sighed. "I saw it at the cinema."

Arefiev made a wry face at the mention of Romeo and Juliet as film stars and thought: it would be nice if they could at least teach girls a bit of culture in school!

But culture was the last thing on his mind. He extracted the briefcase from the pressure chamber and asked Milla if she could walk. She shrugged. He noticed a sterilising kit in the cupboard and opened it. There was some gauze inside. He tore a piece off and held it out to the girl, telling her to put it on. She busied herself with her make-shift skirt and untied the knot at her waist. Arefiev was about to turn away tactfully but he suddenly caught sight of a familiar face on the cloth.

"Why it's Lenin!" he said, amazed. "It's not a table cloth, it's a banner!"

27.

And sure enough, it was indeed a banner of the

"Colleɛtive of Communiſt Labour"

which Kisa had been conscientiously saving for better days.

"Well, what do you know, even a banner can come in handy," said Milla.

She stepped over the cloth as it lay on the tiled floor and reached for the gauze, not in the least bit shy although she had nothing on under Kisa's top.

"What would you say if I asked you to take a look at what's there?" she said, pointing her little finger at the lower part of her belly.

"It wouldn't be anything I haven't seen before," Arefiev said sternly and turned aside.

"I meant the tears. After all, you are a doctor…"

Arefiev sighed. Remembering his days as a trainee medic in the gynaecology ward, he overcame himself.

"Nothing serious," he mumbled. "You've got two tears towards the anus, about two centimetres long."

"Ah", said the girl, and bit her lip.

"Does it hurt?" he was surprised. "I didn't even touch you!"

"No, but you're looking and it's turning me on," she replied. "I could have done it with a threesome, only on my own volition, not like that, with those brutes. I'm very sensual, you know, especially since I drank that Solution B."

"What?!!" screeched Arefiev and abruptly sat down on the floor.

"But you said yourself it increases potency and lactation in monkeys, so I decided to try it."

"But it's full of vitamin E! You could ruin your metabolism."

"Yeah, there is something wrong. I used to love onion and garlic but now I can't eat them at all."

Arefiev still didn't understand whether she was joking or not.

"But why?" was all he could say.

"My breasts are small and I wanted them to be bigger. It's actually helped a bit, hasn't it?"

She pulled up her top and showed Arefiev her lightly freckled bust.

"Well, today's really turning out to be a striptease day!" he frowned. "But we'll have to sew up those tears all the same."

And he began looking for some surgical thread. He found a sealed packet and popped it in his pocket. Meanwhile the girl put the gauze between her legs.

"There's only a little trickle of blood," she said. "I can probably walk."

"I wonder where your knickers are? And all your other clothes? Or do you walk the streets like that?"

"They're in my corner," she replied quietly. "Don't be mad at me."

Arefiev softened and felt sorry for her, the poor thing. He stroked her fluffy black hair, and she hid her face in his chest.

"OK, OK, it's time to go now," he came to his senses almost at once. "I wonder what would have happened if you'd drunk Solution A."

"What does it do?" she smiled.

"It induces multiple nippledness."

28.

Glazed floor tiles, black rhombuses on the yellowish back-ground. Two rhombuses were equal to three steps, and walking was far from easy…

They made their way through the dim corridor and arrived at a low metal door. It was open a crack. Arefiev was about to grab the iron handle when a voice came from outside:

"I'm going to the bog."

The girl clutched Arefiev's hand, frightened.

"Get back," he whispered through her masses of hair into her ear.

But then there was a second voice.

"What the fuck do you need that monkey bog for? Not enough space here?"

"You're right," the reply was heard, and a stream gushed forth. But the voice went on: "It's not right somehow, this being an institute. Science lives here."

"Not any more it doesn't. We drove it off in the bus."

"Yeah, but it lived here 'til then." The voice went silent and the stream dried up.

"You know, I wounded a bro today."

"Where had you fought with him?"

"In Afghanistan."

"How could you?"

"Well, I didn't know he was a bro. I took a swing at his shoulder but he stares me right in the eye and says: "Hey Vasilich! Why are you beating up one of your own?" He recognised my voice! And I remembered I'd seen him out there, in Afghanistan. He was serving in the bomb disposal unit. And I nearly killed him today."

"Feel sorry for him?"

"Yeah."

"And if he'd not been a bro would you still be sorry?"

"No. I don't pussy foot around."

"Would you've killed him then?"

"Yeah, but I didn't."

"And you did right. A man needs to know he can kill anyone. Except his own, of course. It boosts your confidence. And you can always kill them later."

"That's right, like taking a fag break. You can always do that later, too."

"OK. Let's go."

It went quiet. The girl let go of Arefiev's hand, and it was only then he felt pain where her nails had dug into his palm.

"Shall we go?" she whispered, and began licking his ear with her little tongue.

And he desired her, but then forced himself to quell it; this was not the time or place.

"Horrible guys," he said huskily. "Just as well they've gone. You know what, I'd like to go and check up on the monkeys."

And they went back to the vivarium. The monkeys were scared and squealing, and they squealed all the more when they saw Arefiev. One macaque had been hurt and was licking its wounds. A knife was lying nearby.

"Those scoundrels flicked a knife at it," Arefiev said to the girl.

"Let's get out of here. I've got a funny feeling about this."

Arefiev had a funny feeling, too. There seemed to be more monkeys than he remembered. Some unusually large specimens were staring out at him from the baboons' cage, and he was sure they hadn't been there before. Arefiev swore he recognised Kannabich's gaze. But which one was staring at him like that? This one or that one? Neither suit nor straw hat… He hasn't donned a monkey skin, has he?

He examined the wounded macaque. The cut wasn't deep.

"I think it'll be all right," he said to the girl.

And they hurried out of the vivarium.

"Ah, it's so nice to be outside!" she said, stretching and turning her face to the sunlight.

"Could be nicer," he said in a low voice, and pointed at a

black car near the gates. Further off, someone was standing outside the bureau de change. He had his back towards them, but as they watched he began turning in their direction…

29.

"Let's go via the chapel," the girl suggested and, cautiously skirting the building, they went into the gothic chapel with its time-darkened, almost black bricks.

The building which now housed the institute had been a hospital before the revolution, and where there is pain, there is always a church, or a chapel at least. Now that chapel served as a storage space for reagents, hospital furniture and various instruments. An underground passage led from it to the bank of the little river nearby, and in the summer the lab assistants would scoot off along it to go sunbathing. A big padlock had hung on the entrance hatch in Sikofantov's time, but the entrance had recently been reopened.

"So where's the hatch, then?" asked Arefiev; it was five years since he'd been here. He shuddered; the chapel was chilly.

"Here. I could find it with my eyes closed."

She took Arefiev's hand and they began their descent, closing the hatch behind them. Turning off somewhere, they found themselves not in the underground passage but in some sort of little cubbyhole.

"Hold on a sec, I'll put the light on," said the girl, and a feeble yellowish bulb flickered to life above them.

"Where are we?" Arefiev was surprised as he looked around the cubbyhole with its windowless, dark brick walls. There didn't seem to be any doors, either. "I don't think there was anything like this here before."

"This is the 'place for harmony'".

"What?!" Arefiev was taken aback, but then he remembered and gave a little laugh. "So that's where you… Aha, a bed, that's the main thing. How on earth did you manage to get it down here? … Two chairs, and even a kettle! Did you lay in running water, too?"

"Pavlusha did it all," said the girl, and the mention of this man's pet name grated on Arefiev. "There's no running water, but there's a little barrel of fresh water under the table. We can sit it out here."

"How about food?" Arefiev wanted to know, practical as ever.

"There should be some crackers somewhere, but that's all. Are you hungry?"

"Not yet."

"We can go on a reccie later."

Arefiev imagined all the dangers which might be lying in wait for them, and he felt the fear of a primitive cave-dweller wriggle inside him like a worm. Maybe this was the first time in his life he had plumbed the depths of this vulnerability, a vulnerability shared by all in this world which is still primitive.

"How many people know about this den?" he asked warily.

"Only me and *mon pauvre* Paul."

"Do you speak French?" he was surprised.

"Well, I did go to school, you know, and I can still remember the odd word or two."

"Did you study in Moscow?"

"No, in Yekaterinburg. I'm all on my own here in this big city. I don't even have a best friend. Even if I sit here hiding for ages, no-one will miss me."

"It's weird to be sitting in here with the light on when it's daylight outside."

"The working day's over," she said, looking at her watch. "Bang on five o'clock."

And she switched the light off.

30.

"Is that better?" she asked.

"Now it's like the middle of the night," he replied, for pitch blackness had suddenly descended. "I'll fall asleep like that. You'd better put the light back on."

"I won't," she said, and he guessed she was smiling. "Sleep if you want to."

"How about you?"

"I'll sleep, too."

And they lay down on the bed as far apart as possible, but the bed was narrow and badly sprung. Beds like that are renowned for one thing: whatever you put on them rolls into the middle. He and the girl rolled into the middle, too.

"I'm sliding onto you," the girl said.

"So am I."

"Shall we try again?"

And they lay down far apart and tumbled into the middle again, bumping knees. But this time he sensed that the girl was naked, just as she had been earlier.

"Have you taken all your clothes off?" he asked, somewhat alarmed.

"They came off by themselves," she said simply.

"I'm not really happy that it was on this bed you and that…"

"Don't speak badly of him. Who knows, he may not be alive any more…" and she sniffed.

"Do you love him?"

"No. I just feel sorry for him."

"So is that why you…"

"I wanted to be with you, but you're heartless. Yes, you are. Heartless." And she punched him on the shoulder with her little fist. "I played my games so often for you. I knew you could see me in the cupboard. But you… I brought Pavlusha there that time to get my own back on you, and then I got used to him. He was very, very sick — they didn't even want to take him for his military service. He was such a simple, tender guy… Oh! I said "was", as though he were…" and she sniffed again.

Arefiev didn't tell her he'd seen the missing Pavlusha's legs.

"So I'm not simple or tender, then?" he smiled.

"Oh, you're awful. Awfully boring, but oh, so clever. That's why I love you!"

And she stroked his head. He groaned as she brushed against a sore spot.

"Oh, sorry!" she said. "They got you today, too. You were trying to protect me. No, you're a real dear after all."

She moved even closer, although it didn't seem possible to get any closer.

"My dear fellow, the girl is already naked and you…" Her rudeness was deliberate and he thought she was probably putting it on.

"But you shouldn't. What about the tears?" he pointed out.

But her face was already rising, like the moon, and her hands had already visited every inch of his body, and his skin was already feeling her warm touch.

"You've undressed me!" he asserted in amazement.

"Shocking!" she said sarcastically, and began to kiss him.

And at last he remembered he was a man.

"You carried me today," she said, "and now I want to carry you."

And she carried him into the heart of the darkness. Blue sparks were flashing; the water was boiling and cooling all by itself. Then he swept the girl away to the heart of the light, and told her what he felt, and she spurred her steed on and went galloping after him at full tilt.

"We're in the prairie," she told him.

"Hey, racehorse, doesn't it hurt?"

"What hurts is that we could have been together like this for the past two years, but everything turned out differently."

"I meant your…" he began clumsily, but she sealed his mouth with a kiss, and they were in the prairie once more, chasing each other on tired mustangs, and reliving the little cubbyhole's past — a secret refuge for fugitive peasants, or brigands, or lovers.

"If this place had a cupboard, I bet there'd be a skeleton in it."

"Maybe it's under the bed."

Under the bed there turned out to be nothing more than an old hospital bedpan — none too fragrant. A little stream flowed into it, followed by a second a moment later.

Then all was quiet. Then the mustangs, freed from their riders, stayed side by side, nibbling grass and rubbing their withers against one another.

"It's so nice," she said. "Let's stay here forever."

"No. Forever is too short. Let's stay here for eternity, for one day."

"For one night, you mean. You'd better watch out, it's so tempting to rest here beside you that my bones might merge with yours."

"They nearly have already," he smiled.

And they jumped back on the mustangs and rode off without a care. But the sun was already setting over the prairie and they fell asleep on their mounts. With a little whinny of protest, one transformed into a pillow, the other into a blanket.

31.

A buzzer has buzzed in the brain: the body senses the presence of some creatures with tiny trunks, nippers and stings. They are crawling, wiggling their whiskers, biting.

And how do you propose we get rid of them?

And how about the ones which have already wormed their way inside and are wearing us out, skimming our life off, one red drop at a time? We must. We must banish them from inside and straighten up, straighten up before it is too late. Or for a start, we must at least wake up…

But sleep clings. It sits too tight under the arms, too narrow across the shoulders, like something ill-fated. There are no fasteners or laces. You can't get out of it, and the pins prick.

And your sleeping self asks your non-sleeping self: how? And the answer comes: if clothes — or life — cling too tightly, look for an opening for you head, then put your head to work.

He woke up and for a long time couldn't remember where he was. Darkness surrounded him — it was never that dark at home. And what's that under his head? Something soft and roundish, with a pliable knob. Why it's…

He started.

"Are you awake, dear?"

Same as ever, he thought. You just manage to relax a bit then there it is: "Are you awake, dear?"

But she was so gentle that he soon melted and pressed her to him, molten. He felt something cold and damp against his thigh.

"Put the light on," he said. "Seems something's amiss."

"Let's not bother?" she protested weakly.

"Please."

And the light glowed yellow. The cubbyhole was still just as dark and the bed just as white, but a large dark-red stain was spreading out over it from the centre.

"It's up to you, of course, but it should be stitched," he said firmly.

"Well, I'd rather not, but it looks as though we'll have to," she sighed. "Otherwise all the blood will leak out of me and I'll turn into that skeleton."

"Should have done it sooner," he snarled as he switched on the kettle, which had long since gone cold. "I could really do with some anaesthetic and a syringe… Maybe I should go and get some?"

"You'll get caught, and I'll be left here with my blood leaking out. Don't worry, I'll put up with it. They stitch you up without any anaesthetic after childbirth."

"How do you know?" he muttered, and set to work.

"Little snarler," she said, and bit her lip.

The procedure lasted ten minutes but the girl didn't so much as whimper.

"You're a real hero," he said when he'd finished.

"Heroine," she corrected him. "Haven't you noticed, I'm very feminine? While you were sewing me up, I probably came about five times."

"Aha, so that's how you get your thrills," he joked. "I'll make sure I always have a needle to hand."

"Don't bother. I like to get my thrills in various ways, and lots of them. Which reminds me," she tossed her dark mane. "Just think, I had four men today, like Messalina."

Arefiev looked painfully at her peaky face. She's trying to joke! Such a courageous soul, who would have thought it! And he'd taken her for nothing but a fluffy-haired floozy.

It never entered his head that if that which had passed between them had not happened, he would have continued to think of her as a fluffy-haired floozy and her last phrase would have jarred on him so much that he would have pulled one of his famous grimaces of disdain, the one the whole institute was so familiar with.

32.

She dosed off, but woke at once.

"How are you?" he asked.

She gave a guilty smile.

She has such a delicate face! he thought. Where has this spirituality suddenly come from? Why didn't I notice it before?

"Shall we stay here 'til the morning?" he asked.

"Is it evening already?" her reply was a question, but she glanced at the clock as she asked, turning over in bed with difficulty. "So it is. Tomorrow we'll see the dawn of a new life, if nothing goes wrong."

"What could go wrong?" he asked, looking at her cheeks. Were they pale? Yes, pale. "Aren't you hungry?"

"No," she said, and he knew she was lying.

"I'll go and get something to eat," he volunteered, but realised at once he wouldn't go anywhere without her.

"Let's not part," she said looking at him meekly.

"Agreed," he smiled, and kissed her.

She flopped back onto the pillow weakly.

"I think we need to get you to hospital," he said. There was a note of concern in his voice.

"Maybe you're right," she said, her voice barely audible.

He wrapped her in the blanket, carefully lifted her into his arms and together they clambered out of the little cage into the underground passageway.

They had a long way to go. Initially the passage descended for a long time. Roots stuck out here and there, and Arefiev had to watch where he was putting his feet.

"Just as well I'm so petite. Imagine if you had to carry Kisa."

He imagined it vividly, burst out laughing and nearly fell.

"Oh, please don't make me laugh," he spluttered, with a hint of reproach.

"Sorry. It's just that no-one's ever carried me before. I like it. Just floating along without thinking about anything. If it weren't for the pain down below…"

"Oh God, what did they do to you?" He stopped.

"They had a bottle, you see, and they…"

"Brutes!" he exploded. "Bastards! I'll call the papers! I'll take them to court!"

"And who are you going to accuse? The whole police force? They're all masked."

"You're right," he said hollowly, and set off again. "And now we're hiding from them, as though we were the ones who'd broken the law, not them."

"It's the strong who make the rules in this country… Careful, there's a narrow bit here," she warned him.

"Have you been here before?"

"Oh yeah, loads of times. We come this way to go swimming when it's hot."

"Do you swim naked?" he asked suspiciously.

"Some do, some don't. I personally swim naked. But don't get jealous."

That word rang in his ear. Me? Jealous? It was accompanied by another thought: Me? Loved and happy? This can't be me!

"What are you thinking about?" she asked.

"About us," he replied, glad he could say such a thing.

"Really?" she brightened up. "Hey, I think we're coming out now!"

And sure enough, the tunnel suddenly grew lighter.

"We're already outside," he replied in a whisper.

They were standing on the spur of a smallish gully which sloped gently towards the river. The river itself was still some distance away.

The sunset was a blaze of red; the disc with its triangular hat were both the colour of blood. Two crumbly airplane tracks traced the sides of the triangle.

"That's where we go swimming." She pointed. He looked, and saw a dark silhouette against the red rays below them. Someone was crouching right by the river.

"Can you see him?" he whispered to her.

She nodded.

They retreated back into the underground passageway.

"Let's see what he's going to do," Arefiev whispered. "We've got a good view from here."

It looked as though the man was filling his flask. But then he stood up and they could see his military fatigues. He was unmasked.

"We have to go back," Arefiev whispered, and they staggered up the underground passageway.

The way back was even longer and more tortuous. Milla tried to walk by herself but she could barely move her legs. Arefiev picked her up again. Neither of them spoke.

They reached their cubbyhole at last.

"I want to stay here," she said, and he lowered her carefully onto the bed.

"What are we going to do?" he asked. "You need a doctor."

"I already have one," she countered, and put her head on his knees.

"No, you might need an operation. This is serious. I'll go up and call an ambulance. Those guys won't dare…"

"Yes, they will," she said, and looking at her he understood that nothing was beyond those guys. Especially as she was a witness; they would never let her go. I wonder what kind of forbidden things were going on in our institute, he thought, and then re-membered the briefcase. Yes, Wolfson was evidently hiding something. But what? Arefiev was about to open the briefcase but then looked at the girl. She was lying there weakly, her eyes closed.

33.

Know yourself. Know what you can do. And then the icy,
transparent darkness will crack, and black overripe oil will
ooze its way through the chink. You can put it towards
the cost of being your smiling self…

He opened the briefcase up in the end. Inside he found about a hundred thick glass test tubes and a note, typed in the now familiar font.

"Whoever reads this should know: I am now unable to act myself. For your information, the test tubes contain samples of liquids. One of them opens the entrance into another world, the world of shadows. This is not make-believe; it is true. Some have already used my discovery, but the samples were deliberately mixed up in order to prevent further incidences. However, the said liquid can be identified chromatographically. For that you need…"

A sigh came from the bed. Arefiev looked up and saw that the girl had lost consciousness.

He dropped everything and ran up the passage. Ah, the chapel at last. The darkness inside had thickened into pitch blackness but the sky was visible through the arched windows. He got his bearings and went outside. The fresh air made him stagger but it also renewed his strength.

Arefiev went warily round the corner of the chapel. Just as he thought: a man in uniform was patrolling the gates. But he could slip along to the cellar door unnoticed. It was still open. It was dark there and the monkeys' green eyes stared out from the vivarium. Had he been dreaming back then when he'd seen Kannabich among the monkeys? There was no time to ponder that now — he had to get to the phone.

Now he was already on the first floor. It was dark. Glass crunched underfoot. The closest door was Wolfson's lab. But where was the phone in that maze of rooms? He thought he remembered one on the desk.

Arefiev entered Wolfson's ransacked office and saw the connection had been smashed, too. Where was there another? In Kisa's room, and in the director's office.

He ran through the board room into the director's office. He couldn't bear to see Kisa's sofa again. The darkness in the director's office had thickened just as it had in the chapel. Arefiev groped for the switch and found it at last. There at the desk, illuminated by a golden crown of electric light rays, sat a huge black baboon, studying some documents.

34.

Arefiev recoiled. The baboon looked up slowly and pointed his clawed finger at the armchair.

"Adalbert Franzevich…" Arefiev blurted out, thunderstruck.

"Ah, so you've remembered my name and patronymic," grinned the baboon. "Sit down."

"The phone…" Arefiev panted.

"There," the baboon pointed to the far end of the desk. "But who do you want to call?"

"An ambulance. There…" Arefiev was overcome by a wave of dizziness.

"It's too late."

"Too late?"

"Yes. She's already dead."

"But that can't be! I was with her a moment ago!"

"No, it's me who was with her a moment ago. You've been wandering around the institute for ten minutes. I'm telling you, it's all over."

Arefiev didn't say anything. There was nothing to say. He was imagining how she had gone out there in that little cubbyhole, the only living being to whom he was dear. And they hadn't even said farewell. Why had he gone running off? What for? Now there was no need to run anywhere…

He folded his arms on the desk and buried his head in his hands. No tears came. He didn't even notice the huge black shadow slither out of the room and the light in the office go out. Arefiev was not asleep, nor was he conscious of anything. The black, suffocating fog of grief overwhelmed him. Then a vision came: the girl was being buried, and music was spreading through the imagined church. Mozart's Requiem. And when *Lacrimosa* began, tears came at last.

35.

Night shuffled past, or maybe it was only a part of the centipede night. He was still but not asleep. He was numb. Then a thought surfaced: I have to go to her. He went out of the institute on unsteady legs, by the main exit this time; the man guarding the gate was completely forgotten. There was no sign of him, anyway — he'd probably decided to take a break.

The chapel. Now to find the hatch. He was giving himself subconscious commands, leading himself to his final goal. The hatch was hiding from him, and Arefiev had to do several laps round the chapel before he stumbled upon it. The cubbyhole was dark. Let it be dark. He hadn't the strength to see. The bed. And on it… Yes, the body is motionless. Life has forsaken it, but it is her none the less. The only one he had ever loved.

Entrance, exit — those are nothing but fairytales; this body is what's real. He switched the light on for a moment. The white, bloodless face of the girl was reminiscent of the pale countenance of Giotto's Madonna. Ah, it was the saintliness of death, Arefiev realised. That's why she'd changed so much on her last day…

He leant towards the body and he, too, became motionless. Thoughts no longer came, and feelings dried up.

Suddenly he felt someone's breath on his forehead; condensed air. A whisper.

"Darling."

He started and opened his eyes wide, as if piercing the air with his gaze.

"Is it you?" he mouthed. It was a crazy hope.

But the body under the blanket remained motionless.

"I'm here." The words came through the darkness faintly.

The voice, or rather the rustle, was somewhere above him. He felt his sanity beginning to slip.

"What's going on?" he asked sharply, and reached for the light switch.

But something blocked his hand.

"Don't be afraid, darling. It's me." The words were clearer now. "I'm completely different now."

"Are you invisible?" he asked softly.

"No. I just haven't decided which outfit to show myself to you in."

"Can I see you?"

"That depends on me. If I feel like it, then you can."

"Please feel like it!" he smiled for the first time in the last few hours.

"You haven't said which outfit you'd like to see me in."

"In Kisa's top and the banner with Lenin," he said, remembering.

"I can appear with nothing on at all."

"Aha, so the striptease continues!"

"Or I might appear in the guise of a little monkey… OK, OK, let's stick with your first choice. Switch the light on, please."

His soul devoid of hope, he flicked the switch.

She was sitting on the chair, just as she had done before, in the same strange garb.

"But who's lying there under the blanket?" he exclaimed.

"A certain friend of mine… No, seriously, that's the real me, that which is no more."

"Who are you then? I like you very much," he smiled at her.

"I'm also her, or rather, her shadow. I'm not quite flesh and blood."

"You won't disappear, will you?"

"Only if I get fed up of you… Don't worry, silly!"

"But what happened?"

"I drank the liquid in the test tube," she said, pointing at the ransacked briefcase.

"But there are almost a hundred test tubes there! How did you find the right one?"

"A very sweet baboon paid me a visit. For a monkey, he spoke very good Russian. He gave me the test tube."

"I know I'll get used to you, but you're not quite her. Or rather, you are and you aren't, both at the same time."

"Really? How interesting. If that's the case, don't call me Milla but Illam."

"Yes, that name suits a disembodied spirit."

"It's a real pity we were together for such a short time," she sighed.

"But we're still together," he reassured her.

However, this was something utterly different, and he was well aware of it.

36.

Towards morning they decided to leave.

"I'll turn into a siren," she said, "and distract the guard on the river bank."

A melodious voice floated over the shallow stream. Then —

to the great surprise of the man in military fatigues — up swam a siren, complete with a fish tail. He rubbed his eyes in disbelief, then took off his boots and jumped into the water. The siren glided right in front of him, then slipped away, smiling and singing and diving, and the man in fatigues dived after her. But she suddenly turned into a huge bird with a human face. Wet through, he began jumping up to chase her, and she led him away from the gully. Two minutes later, Arefiev, who had initially been observing this scene from the underground passageway, then from the rim of the gully, found a companion by his side. She was wearing a Pierre Cardin dress.

"I'm turning into a witch," she said. "I wanted to drown him. If he'd been one of those three, I would have done."

"That's understandable."

"Well, he wouldn't have been the first to be brought down by otherworldly vengeance. So now you're friends with a dangerous being. Aren't you afraid?"

"No. Now you're part of me, my inner voice. No, that's not it. You're my confident, the only one I could ever need or dream of."

"Are you sure you won't want another girl, an earthly one?" she gave him a sly look. "If you do, just tell me. I can disappear for any length of time, for as long as you like."

"Don't disappear," was all he said.

"Do you like my outfit?" she asked, changing the subject.

"Yes, but how did you do it?"

"I'd made a mental note of this fashion and now it's come in handy."

They made a contrasting pair — a fashionable girl with a dishevelled, under-slept man in a crumpled suit. Passersby turned and stared.

"Where are we going?" he asked.

"Wherever you like. Now we're like the sky and the stars — always together even if you can't see them."

But she forgot that he, unlike her, was visible to anyone who wanted to see him or keep an eye on him.

37.

*The impossible is possible. It gladly clambers out of any
crack for anyone apart from those who watch the course
of their own life, who know the furtive lightness of the
empty shells of humans but who, burdened by the ballast
of their heads, reach the same heights of their own
impossible transparency...*

Nobody showed up for work that morning. There wasn't any work to show up for. Everyone was informed that the Institute of Useful Mutations had been disbanded. Admittedly, the no-goodnik employees of the formerly useful institute had been released as early as the previous evening because there were no cells to hold them in. In Russia there is a general lack of cells but an abundance of those arrested. It is thought that arresting someone does him a power of good: he is given an extra chance to meet the authorities, you see, so hopefully he won't get himself into trouble again.

A few days later a brassy plaque appeared on the outside of the former institute:

NUTVOR Ltd.

One of the ex-employees decided to check what sort of newly-hatched company it was, so he parked his car opposite the main entrance early one morning and began to wait. A black Mercedes soon pulled up, and out stepped the same broad-cheeked man who had led the storming of the building. He went inside as if he owned the place.

38.

*Bulldogs, policemen... The mere sight of them is enough
to put you on your best behaviour. Because they might
attack first. And not in self-defence.*

Wolfson spent a night in a cell, too. He was put in solitary confinement, not with twenty other detainees as might easily have been the case. He was used to it. In the early hours a dream came to him: he was walking in a meadow drawn in green felt-tip pen. A little path ran down the middle, dividing it into two halves. Purple cows grazed on the left, red sheep on the right. The path led to a pen. Wolfson didn't want to go into it; confined spaces made him uneasy. But the pen was tempting him with coolness, a stream and a carafe standing on the chairman's desk. He went in and rang the bell. Someone at once made a speech which came straight from the heart — no words, only emotions. The listeners were being woken and told that briefcases with sets of keys to this life were being distributed in the foyer. He didn't go to pick up the keys. He already had a key to life, and this life was nothing but weariness and strife, uncovered defeats followed by victories you can tell no-one about, others' stupidity and his own never-ending patience. He turned the key in the keyhole and the partition separating dream and waking reality receded into non-existence. And waking reality, of course, sneaked and spread everywhere, which it does only too well.

"Well," boomed Reality in a deep voice, "we have information that you have been masterminding the illegal transfer of citizens abroad."

There was no reply.

"If you admit it, sign here," Reality said. The voice was different this time, more like that of a weak opera tenor.

He was watching Reality's eddies with lively interest, trying to guess which direction the next loopiness would take.

"Don't be like that," Reality sighed. "You'd better co-operate with us."

"I've not been co-operating with you since 1947 when you came up with your first proposal," he replied in the language of Reality.

"And are you happy with the outcome?" Reality asked ingratiatingly.

"Quite happy," he cut Reality short.

"And so you wanted to earn a bit on the side through illegal emigration?"

"I was engaged in science. I studied mutagens."

"Aha! You were creating the exemplary builder of Communism."

"No. Our scientific board had set us a different task, back in '87: the study and selection of mutations useful for the human organism."

"So you believe that this human organism would be better off in the West, do you?"

"Maybe, if it's not asked stupid questions there."

"Do forgive us!" Reality flattened itself to the earth like grass. "Tell us, where did you really send those people?"

"When I was studying mutagens I chanced upon the discovery that a certain substance produces a very odd reaction in mammals: it removes their body leaving only the shadow and the voice."

"Where does it take the body?" Reality splashed like a little brook.

"The body becomes lifeless and can be buried."

"So the guinea pigs died?"

"Yes, in a way. But their shadow remained, and the shadows could speak. And speak the truth. Without fearing anything."

"So you were moving people to the other world. Very nice! But that's murder!"

"Not at all. Everyone who tried this remedy did it voluntary. None of them regretted it later, like the young man who parted with his body in order not to be conscripted into the army. Your army."

The faces of the two indistinct figures personifying Reality became like the man on the laxative advert.

"These people — if you can call them people," Wolfson went on, "can think and feel, but they don't live a corporeal life and so are beyond time's control. They can substitute anyone or take on any guise. They are free individuals and have paid for this freedom with their corporeal lives."

"Some kind of shadow theatre," Reality hissed like a pierced balloon. "That means that anyone, let's say, could take the place of our President?! No, no, this is dangerous! We forbid your research. Your Institute is disbanded and you shall be put on trial."

"Let's continue our conversation in the green meadow," he said, and came out of the pen. "Excuse me, which of these brown cows is you?"

"Where is he? I can't see him!" Reality gurgled.

"Or maybe you're a purple sheep?"

"He's taken his remedy!" they guessed. "He's an omniscient speaking shadow now."

"I'd like to bid you farewell, gentlemen," said someone appearing as a dzhigit against the backdrop of the bricks and mortar of Moscow's high-rise mountains. "I can no longer remain in your company."

And the dzhigit turned himself inside out, becoming a crumple-capped Lenin.

"Live a straight life, comrades!" Lenin called with his burr as he soared in the air. "And by the way, comrade Dzerzhinsky* has something to tell you."

And so Dzerzhinsky walked up to — or to be more precise, soared up to — the heights of a monument to himself, played with his lead Adam's apple and rapped out:

"So you think you're proper members of the Soviet Secret Service, do you, you sons of bitches?"

39.

*The edifice of history constructs itself. Sometimes in the way
it was conceived.*

But why all those inconsistencies at the seams? Why those cracks and crumbling soil? The imperfection of design, you

---

* Founder of the fore-runner to the KGB.

might say, but hey, who planned it all and why such things were allowed to happen? Or maybe there was no design, and the process developed according to its own laws, i.e. everything has been falling into pieces from the very beginning? But how can it be?

Reality wanted to watch them and watch over them. The couple watched their steps, too, keeping a sharp look-out. But how can you spot a needle in a haystack, even if it is not a needle but a fisherman's hook with blood sucking, wriggling bait dangling from it? It was like a game where you have to choose a little square for yourself on the big board, but the squares are crossed out one after another and the big board is already almost full, then completely full. Where was there a place for them? She was with him, an invisible, secret second soul. But the squares were being crossed out. He wanted to leave, but at the station a beggar came up to him, took the offered coin and said:

"I wouldn't waste your money on a ticket if I were you." And to back up his words he took a snow-white envelope from his dirty jacket, thrust it into Arefiev's hands, and bored his way into the crowd.

"It's from them," said his invisible companion.

"It's a summons," he announced, once he'd opened it. "They're inviting me to come of my own volition."

40.

"I've come to a decision," he said when they were strolling together in the Alexander Gardens, in the very heart of the mother-state so cold to her children.

She immediately guessed what he was hinting at, and began talking him out of it.

"No, I don't have a life here, and I never will. They're everywhere now, the new kind and the ex's. But you know what their boss says — and we elected him ourselves: there's no such thing as an ex-… They're always on duty. You can't get away from them." He paused and added: "Besides, I want to be like you, so that we'll be on equal terms."

She looked into his eyes and saw in them the Kremlin's prison walls, the pale grey sky, and a firm decision.

They boarded a metro. A pale, black-haired beauty in a lilac dress and a man in an old checked jacket, with a nervous tick in one eye. He was saying goodbye to the landscape beyond the carriage windows, to the city and to the world. Then the train dived down.

The metro let them out at the edge of the forest, handed them over to the lilac bushes and then the elms, the maples, and the aspen. The trees surrounded this strange couple, spinning them and playing hide and seek. For a long time the two figures searched for that glade with its little hill.

And then the forest was deprived of its two play things, and it rustled and hummed huffily, and only what was written became obvious, while what was lived followed in the footsteps of all those who have lived, went the way of generations, and generations of human beings.

PART TWO

I.

The university of the German town of Münsterstadt — which many called Musterstadt, or exemplary town — had an exemplary Biology Faculty, and in that faculty there was an exemplary professor, although his name was not Mustermann, as you might expect, but Ostermann. He was studying cases of atavism among humans, and was particularly interested in phenomena such as excessive facial and body hair, multiple nippled-ness and the presence of tails. At one time the professor had thought of adding "excessive sexuality" to his list, but then imagined all too vividly how many maniacs he would have to welcome and study, and that soon put paid to his idea.

The professor had a wife, who did not suffer from multiple nippled-ness, but was just the sort of wife a professor should have: patient, sluggishly calm, and faintly foreign. Vanda (for that was his wife's name) was of Saxon-Polish stock; the Saxon capacity for hard work (and the ineradicable accent) peacefully co-habited with the ability to show herself off, inherent in all Polish girls. She didn't merely spend a long time perfecting her high hairdo, she also spent a long time living at the country cottage.

The professor devoted his free time to scientific research and any free time he had left over from that was devoted to other avenues of research. Today, for instance, he found himself in the university canteen at the same table as a young female student. She was not even studying in his faculty but in the Philology Faculty, and she informed him that she had recently seen a man with a tail. The professor delicately enquired which side the tail was on, but everything was in order: the tail was at the back. The smile with which the girl accompanied this assertion was not exactly promising, but neither was it hopeless.

They arranged to meet that evening to go in search of the tailed one. Having drunk up their coffee and handed their cups and tokens over to the canteen lady, they were handed back two euro which they popped in the purses with a synchronous movement, and simultaneously pronounced the farewell "Tschu-uus".

2.

They met on the platform of Münsterstadt-West railway station on the town's western outskirts. The platform was on a high bridge and gave a good view of the skyscrapers and TV tower of nearby Frankfurt. Although Frankfurt was not far from Münsterstadt, the two cities were rivals and did their best to ignore one another. Münsterstadt-West was in an industrial part of the city which was peopled during the day but deserted at night. The people left in search of a different life, a domestic one, and only the buildings were left, though they might have preferred to leave, too. But buildings don't have a private life; they are always busy, always at work until their bricks or breeze blocks collapse.

They met at the free gravel car park, and barely recognised each other. Then they set off on endless wanderings through the empty streets, past storehouses, barbed wire fences and filling stations. Their route was like a tangled ball of string, and their thoughts wandered along intricate trajectories, too. Nobody disturbed the couple or their thoughts. They didn't catch sight of the tailed man, nor of anyone else, for that matter.

The hardworking German wind was blowing, sweeping the grey city grit along the tarmac. They went as far as the graveyard, and stopped by its brick wall, right opposite the lych-gate. A green coldness splashed out and doused them a chilling whiff by way of invitation. Alter Friedhof: old graveyard. Someone was out there, in the darkness, by the gravestones. A shadow. Maybe more that one. But it would be unthinkable to disturb people in such a place at such a moment.

They turned back. When they were almost at the station, a tavern gave itself away with lively sounds. It was called "Zum Laternchen", or "The Little Lantern". The tavern's doors opened and revealed the lantern. And so they rounded their evening off at "The Little Lantern," drinking Frascati, talking, and discovering those fundamental things which determine acceptance or rejection. He was clearly attracted to this girl, Magda. But another little lantern was burning somewhere… almost nowhere. A red light – no, not danger but apprehension. And the professor couldn't work out why.

They agreed to meet again in three days' time. As they were leaving, the professor accompanied his companion to the door, and when they opened it, they almost bumped into someone walking past. For a second his face flashed before them– raging like a tiger, and covered in brown fur. It was an almost inhuman face, yet wantonly-human at the same time. The face of a beast dressed in an expensive soft coat.

3.

They froze on the spot.

"Did you see that?!" he whispered at last, right into her ear.

"Yes," she said softly, and her breath was hot. She slipped her hand in his. "I'm frightened."

"We should follow him," said the professor, and literally dragged the girl after him.

The figure in the overcoat didn't turn around when it reached the graveyard wall but leapt over it nimbly without breaking its stride. They stopped — the wall was one and a half metres high, so it was rather difficult for them to copy his feat.

"I think there's a gate here," said the girl.

And indeed, a lych-gate enveloped in a pale green light offered itself to them. But it turned out to be locked.

"It's not so high here," the professor said, and somehow clambered over to the other side. "Give me your hand."

But the girl was in better shape than him, and was already standing beside him.

They hurried along one of the avenues without much idea of where to go. They didn't want to split up. It was almost dark and the graveyard's little red lamps stood out strangely against the green of the leaves of the surrounding trees. Angels with peeling countenances peered out at them from the tall roofs of family tombs.

"I can't see anyone," said the professor finally, after they had gone all round the edge of the graveyard. "Let's go down the central avenue. We should be able to see everything from there."

But the person they were looking for was not in the graveyard. There was no-one at all in the graveyard, except for the little red lamps and the green leaves which danced with each other in the wind creating dapples and rustles almost as though they were giggling conspiratorially.

"What if he's inside one of the big tombs?" asked the girl.

The angels shook their heads disapprovingly.

"Well, these family tombs usually all lock," the professor remarked thoughtfully. "But we can check."

"I think I'm going to die of fright," said the girl in all seriousness. "Why on earth did I bring you here…"

They set off down the avenue again, tugging at each wooden handle as they went. All the tombs were locked, of course.

"He could have jumped over the far wall," said the girl.

"I suppose so. Or maybe he's sitting in the branches right now, listening to us."

And at that very moment something heavy fell out of the branches and the girl gave a stifled scream. But it was just a large bird. Working its sleepy wings, it slowly dragged itself off somewhere beyond the city.

"No, he's not here," said the professor. "I can sense it."

They left by the main entrance. The lights of cars racing along the ring road gleamed on the left, the neon lights of the railway station shone violet to the right.

"Oh, good. People again," the girl whispered. "I won't be able to sleep tonight. I'd have nightmares of that terrible face."

And so they decided to drive to his place, leaving her terra-cotta-coloured Volkswagen to spend the night in the car park next to a minibus belonging to an office supplies company. Its owner's name was painted on the side, yellow on blue: Torsten Bulka.

But they had only just set off when the girl said she had a headache, so they drove back to the car park.

"We'll see each other tomorrow, won't we, at the same place?" said the girl as she blew him a kiss from her car.

Dangling on a thread between her face and the windscreen was a little African god. Or maybe a little devil.

4.

If a sweetie is hanging temptingly in front of you, there is no guarantee you will be able to reach it. Even if you stretch up to the right height, there is no guarantee that the sweetie won't float higher at the last moment. Even if you manage to catch it in your hands, there is no guarantee that you have caught anything edible, and not just an empty wrapper, a hollow model or a fishing hook in disguise.

The professor went home rather vexed by the girl's capriciousness, but in the morning he came to the conclusion that girls will be girls.

He forgot all about it when he arrived at the university, and after his lecture he began surfing the internet for information about hairy people in Germany. There were not so many of them. One lived somewhere in Friesland, but it was a long way from there to Hessen. And the age didn't match, either — a sixty-seven year old wouldn't be able to scale a wall so easily! No, it had been somebody else, someone in their prime, and with decidedly negative vibes.

By the time he got to Münsterstadt-West station, the girl's car was already parked in the car park, next to the Torsten Bulka minibus again. There was no-one in the car.

Aha, he said to himself, and headed off to the "Zum Latern-chen" tavern. But the girl was not there, either. He walked round the nearby streets. Everything was as deserted as it had been the night before. Surely she hadn't gone to the graveyard on her own? Although it was still quite light.

He hurried over to the graveyard. There were the main gates. Why was there an instant sensation of cold and damp when you went through them? He walked along the central avenue. No, there was no-one to be seen. Then he decided to walk round the edge of the graveyard. The walkway was empty and he could see a long way in front of him. But there was no-one around. The perimeter paths met at the avenue lined with tombs. Maybe the girl had gone inside one?!

He began trying the handles. They were locked, as they had been yesterday. As he reached out for the next handle, he sensed something hanging over him. He started violently and looked up.

It was the stone figure of a girl, growing out of the vaulted arch into the tomb. There was something uncanny about it…

He took a step back to get a better look at that cracked stone face. Why, it was Magda's face! Yes, yes — her face, her neck, her bust, and then…. the archway into the tomb. So that's who she was – the gate-keeper!

She hadn't turned to stone, had she?

The wind whispered something in his ear, but the whisper remained enigmatic.

So she was the gate-keeper, but where was the gateway?

He went back to the car park. The girl's car was still parked in the same place. He waited another half hour, but nobody showed up. He drove home.

He made a brisk detour on his way to the university the next morning and drove into the car park at Münsterstadt-West, gravel crunching. Magda's car was still there, gleaming in the morning light.

5.

We know that every exit is an entrance, but not every entrance is an exit. Not everyone who comes in is entering or exiting; not everyone who comes into this world is an animated object which can be named "human" at its birth.

First of all, let's examine the dimensions. The aperture in a pencil shaft is not the entrance for a ballistic missile; the aperture of the sky, for all its boundlessness, is not the entrance for an object or subject without wings, be it a tractor or the accountant Ivan Ivanovich, alias John Johnson, or even Séan Shaughnessy. But as for Séan Shaughnessy's thoughts about the boundlessness of the heavenly expanse or even about buying a new fridge, well, the entrance is certainly open to them.

Like a diligent bird clinging to one perch or a single theme, Professor Ostermann's thoughts clung to one subject: his own Waterloo with the girl. Sometimes, just for a change, his thoughts shifted to the girl herself, and then anxiety would overwhelm him. It was in one of those moments that he telephoned the dean of her faculty and tried to make an enquiry. But the enquiry back-fired like a faulty gun, shattering the silence with the words: "There is no such student here!" "How about earlier?" "There has never been a student of that name here since the founding of the university!"

It was a relatively modern university which had only been opened in the time of Kaiser Wilhelm prior to the First World War, but that didn't make it any better. Magda was not registered in any of the other faculty registers, either, nor was she in the phone book. To banish any lingering doubt, he went to the town hall. But he didn't get the information he needed there, either: "You have either misspelt her name, or she is not from this town" he was told by the various very sweet girls there.

Not from our town? What's the registration plate on her car?

And the professor, who couldn't even remember his own address, dashed over to Münsterstadt-West.

The car was where it had been, and the registration plate began with "Mü" — Münsterstadt. And the car was such a homely pink colour that a baby was even rioting on the back seat, and here are two adults walking over to the car with the obvious intention of getting into it. Two adults who were obviously not the criminal type.

The professor was only a stern professor during exams. At other times he could be a very endearing professor, and he used that skill to his advantage. He had the smile of an overgrown little boy, and the little boy inside him felt at ease and very comfy in his John Lennon glasses. So he put his sunny smile on now and asked the couple about the girl. No, they didn't know her. They had been to Bremen for the week and left the car here — it was quite safe as the car park was, supposedly, under surveillance. Someone had got in the car? Well, that was most surprising. But at least they hadn't driven it away! Maybe it had been a different car? Maybe, the professor agreed meekly, and apologised; for when there is nothing left to say, it's always good to apologise.

He went back to his own car and sat behind the wheel. That was the terra-cotta-coloured Volkswagen filing past now. The driver raised his hand and waved goodbye, and brushed the African devil-god. It swung indignantly on its little thread.

6.

Ostermann was strolling in his garden wondering whether he should cut the grass immediately or wait a few days. The garden path under his feet was soft and subsided slightly, as though it was going to sink into some other world hiding beneath the grass. The soles of his shoes stuck to wet brownish soil of the bare, grassless patches.

On the other side of the brand new grey-brick wall was a bench, and at that very moment a cyclist sat down on it to take a breather. His old Raleigh bike was leaning against the end of the bench. A German whistled past on a brand new bike, all kitted out in sporting lycra. The old Raleigh shuddered, then swayed and collapsed on the tarmac with a clatter.

"Damn!" The cyclist couldn't contain himself.

The back wheel started to rotate mockingly in the opposite direction. Ostemnann, who was about to turn away, gave a start, looked over the wall and stared at the writer.

"Good Lord! Mr. Swidersky!" He said, in pretty good Russian. "Is it really you?"

The rounded, red-haired fellow in a jaunty baseball cap, with his cheeks ruddy from the fresh German wind, gave him an inquiring glance.

"I'm Heinz Ostermann, Professor Ostermann. I visited your step-brother, Dr. Arefiev, in Moscow. Does that ring any bells?"

"Ah, you are the professor of biology who came to my reading!"

"That's right. I still remember the story you read that night about Moscow taverns."

"Well, I lead a very healthy life here," said the author shamefacedly.

"Quite right, quite right!" laughed the professor. "Mmm. Transplanting to new soil... Are you over here for long?"

"For ever, so to speak. I have emigrated."

"I didn't realise you were from a German family!"

"My father was half Polish. But I am here thanks to my Jewish blood: both my grandmothers were Jewish."

"I hardly dare ask about your other grandfather."

"He was born in Ireland but moved to Moscow at the beginning of the nineteen twenties to help them build socialism. He worked as the director of a printing-house. In 1940 he was arrested and sent to the camps as an "English spy". He spent thirteen years there, until Stalin died."

"Your genes are not exactly typical for a Russian writer."

"More like very untypical," smirked Swidersky.

"And how are you enjoying living here?"

"It's rather boring," Swidersky admitted frankly.

"Do you ever go to the theatre? Though, er, maybe you still find the language a bit difficult. How about the opera?"

"I went once to *The Barber of Seville*. It was wonderful! But the tickets are expensive. Concert tickets are pricey, too, so I can't afford it for now."

"I suppose you're not working yet?"

That morning Swidersky received a job offer from the authorities, and so he told Ostermann what kind of work they had offered him.

"A steeplejack?" laughed the professor. "It's hard to imagine you as one. Are you sure you understood the letter correctly?"

Swidersky took the letter from his inside jacket pocket.

"Well, yes. Washing the façades of high buildings. Wouldn't you like to wash the façades of the German state?" winked Ostermann

"No, I wouldn't," smiled the writer.

"Then go along to the doctor's. He might find something and give you a medical note. How is your heart?"

"Everything's fine, apart from arrhythmia."

"Arrhythmia is serious. Have you had it long?"

"Since my step-brother went missing. You heard about it, didn't you?"

"Yes, vaguely. Russia's not the safest place to live... Forgive my curiosity, but did you and your brother have the same father and different mothers?"

"That's right. My brother took his mother's surname, that's why we have different surnames. He doesn't have a drop of Irish blood, by the way, and we are not really alike, neither physically nor in terms of our characters. But we always got along well and looked out for one another. I really miss him…"

"I can imagine," the professor said sympathetically, shaking his head.

7.

In this day and age of unceasing man-made rocking,
we are all pendulums.

In the past, thanks to the synchronicity of their rocking, the pendulums marched in step. Later even they were touched by dissent. Out of sync swinging became a symbol of a free society of pendulums. Of course, there are crazy pendulums, too, swinging in loops instead of the regular citizenly "tic-toc." But even the crazy pendulums reach a state of balance. And that is not necessarily death; it could be something quite different. And a crazy pendulum will not necessarily find its static balance resting in the equilibrium position. What would happen if the crazy pendulum took it into its head to ponder the meaning of movement while displaced from that position?

Swidersky thought: that's exactly the position I've got stuck in because there is no gravitational pull. My native land doesn't pull me into a vertical position, and here — well, here, I could just come to a standstill at any angle. At least there is an atmosphere I can breathe — the air of my native alphabet and even the punctuation marks. I live in the landscape of my own language. That is my environment. And it is an environment of silence, forever and for every day.

He recently organised an evening of Serbian and Albanian poetry in Moscow — right at the height of the Kosovo conflict. He thought it important… In fact, it was a miracle he had managed to pull the evening off at all — they hadn't wanted to rent the hall to him, the municipal authorities had rung him at home to plead with him threateningly and threaten him pleadingly. He had said: if you don't give me the hall, I shall hold the evening on the street, right outside the hall, and I shall invite the foreign journalists. After a short period of silence, one of the very important bosses rang him at home and said: OK, have your evening.

And he had had it, but then the problems began. The journals suspended all publication of his work until better days, the bosses in the Writers' Union gave him dirty looks, and his acquaintances just looked straight past him. To cap it all, the journal where he worked as an editor went bankrupt and stopped paying its employees. Then they fired him completely and he found himself out of a job. Several nationalist-minded voices repeatedly made threatening phone calls to him. What, was he trying to reconcile our Serbian brothers with some shitty Albanians?! Absolutely unforgivable…

The time came for him to prepare for his departure. There was something rather desperate in those preparations. The neighbours watched from the windows as Swidersky threw out his archive of notes and letters, right down into the square skip. Dust and sheets of paper whirled around…

Next he rid himself of his old photographs. "I'll never be like that again" he said to himself, and the one he said it to agreed. His writer's membership cards were executed in their red, green and dark blue bindings. They had once opened some doors for him, doors he no longer had the faintest desire to walk through. "I won't accumulate certificates about myself" Swidersky traced in the dusty plain of his desk. Then as an afterthought he added: "Down with autobiographies! We shall write our life non-stories!"

Then he went out for a walk. Maybe someone was following him. If they were, they would have heard him humming some strange tune as he walked. That was how he lived his life: he wandered through the city humming his strange song.

Germany floated by outside the windows. It pretended to be Poland for a while, but the square blocks of identical houses and monotonous square industrial buildings soon appeared. No-one knew where it was floating off to, though they vaguely suspected it would drift past everyone, wherever it fancied. The writer Swidersky, however, figured it out: Germany and he were floating in opposite directions. And he didn't like that.

Where am I going? he asked himself. To a country where fully legitimate citizens fully legitimately — though without trial — shot my Polish grandfather and his Jewish wife, and in their own country, what's more, in Poland. What will they do to me?

But he decided to banish such thoughts. Everything flows, everything changes, you cannot jump into the river of history twice, there will not be a second meeting on the Elbe, and even if there is, who knows which planets the civilizations meeting there would hail from...

8.

Not that we are not all residing in an impossible location (or at least our thought dwell there) but the hotel they had housed him in was known locally as Hotel "Nowhere", and the place where it stood was called "Nowhere", "Ausserhalb".

It was in the forest, beyond the town. You could see the little town, though — it was just there. But the town didn't want to include that hotel and its inhabitants and had squeezed it out into nowhere. And it turned out that the multi-lingual guests of the hotel called it "The End of the Road."

The stadium and the hotel were separated by a road which stretched all the way up from the town. Swidersky was wondering where it lead. There's the town on the left, but what's on the right? And the curious Swidersky rolled off to the right. And he rolled up to a place where the road disintegrated completely into a bog.

He had reached the end of the road.

Swidersky turned back and again entered the woods where larches made friends with fir trees and ganged up against the hazel trees, forcing them out to the forest fringes. Two roe deer sprang out not five paces in front of Swidersky and he stared at the undergrowth for a long time: who else was in there? The forest asked the sun to shed light on it for the writer, and the request was granted; but no other beasts were discovered.

Things were freer in the forest. A forest breathes in centuries, not in the measured hours of the working day and the curtailed hours which remain once we are relieved of work. The forest leads anyone who enters it along ways known only to itself, and these are not paths but the veins and arteries of forest life, pulsating with its ebbs and flows, confluences and coincidences.

Then Swidersky discovered a children's playground on the edge of the forest. It was fenced in and wouldn't allow anyone to enter. Finding no legitimate point of access, Swidersky simply stepped over the thickly painted little fence with his short legs. In the middle of the square was a huge sand pit with some sort of wooden construction inside. Semicircular black plastic bowls dangled from long metal chains hanging from it. A chain clanked softly, and the bowl nearest the writer dipped down and collected some sand, then moved off somewhere. Another little bowl took its place, and the whole process was repeated.

Swidersky watched, transfixed. He finally tore himself away and walked off a few paces. He came face to face with a small orange table spinning delicately. It was framed by tiny kiddies' chairs which turned with the table. Beyond that, a swing swung silently, and a seat on a spring nodded its horse's head.

The writer realised that the playground was living its own life, playing by itself. It had no need of children. Or rather, children could come, but the playground would still play by its own rules, and the children would have to follow them. Or just stand and watch.

9.

In his dream he was a bird soaring over the sea's desert, the wind blowing to meet him. He could see for miles around but there was nowhere for him to land and rest. Mist was rolling in from the North. Maybe aeroplanes are hanging there in that mist, he thought. I wonder if it's worse for them than it is for me. Should he envy them or not? Yes, he probably should, he decided, for they have a goal, a landing point, and even if they don't make it to that goal, at least they have somewhere to aim for. Where are my faded wings taking me, he wondered, and would they soon grow weary?

The news from Moscow was not particularly good. His publisher had shelved his book indefinitely. Swidersky then offered his manuscript to a few German publishers; however, it was turned down as soon as they found out where the author was now living. Germany reasoned that all things Russian should come from the mysterious land of Russia which sagely slumbers, and as for those who live with us in Germany, they have been spurned by the great and mysterious Russian culture, and are thus spurned by our culture, too, which maintains reason in all things.

All the same, I must get to work, he said to himself. Because it was important for him to be somebody, because it's important for everybody to be somebody, otherwise they feel small and naked, shivering from cold among the basalt crags of humanity, and listening to the growls of the predators who have not eaten their fill that day.

That night he dreamt of a competition "Attempts at Sound" which was graded in digits of human dimension: a person's height equals five forearms, and one forearm equals five fists.

Some shouted, some wept, but he just sang his quiet song. Since he had not matured to human height, he was given his marks in forearms and fists. For a long time after he woke up he could still feel the naggingly intimate proximity of those forearms and fists.

10.

A blue tit landed on the window sill and spoke in the language of beaks, claws and little wings.

The writer took a piece of paper and inscribed it with: "habits, phobias, idiosyncrasies, three-dimensionality". Then he pinned the piece of paper to the wallpaper. He was going to give his characters these qualities.

Then Swidersky got down to the familiar business: he took a fresh notebook and began to make entries: the blue tit's claws, the twig at the windowpane, the vacuum in which he had lived. The vacuum was called Moscow. It breathed with the early morning dew of the birch groves and begot mutants. And a spider's web of events began spinning itself out over the page. Unknown shadows fell across it, and mysterious gaps yawned there. Gun shots were fired. And Fear lorded over it all. The unpredictable lived in the next little square of space and gazed through the glassy eyes of windows. Everyone wanted somewhere to hide, even if that hiding place was nonexistence. But nonexistence was like a proud realm and wouldn't admit any old Tom, Dick or Harry. It chose its visitors carefully, issuing them with visas.

Finally, he finished writing his story, printed it out, made bullet-like holes in each page and bound the leaves with a black funeral ribbon. The story ended up in a huge and ever-growing file named "The Unpublished".

His other projects flowed along their course on the scanty waters of the writer's imagination. As for the waters of reality, they would occasionally bring quiet moments to his shores.

The soft darkness of the German sky looked like a screen, a backdrop for the motionless dance of the fiery stars. But only directly overhead; the stars were hiding elsewhere, and darkness dominated. He looked up at the highest point of the earth's surface, at the red tiled roof of a distant five-storey building, and suddenly noticed a misty, silvery-steel stork gliding low over the roof.

Yes, it was silvery, not white, and transparent, not solid, and it must be big — enormous, even, if it could be seen so clearly from such a distance. It was hovering in one place. The black clouds parted and flowed round it. It was floating towards him, yet remained motionless, unable to reach him. Like happiness — silvery and alluring…

He went back into his room, lit the bedside lamp, and took the first book which came to hand. It was a German-language book,

The Marquis of Bolibar by Leo Perutz.

A mysterious avenger, Spain, the clash of sables and gunfire in the night. And the tragedy of a person who was left alone in a foreign land and who sold himself to the demon of revenge. It was a sad tale, but then all tales are sad, just as history is sad, too, let alone the tear-jerkers of real life. He was having German dreams now, too, which was also cheerless, in fact…

He had already dozed off and the book was lying in the gap between the mattress and the wall when something suddenly made him wake up. Something was wrong. He looked around the room — everything seemed fine, all the objects were readying themselves for sleep, he couldn't even hear the tick of the wall clock; it must be asleep already. He turned his gaze to the window – and a shudder ran through his whole body: a pale, lifeless face was pressed up against the glass.

He got up abruptly and looked again. Yes, it was a human face, smooth and hairless. It had set like a mask, without a smile. Only a face — where was the rest of the body? There was nothing else to be seen, only blackness.

But then a hand appeared, or rather, the wrist of a hand. It was pale, too. The wrist pointed towards the balcony door, and a questioning expression appeared on the face.

Swidersky realised it was not a ghost, or not completely a ghost, but more likely a guest, and that he, Swidersky, should let the guest in. He threw his lilac terry dressing gown over his shoulders and unlocked the transparent door. The guest flowed into the room. He was dressed in black and resembled the famous portrait of Franz Liszt in a monk's cassock, though unlike the painting, the guest lacked a thick head of hair.

Having adjusted his black cuffs, the guest looked the room over leisurely and took his place in the darkest spot.

In response to the writer's inquisitive look, he introduced himself: "Nemglan, an fiagai. I am at your service for the next lunar hour."

Swidersky made a mental note of that strange word "*fiagai*" which the visitor pronounced as "figgie", half way between higgler and fig-tree, and continued to stare uncomprehendingly at his guest.

"You called for me, didn't you?"

"Called for you?" the writer echoed in surprise.

"You gave me a sign via my heraldic bird. If you look at it for a long time, it will transmit the signal to me. Just like clicking the mouse when you're sitting at your computer."

It dawned on Swidersky that he was talking about the stork. So that's what it is!

"What do you want to tell me?" enquired his guest.

Swidersky looked at his guest's pale lemony, hairless face and wondered whether there was anything he wanted to communicate to this person.

"Is everything all right? Are you satisfied with your life?" his guest prompted him.

As if someone had flicked the "on" switch, Swidersky let out the whining stream of his émigré's complaints.

His guest listened politely, though you could not really say he was paying much attention.

"Is that all?" he asked when Swidersky dried up, worn out by his own profuseness.

The writer gave a weary nod.

"Well, what did you expect? French marzipan and Scottish

shortbread? You have launched yourself into a new environment, and that environment rejects foreign bodies. Look around you. Every other person you meet is a foreigner and an immigrant. They are all strangers here, and everything is strange to them. Aid for refugees is a myth, it is nothing but a country's guilty conscience, the guilty conscience of a country which has filled its ditches and gulleys with the bodies of those it killed. Now it is filling its houses and apartments with the bodies of the living, but things will go badly for those living bodies."

"Why?"

"Because the environment rejects them, too, and the environment always has a clear conscience, because it doesn't have one at all. Every individual is always right about everything, and so he always wants to see around him people he finds pleasing, or at least, people who are similar to him. But he certainly doesn't want to see any foreign bodies. So when the environment comes to the boil this state will turn into a nice jam."

"Oh, nothing will happen. The bureaucratic Moloch can consume any foreign body. And anyway, émigrés soon adapt and are assimilated. It's all just a question of time," said Swidersky, thinking out loud.

"And how much time will it take in your case?"

"I don't know. Not long, I hope."

"Excuse me, but what language are we speaking in now?" the visitor gave a pale smirk.

"In Russian."

"That's precisely my point. And how many years will it take you to speak just as freely with me in German? Five? Ten? Or maybe never? Language is the border between being in or out."

"I'm no linguistic genius, sadly," sighed the writer. "Languages, like girls, prefer the young. But I would like to point out that I have begun attending German classes."

"Then you can cross those six months off your life."

"Are you saying I'll never get where I want to in life?"

"Where do you want to get? Do you want fame? Riches? Women?" the visitor creaked the writer's favourite chair as he sat in it. "Tell me. I can perform a miracle for you."

And he pressed a button on his watch. The watch case opened and out poured thin rays of white light. They began to play, and black rays mingled among them, too. Or maybe they were nothing but the empty sectors between the white rays.

Swidersky thought for a while, then said:

"Since I left, I have only been living on paper. I have forgotten how to enjoy life, and now I only know how to work, how to write. I would like to learn to live again, if possible."

The guest shook his head.

"Only if you give up writing. You can either write, or live. There is no other way."

"Then there is nothing I need."

The lemony face looked admiringly at this rounded, unlovely man who was no longer young, and who had so simply given up earthly vanity.

"Are you sure?" he asked.

"Completely."

"Fine. Very well. Then rest your hopes on luck. Luck is very good at helping those it is hard to help… Does your body sit well with you?" he suddenly asked unexpectedly.

The writer was about to answer with an instant "yes", but then thought that "no" might be a better choice. In the end, he didn't say anything.

"Hmmm. It seems as though you don't know yourself yet. Who knows, things might be easier for you if you were like me, visible but incorporeal. It is like having wings… Oh well, it was nice meeting you. I'll fly back to Ireland… Remember my sign, just in case. It is the silvery stork."

And the stork flew up out of the rays of light, but the stranger closed the lid and everything grew very dark. Even the lamp over the writer's bedstead went out. Swidersky began groping around for the switch, and tugged it, but the bulb must have blown. Then he got up and switched on the light. There was no-one in the room.

II.

*High-flying aeroplanes observe the striped earth that
hibernates under the cotton wool of clouds. The earth
has striped dreams devoid of people; as for people's dreams,
there's a flight without a landing in them —
or a landing without a flight…*

"What a stupid dream!" Swidersky yawned placidly the next morning in his all too compliant bed. The metallic bed springs had twisted his spine at such an angle that it seemed to be sticking a needle in its owner as it untwisted itself. Memories were sticking like needles into the spheres not invested with flesh. The stork… Nemglan, the man with the lemony face… your choice: writing or living… rest your hopes on luck… And that strange word "fiagai." It was obviously neither Russian nor German.

The writer delved deep into his dictionaries and touched the bottom. Fiagai was Irish and meant hunter or predator.

Had there been anything predatory about the visitor? Maybe. But the lemony face bore a constant expression of eternal weariness. Omniscience and weariness. But what would that face be like if you closed your eyes? The features of the face would become little triangles, then squares, berries, pebbles, a rubbish bin, a space rocket; they would take on the colours of sunflowers and come scattering down on little wings like maple seeds…

When he opened his eyes, Swidersky began leafing through his dictionary. Unfamiliar words came and went. At last he found that mysterious name, Nemglan. The dictionary of Irish mythology informed him that it was "the lord of birds and winged souls".

12.

And someone is growing towards me from afar, reaching their green-fingered branches towards me, for our friends grow weary of us and turn their shady tree tops aside, exposing us to the cosmic cold of lonely growth. Even the turning of one leaf is laden with significance, it can mean "yes" or "no", thought the writer, as he analysed his dream, in which the world was inhabited by animated trees that could move and went scurrying around some clusters of yahoo leading a plant-style life.

"An interesting dream. I don't particularly want to wake up," Swidersky thought, already waking up. It was five o'clock, the time when his Ethiopian neighbours rushed off to their legitimate or illegitimate work as dishwashers and waiters. This was a process accompanied by the cannon-like banging of any and all doors which could be banged.

Occasionally it was quiet in the afternoon and Swidersky would work, dotting chaotic notes across his countless notebooks. One day, sometime later, they should come together in a Single Whole. It was hard to work in the evenings, for whether you closed your door or not, the boom-bang was always there. His neighbours would leave their doors open, talk to each other across the corridor, pop in to see each other every five minutes. They loved music and listened to it turned up as loud as their own ear drum membranes would allow. And then there were Saturdays and Sundays, with prostitutes invited over the phone to the neighbouring rooms...

On days like that, Swidersky would go cycling along the bank of the Main River. Large barges conveyed themselves along it majestically while little cutters scudded about in all directions. The only thing missing were fishing boats, but the German fishermen fished from the banks. The cutters were all local but a whole range of flags fluttered on the barges — Dutch, Belgian, French, Austrian. He even glimpsed a Hungarian flag once. The writer saluted them all with his left hand, keeping his right hand on the handle bars. But there was no reply from the barges; they simply glided on their way, fully aware of their grandeur. Ships have motors but a bicycle has only two human legs and a tired, busily beating battered heart.

When he needed to rest he would pedal unhurriedly to his favourite bench. It was a simple wooden bench, not painted, and hid in the grass on the high river bank. The view from there was wonderful: the dam cutting the river in two and the Phillippsruhe – or "Philip's peace" — castle in the distance. The word "peace", in the context of his new life, sounded a bit ambiguous…

What does a person need? Peace and quiet. And that comes at a price which not many can afford, and so on and so forth. And so we live too close to people who are not close to us, and even study them as though they were representatives of some foreign tribe. It's worse for plants. They have to grow where they are planted. And gardeners are rare and rather careless.

When prose was writing itself, Swidersky was a plant. His tip had long since burst through the ceiling of his allotted cell and was waving thoughtfully in the cloudy — and occasionally heavenly — space. And the branches rustled their paper leaves no less thoughtfully.

Oddly enough, Swidersky didn't live in Germany; he lived within himself and his room. A person in a landscape of clouds, where the clouds originate from mental activity. Why shouldn't he live in a heavenly landscape? Is it any worse than an earthly landscape?

There were certain changes in the earthly landscape in which his corporeal self dwelt. In those days the writer led a German bicycle life. His shopping now let itself be caught easily, and his prey lay docile in the basket behind his saddle, and then it was just a case of turning the pedals! And once you've off-loaded the shopping at home, you can cycle further. You can even go to the next small town. Or along the road, or take the track through the forest, like this one where there's no-one around, nothing but prickly blackberry bushes on either side. Well, let's carry on. So he went further, and further, and then closer, and closer: there was a young woman with a little three-year-old just about toddling along beside her.

Swidersky yanked on the worn-out brakes, and came to a halt next to them. When the girl turned around she saw a broad face overgrown with ginger stubble, shaded by dark glasses and crowned with a baseball cap. Only the night before the girl had read an article in the local paper describing in great detail (it was a German newspaper!) all the rapes and murders which had taken place in that forest over the last twelve months. And so she came to the logical conclusion that something very unpleasant was about to befall her, and she steeled herself.

"Excuse me, can you tell me the way to Niederhausen?" enquired the face in dark glasses.

When she heard this half-German, the poor girl became quite distraught, for she remembered the statistics in the paper: fifty-five percent of all crimes in Germany are committed by foreigners. Asking the way is a ploy to distract me, she thought.

"Take the first turn on the right," she said sharply, wondering whether he would attack that very instant or a fraction later.

But the head in the baseball cap uttered something reminiscent of a "thank you" and gave a little bow, after which the suspicious-looking fellow disappeared off into the distance with a squeak of his bicycle wheels.

The girl couldn't believe her eyes. She caught her breath, then pulled the little boy out of the bushes he had toddled into. "So easy?" she thought. "Maybe he really was just lost?"

There was nobody to explain to the girl that the man was neither a bandit nor a rapist, but a Russian writer.

Russian writers are only a threat to those around them when they are in their own lair, not when they are out in the forest.

13.

All accommodation is temporary.

We borrow the weeks and months from eternity. We borrow time, although actually it would be far more logical to borrow space, as time is limited anyway. But we are concerned with time, and so we are crammed into cages where we become stooped, gradually losing our upright thoughts and bearing. Sometimes we squeeze into those cages voluntarily…

One night Swidersky dreamt he was a professor of zoology and had somehow and for some unknown reason been locked in a cage with apes. The apes tried to make him see reason: "What do you need a computer here for? You don't need a notebook, either, nor your burden of memories, nor even — perish the thought! – clothes. Learn to express your emotions with your hands, professor, and your thoughts with gestures. Become a traveller without luggage. And go on, bite someone — we can see that our naturalness irks you. After all, we have here all that you struggled for: the freedom of easy words, a variety of healthy sex and masses of free time. See how carefree our life is, but don't slip on a banana skin. We respect you, professor, we are proud of you. Every cage should have its professor. Even our planet is a lonely professor in a cage of wild constellations!"

The writer woke in a cold sweat.

14.

Telephone Halloo is fluffy and cuddly. Also transparent, and therefore invisible. It sneaks up on you, rather cautiously. Is there any point in asking yourself where it comes from? The main thing is that it's here.

"Are you still being published in Russia?" Professor Ostermann asked Swidersky over the phone.

The writer flapped his hand hopelessly.

"Who needs émigrés there…They only publish the ones who are safely buried. They published the living a few years back, too. It was fashionable. But now that's over."

"Do you divide people into the living and the dead?"

"No, but nature does."

"Are you sure?" asked the professor in a rather strange way. "I've seen a couple of chaps who aren't so easy to classify with certainty."

"Ghosts? Where did you see them?"

"In the graveyard," came the reply.

"Mm… On the ground or under it?"

"That's not so easy to say, either. I think your half-brother would have been very interested in one of them."

"Aha, atavism…. Had a tail, did he?"

"I don't know. But he was very hairy."

"He wasn't an ape, by any chance? My brother told me he'd seen an ape in a suit and tie in the forest near Moscow."

"This one was wearing a suit and tie, too. And an overcoat."

"I'd like to take a look at him."

"We can arrange it," said the professor. "I'm free on…. let's check the timetable… Thursday. Let's meet at Münsterstadt-West station at two pm. Can you make it?"

"Strange how they all arrange things a whole week in advance here," thought Swidersky. "No chance of that in Moscow — everyone would forget!"

The doctor gave him a medical note, and prescribed a medicine for arrhythmia. Swidersky was glad that he could just send away that note, instead of going to one of the places where you come for want of something but all they give you are words, and not the kind of words that may satisfy a want. You come there with a smile, but you leave with a stamp on your forehead. You arrive and stand on the threshold up to your full height, but you leave as your diminished copy…

"Shame the doctor can't cure me of anonymity. Give me a name. I've seen name shops where they sell names, weighing out the letters on scales. Critics plant names in flower beds and water them with the tears of the speechless. But where is my unconventional, un-lettered name? Secretive and silent? On which tablets is it written? On whose heart is it emblazoned? I want to buy my own name. I have paid for it with years of letter-less life…"

15.

We are all half-brothers and sisters, or if not, we are someone's descendants, and sometimes descendants of each other, or sometimes even descendants of someone famous. Stalin is a descendant of Ivan the Terrible, and Lenin a descendant of Maimonides; Churchill is a descendant of *Marlbrough s'en va-t-en guerre*, and de Valera a descendent of Valerius Maximus who collected maxims, i.e. anecdotes, and also of Emperor Valerian, who was captured by the Persians and furnished the Romans with fodder for those anecdotes.

It's important to find an ancestor as a role model.

We can all easily imagine what our ancestor must have been like, so all we have to do is compare available ones to our ideal.

A popular campaign: "choose yourself an ancestor" unfolded in the writer's dreaming intellect, and the sleeping Swidersky chose a sunflower face as his ancestor, prompted by a sunflower which was growing under his window on the second floor and kept asking to be let in. As for other characters in his dream, they selected trilobites, crocodiles and Neanderthals.

"Looks as though I have chosen more wisely than others," thought the writer — or rather, his dream manifestation: "you can even sow my ancestor. And then the future will grow and there will be a place in it for the past we have chosen… And that past will try to change us…"

If you squeeze a bar of plasticine you'll get a pliable clod; if you squeeze a man you'll only break his bones.

The environment tries to change us, tries even to interfere with our genetic code, though that is unbreakable. It is something akin to the Great Flood; that, too, was an attempt at re-creation. But however successful the environment may be at re-creating things, the re-creation of man can only produce chimeras. So, leaving behind its plans for a flood, the environment turns to musing about perfection, even though all goings-on at any given moment prove non-existence to be the apex of perfection...

Swidersky's German life, slow and gastronomical, dragged on. Pictures of numerous naked young girls appeared on one of his neighbours' door; he'd cut them out of a glossy magazine. They looked very similar, and were very small. And they were multiplying. It's crawling with them, thought the writer, like ants. Crawling humanity. A little stream with sticky fingers flowing over signet rings, trunks and bodies, occupying the empty forms of heroes, chieftains and lovers with their homogenous flow of flesh, creating the impression that space is populated with a perfected biological species which goes by the promising self-name "human".

The writer put a CD into the old CD player and let himself be carried away to another time and place by the Irish flautist Matt Molloy.

16.

The week completed its trip from the present into the past. On Thursday, having cycled dashingly down the slope to the Münsterstadt-West station, Swidersky fettered his bicycle in the steel stall.

Professor Ostermann was already pacing the platform.

"Let's pop into the tavern near the station for a coffee," he suggested.

The "Zum Laternchen"'s very yellow lantern — which never went out, even during the day — was already beckoning. The coffee was almost home-made, with milk, and the pastry horns they had with jam were almost like Russian ones. Swidersky didn't want to go anywhere.

"It's not far," said the professor.

"What are we looking for, by the way?"

"If only I knew… But there's something going on here, I can feel it. Intuition, you know…"

Just then Swidersky looked out of the window.

"Aha! Did you see that?" he said, suddenly livening up.

"No. What was it?"

"A man with keys. He had at least a thousand keys on his key ring."

They jumped up and ran out of the tavern.

They caught sight of a dark silhouette disappearing at the end of the street.

"There he is!"

They gave chase. The man with the keys seemed in no hurry, yet it wasn't easy to catch him up. It wasn't until they were at the graveyard gates that they gained on him.

He turned around. A pale bloodless face and watery eyes, and keys, lots of keys on the key ring hanging over his shoulder. When he saw they'd caught up with him, he slipped through the little gate into the graveyard.

They had to hang back for a few moments to let some people out, including a middle-aged couple with children, but at last Swidersky and the professor rushed into the graveyard. Three walkways spread out in different directions. The man with keys was already some way off, in the walkway on the left, and was just turning the corner, heading for the tombs, if the professor remembered correctly.

There was no longer anyone in the avenue by the time they reached the tombs. The door of one of the tombs was half open, creaking in the wind.

"He's in there," they said to each other, and went inside with some trepidation.

But there was no-one in the tomb. There had not been anyone inside for many years, maybe even many centuries. It was unlikely anyone had touched that headstone with its worn away dates and indecipherable names.

They went out into the fresh air. No-one. Only the wind, whining and clanging. But what was it clanging? They both looked up at the same time.

Ten metres away, a huge pine tree was bending its green leprechaun hat of needles towards them, and something was dangling from the topmost branch: a key ring with a thousand keys, swaying mockingly.

17.

As a result of a certain strange and even illegal exchange, a young writer had become old and venerable, and an old and venerable one had become young. The former had sufficient sense not to publish so much as one more line, and this did not result in so much as the slightest financial loss for him. The second, the venerable one, created several literary masterpieces in the secrecy of oblivion, in the hopes that he would be able to publish them in his old age.

Both writers were satisfied. The only dissatisfied ones were those who hoped to reap some harvest from these literary fields. Shall we plough the soil yet again? These people pondered, but then decided fencing the fields would suffice.

This newly-written mini-essay of Swidersky's heralded a rather unexpected excursion into local literary circles.

Professor Ostermann called him that evening.

"How do you fancy coming along to our 'Literaturhaus' here in

Frankfurt? It's not far from your place; you can take the local train. You haven't been yet, I take it? There's going to be a conference on 'The globalization of literature in modern Europe'."

The "Literaturhaus" was in an old-fashioned mansion not far from Frankfurt University. The back yard was fenced off from the street by ivy-clad walls, and the literary cafe felt very snug there. Professor Ostermann had a keen interest in literature and told Swidersky, in a whisper, about contemporary German writers and their novels.

"Are there any poets in the land of Goethe and Schiller?" the writer enquired.

"Well, there are some poets, too, but poetry is not prestigious here now. Literary criticism, however, is quite another matter. Everyone here knows the critic Reich-Ranicki, for instance. By the way, there's a Russian critic here tonight, a lady. She's going to speak soon."

According to the press release, the Russian critic-ess lived in England and taught Russian language and literature at a university. Her paper was entitled: "Brodsky and the globalization of poetry." Swidersky liked the concept of it.

"Do you want to go and talk to her?" Ostermann whispered during a break between papers. "She's talking to a German critic I know."

And so they went over. The German critic introduced his colleague to the professor, and he in turn introduced Swidersky.

"I'm from St. Petersburg," said the criticess. "Where are you from?"

"Well, I'm a local now. I live in Germany."

The four of them went out into the courtyard and took a seat under an enormous linden at one of the tables in the literary cafe. The foursome immediately split into pairs. The German critic spoke to the professor in German, while Swidersky spoke to the criticess in Russian.

"So you're a writer?" the criticess probed. "What's your surname?"

Swidersky told her.

"Mmm. I've heard something about you. Whose court are you in?"

"What do you mean?" said Swidersky, somewhat taken aback.

"Well, you know how it is. There are famous writers and there are retinues. In other words, which of the greats are you friends with?"

"I am friendly with many, and I seek friendship with neither great nor small. I don't think success is the right criterion to choose my friends by. As for retinue, I'm not a part of anyone's retinue, nor do I have any intention of joining one."

"Then you will have to be a self-sufficient person," said the criticess with a self-sufficient smile. "Forgive me for asking, but how many languages have your books been published in?"

"My short stories have been translated into several languages and published in various journals. My books have only come out in Russian. But I don't suffer from an inferiority complex."

"So how did you get on with the criticess?" Ostermann wanted to know as they were going up the steps to the conference hall.

"Not very well, I fear," said Swidersky morosely. "She's a very snobby lady."

"You should have seen the other Russian criticess who was here last year. She kept harping on about the need to distinguish between Jews and Yids. According to her, Yids are Jews who are successful in life at the expense of the natives of the country they live in. Even our Nazis would have seen her as a lady with radical views."

"I bet she's a member of our nationalist Writers' Union."

"No, my friend, you are wrong, she is in the same union as you are, the one you hold to be democratic. I was introduced to her by the Chief of Staff of the Russian President in Moscow."

"Nothing surprises me anymore," commented Swidersky darkly.

18.

*The Sun and the Moon played a game, and the score
was even, because the weather was fine and the number
of cloudless sunrises was equal to the number of majestic
moons that got sunk in night's dark waters.*

One morning Swidersky got a letter inviting him to a literary festival in Ireland. It was written on pretty greenish paper with a Celtic harp. The festival was to take place in two month's time.

A silvery green Irish víosa, i.e. an entry visa for Ireland, appeared in his passport a fortnight later. That evening the West glowed with the ghostly gold of Celtic kings while darkness spread menacingly in the East. But it was not frightening. And things no longer seemed hopeless.

Maybe things would be better for me in Ireland, he thought. After all, where am I now, how did I end up here, and, most importantly, what am I doing here? If you start moving in a certain direction, you always end up somewhere you didn't want to be at first because you haven't arrived yet, and then afterwards you may already be in the wrong place. The main thing is to know when to stop, to find the point between "not yet" and "already". If only I knew where that point is, and precisely when I should stop…

The grass is greener on the other side, and love is stronger than justice, but what's a man supposed to do if he can't get either?

But what should he do next? Should he come back from Ireland, fight the "amts" and dive into the depths of language-lessness and unemployability?

"Do not return, of course not," Swidersky's new acquaintance said to him. He was an old professor from St. Petersburg, a former medic who had recently come to live in the same small German town. "Here the "amts" are a little greater than the Tsar, a little lower than God. On the same level as the Pope, let's say. And as we all know, it's a bad thing to live in Rome and quarrel with the Pope. Is there anywhere you could go?"

"I'm not sure. Why?"

"Think about it. I don't expect you would go back to Russia; one doesn't return to Russia after Europe. But maybe you have relatives somewhere in Germany?"

"No."

"No relatives at all, anywhere?"

"I might have some in Ireland. But I don't know anything about them."

"Well, we Jews did go a long way!"

"They're not Jews, they're Irish."

The old man gave the writer a very particular look, then said: "Are you joking?"

"No."

"Aren't you Jewish?"

"No, funnily enough, I'm not. I'm an atheist. Or an agnostic, if you prefer."

"But were your forefathers believers?"

"My forefathers were a mixed bunch, both Jews and Catholics. But I get by very nicely without any religion."

"Ah, Catholics! Those who jealously guard the purity of our race would not like that at all. I don't know whether you would be accepted into our community or not."

"Well, I'm not exactly pushing to be accepted."

"And that's where you're making a mistake, my friend. You're missing a real show!" said the old man, parting his yellowy skin with a little laugh. "You'd do better to come and watch how they wage war in our synagogue."

"In the synagogue?"

"Yes! They have a religious tax here in Germany, and you have to pay it whether you're a believer or not, and then the Germans channel the money into the different confessions. The Catholics and Protestants get most, but the Jews get some, too, and they divide it up. Not long ago there was an election for the synagogue authorities, and a Moldavian Jew got into a fight with a Ukrainian one. They ripped each other's shirts. The two old scrappers had to be forcefully thrown out. You should have gone to watch."

"I'm not so interested."

"Well, go watch some Irish fighting then… Is Ireland part of Britain?"

"Not any more, thank God."

"It's somewhere up near the Polar Circle, isn't it? Surely it's too cold up there!"

"No, that's Iceland, not Ireland. It's quite mild in Ireland. It hardly ever snows."

"Well, off you go, then. And don't come back."

"But who will let me stay there? I hold a Russian passport and they don't issue visas for longer than three months," said the writer, thinking out loud as he sipped his German fruit tea and nibbled a biscuit which was actively crumbling itself onto his knees.

"Go for three months and try to get yourself an Irish passport. Get your relatives to help you."

"I don't even know where they live or whether they're still alive. They might have all emigrated to America, for all I know."

"Well, marry someone then."

"Who, for heaven's sake?!"

"Find someone, maybe on the Internet. Then you go over and meet her. Who knows, you may even find the love of your life!"

"Hmm, love," said Swidersky and brushed the crumbs away.

"By the way, did I tell you how one of my colleagues went for a date in a park in St. Petersburg? It was winter, there was snow everywhere, and the two of them got talking. Suddenly his denture fell out, and the two of them spent a whole hour looking for it in the snow."

"And how did it all end?"

"I don't know. But that's not the point. What I'm saying is, you should apply for citizenship or if the worst comes to the worst, get married. But in any case, make sure you take all you need to hold on for six months. Then you can come back for the rest once you've established yourself over there."

"You're so sure I'll be granted Irish citizenship but it's practically impossible…"

"You will be if you really want it."

"It would be a miracle… But I can't hope for miracles."

He dreamt of cosmonauts living on the moon. They were looking down on the earth, stroking the handle of the telescope. They were far from home and from their loved ones now. There was no-one to advise them; the morning papers weren't delivered, they didn't know who had won the most important football match or who had been elected to reign over souls. They could make a bit of music, play a harmonica, or train in the slow jump, or write letters and store them up in cardboard boxes.

19.

Foreigners and criminals pay double for everything, so that they can rise above hate-ridden commonness. The former count out meticulously their red blood cells whereas the latter carelessly throw on the counter years and years cut out of other people's lives. In their absence, a written tick flies into their houses and, its ink-wings flapping, aims at the white purity of their doors.

Once in a while the statue of the State requests their attendance for a talk, and says to each of them, flexing her bronze muscles, "I can play every dirty trick in the book on you. You can't possibly imagine the things I am capable of doing to you, however I do nothing of the sort. Aren't you fond of me? I mean, really…"

So this is the end of a German cycle track. You pedal and pedal along the track, everything is fine, the tarmac is smooth, and then suddenly there you have it, a sign:

"ENDE".

And there is nowhere to go, and nobody to be seen, just nettles to one side and cars whizzing by terrifyingly on the other.

"This is the first time in my life I have bought a one way plane ticket," the writer thought. "There's something irrevocable about it, or maybe inescapable?"

Professor Ostermann kindly agreed to take his other bags and keep them in his cellar for a while. The writer packed his books carefully, with layers of cardboard and polythene so they would not get damp. He would come back for them!

O ye who seek in life what can only be found in books,
is your happiness greater than that of those who seek
in books what life has in abundance?

"O madmen who live amongst us, how do you see the world?" thought Swidersky. "Do you see its contrasts as monotony, its complexity as simplicity, its harmony as distortion, and its beauty as squalor? Is it easier for you since your world is different, unreal? And is it real, this world which we seek to comprehend with our imperfect reasoning?"

"God preserve me from madness, for I think I am sane, even if that is not actually the case. How can I be the judge of that?"

"In this instant of madness, who would say I am sane, as I pack my whole life into one suitcase, albeit a large one? Where am I taking these things? Where am I taking myself? Who would recognise me in that double refugee? A person seeking refuge in Germany and a person seeking refuge from Germany, and both of them united in one face. My face. A face I do not want to see in the mirror."

"Customs officers judge a person by their luggage. What would they say about me, a man with a huge suitcase stuffed with Russian books and German CDs of classical music? And with a sports bag full of manuscripts: a novel stranded midstream, poems, short stories, my aunt's unpublished book about John Field which I've edited and prepared for print, though who knows who would ever print it… Has my whole life really fitted inside that suitcase and that bag? He remembered a banshee's words to Ireland's legendary king Conaire Mór. "No matter where you go, you will always remain within your own skin. And if you go anywhere, you will be able to take with you nothing more than a bird can carry in its claw."

And there it is again, not for the first year, that strange sensation of being a grain of sand in the sea or a drop of water in the desert. That grain has no desert, nor is there any ocean that drop could call its own.

20.

> *The goddess of everyday has left the town; her castle*
> *is occupied by the echo of emptiness. Mandalas grow*
> *dim, the ziggurat is turned upside down. Minutes*
> *melt inside the clocks, ooze down to the ground.*
> *Days borrow themselves from the future…*

Ostermann rolled up in his Opel right on time, and the five suitcases just fitted into the boot and the back seat.

"I'll just lock the car and we can nip into the Bavarian Court."

The Bavarian Court was an inn where they served Bavarian food. Even the tablecloths were blue and white checked in keeping with the national colours. A lazy waft swung in the air, and a strange calm reigned, with none of the not-so-unusual local beer putsches.

"How do you feel now in the days leading up to your departure?" the professor asked.

"That's a good question. Like Lenin crossing the ice of the Gulf of Finland."

"Did he really cross over on the ice?" The professor was curious.

"I don't know. Lenin is a legendary figure in Russia, you see. Few people know what he really did or said."

"Have you seen his mummy in the mausoleum?"

"Of course not. I'm not a fan of such spectacles. Why can't they put him in a closed tomb?"

"Talking of tombs, how do you fancy a farewell visit to the Münsterstadt graveyard? There's always something interesting, or even odd, going on there, if you remember."

"Why not?"

21.

We invent ourselves and, once we are done, send the newly
invented personality travelling along a tarmac road
or through the countryside, or even across a page of a book,
and the Sun of the dreamers shines as brightly as it can.
Sometimes we supply that invented personality
with a map, sometimes we don't.

The shadows were talking in the forest. Green and blue, transparent and opaque, like diluted milk. There were no words, only movements. The light burned green as they strolled along — the sun on grass. Don't be late. Don't miss the moment when the little red lamps are switched on. For that is the entry signal, said the passing wind. But no-one cared to listen, much less understand.

The wind ruffled the grass indignantly. Far away the town rustled people; the paper life went on. The various "amts" rustled human fates, but the shadows were indifferent to all that. The forest peeped over the graveyard fence, but didn't find anything alien there, so it quietly withdrew. Sometimes the forest paid a short visit to the sleek little gardens, and vengefully snapped a few branches. It churned up the soil with fat, snake-like roots, sowed weeds and hogweed, egged on the birds to defecate on the wicker pergolas, red plaster gnomes, and sometimes on the pale but live garden lovers, if they were unlucky enough to stand under the path of a shit-firing apparatus. The height of perfection for the birds was a direct hit on the shining bald head of some nasty old man with a dubious Nazi past — or sometimes with a doubtless Nazi past. To the birds their freedom, to the people their care. And so they buy excess washing up liquid and shampoo for bald spots. Industry is working, money goes around, everyone is happy and as a sign that they are firmly cementing the living foundations of the state with themselves, they buy more and more plaster monsters for their gardens, and that means that new targets open up for the birds' bombing raids. The circle closes right there in the heart of the Japanese flag, just as if somewhere in the heavens someone gives a round smile, also Japanese, although everything all around is unmistakeably square.

The sun smiled, too, brightly and just as roundly. On the edge of the wood a certain hairy-faced chap straightened his red tie. He was quite serious, as today he had a responsible, almost diplomatic, mission.

Swidersky and the professor drove up to the car park we are already familiar with.

"Aha! Torsten Bulka is still here!" said Ostermann with a little laugh, and told the writer about his adventures with the girl.

"Surely she didn't turn into a stone statue?" Swidersky asked, rather perplexed. "A kind of miracle. I'd like to have a look at that statue."

"That's exactly where we're going."

The wind over the graveyard was red with sunlight. It rustled playfully. There was hardly anyone there. The setting sun painted the leaves red and coloured the gravestones with a raspberry hue. The writer and the professor turned down the avenue with the tombs — and the very next second the professor froze on the spot. Swidersky sensed something uncanny. He looked ahead and saw a female figure dressed in a white tunic at the entrance to the already-familiar tomb. A question was about to burst from his lips when he glanced back at the professor and realised that there was no need to ask: it was her, Magda.

At this distance the figure looked completely lifelike, although it was motionless. But suddenly it raised its hand and made a welcoming gesture, bowing its head simultaneously.

They understood: they were being invited inside. They exchanged glances, and then, without a word, they both took a step forwards. The girl moved aside, letting them into the tomb. Or was it a tomb? A neon light was burning, the walls were hidden behind lemon-yellow silk drapes, and a long corridor stretched out ahead. But where did it lead? Someone was coming towards them along the passageway, someone dressed in a very civilised manner, in a black suit and red tie.

"Allow me to introduce myself. I am Sylvan," he said, showing them a smile the likes of which might have been seen on the faces of salesmen in Old Russian firms. It was a face which caught their attention, for in fact there was very little face at all: it was all covered in black hair.

"I hope you will excuse me for speaking Russian," said the man, addressing them both. "You do both understand Russian, don't you? I can speak in any European language, so if you prefer, say, German or English or French, I shall be only too happy to oblige."

"Russian is fine," said the professor rather automatically; he had not quite come to his senses. "Forgive my asking, but where are we? Are we in the tale of "A thousand and one nights"? And who are you?"

"I am the master of ceremonies. My name is Sylvan, although actually that is not a personal name. There are many of us sylvans, and you may meet others while you are walking in the parks or maybe in town. But first we must make the most of this chance to enter a place where no living human has yet set foot. You have been to the gateway several times, and your persistence was noted with approval, and has now been rewarded. Follow me."

Swidersky was about to say something, but the professor quietly pushed him ahead and they walked along the corridor which was filled with a pale light. The corridor seemed endless. The same silk drapes and neon lamps were everywhere.

"It's like a hospital," Ostermann whispered to the writer.

He nodded. It was only now that they realised Magda was following them, floating along without moving her feet.

The light grew brighter, then unbearably bright. And everything drowned in blinding whiteness. They stopped, not knowing whether they should go further, not even knowing whether there was a "further".

"Welcome to the other world," said a disembodied voice which they both found vaguely familiar.

PART THREE

I.

They were standing on the square of an unfamiliar town. The rectangular façades of the houses leaned off in different directions forming strange rhombuses. The lines which should have been straight wobbled, as though warping with warmth.

It was a fluid world. Matter and the criteria of existence were in suspension.

The air was transparently lilac, the sunshine was green, and there were even two suns, at opposite sides of the sky, although, of course, it was unlikely to really be the sky.

"Yes, we installed lighting here," said a voice. "Otherwise everything was rather on the underground side."

There was no birdsong, not a breath of wind. Only silence, and the voice.

"There is no wind underground," the commentator went on.

Basalt was under their feet. It was polished and shone with a blackish gleam. The green suns were reflected in this mirror of blackness so it seemed as though countless green eyes were watching whoever stood on the square.

The motionless silhouettes of the two visitors still stood out darkly in the very centre of the square. They were trying to understand where the voice was coming from, to catch a glimpse of the speaker, but their eyes, dazzled by the white glare, were unable to register anything at first.

"Allow me to introduce myself. Alfonce Afonsky, academician," said a silhouette, and the visitors' eyes, gradually floating out of the inextinguishable silvery-white and fiery-orange circles, saw a face which school children knew from the front of their biology textbooks and art lovers beheld in Nesterov's copy of his own *Eureka* painting in Moscow's Tretyakov gallery.

"Pleased to meet you," said Swidersky, in Russian, for that was the language he had been addressed in, and in which he felt duty-bound to answer, since he was a native speaker.

Academician Afonsky was not out and about naked this time, as he was on the portrait *Eureka*, but was dressed in a very smart swallow-tailed coat dating from the brief period of Soviet academic renaissance. Nor was Afonsky sticking his tongue out and his hands were not pressed to the sides of his head making them look like elephant's ears, although the mischievous expression on the academician's face was just as ascetic yet Tolstoyishly carnal. His facial features had undergone certain changes, a lush grey beard covered his cheeks and grey hair framed his face on all sides forming a kind of halo around this famous face. The academician's head was huge, round and somehow very sun-like.

"Sylvans! Fall in!" came the command, and the square was filled with a parade of people in double-breasted jackets and red ties, their faces grown over with bushy stubble. "Greet our guests!"

There was a short outburst of something like: Hurrah hurrah hurrah hurrah Khrushch! which was usually heard at Soviet military parades at the beginning of the sixties. The words may have been different — they most probably were — but the sound hadn't changed even though Khrushchev was no longer at the helm.

Suddenly there was some kind of commotion and the lines of sylvans unexpectedly broke formation. Right between the academician and the sylvans standing to attention, some sort of very monkey-ish creature was scuttling about on the square. It was pulling faces and made a little pirouette without slackening its pace.

"Another illegal penetration!" said the academic looking rather offended, and then yelled: "What are you standing around like statues for, sylvans?! Catch it!"

The sylvans scattered and rushed after the monkey, which is exactly what it had been waiting for. With a satanic guffaw it began racing around the square, darted up behind the sylvans and tweaked their coattails, then when they turned around, it ripped off their ties. At last it bounded up onto the roof of the nearest building, tied the ties into a rope and knotted one end of it to the chimney before jumping off the roof and swinging on the rope as if it was a liana, shouting:

"First of May, first of May, monkeys getting their own way!"

Leaping onto another building, it shot off at top speed with the sylvans in hot pursuit as they bustled noisily on the basalt.

"Please excuse this spectacle," said the academician sorrowfully. "Another infiltration from the closed territories. How do they do it? We erected plexiglass barriers everywhere. It was such an effort…"

The visitors shrugged sympathetically and synchronously.

"Please excuse us. We are unaccustomed to visits from corporeal people," the academician went on. "I expect you need to rest. We never rest here. We don't need to, you see. We don't even need to eat. We are more like bodily casings than living beings. So we don't have any bedrooms here, nor even any chairs… by the way, do you fancy dressing up in a casing? Temporarily, of course."

"How does it work?" asked Swidersky suspiciously, his wary self-control waking up. "Does it mean separating from our body?"

"Something like that."

"I can't speak for my colleague, of course, but I'm not sure," said the professor.

"Well, it's nothing to be afraid of. Maybe you'll change your mind later. For now we'll prepare somewhere for you to stay. Do you have many things with you?"

"No. Actually, our arrival here was quite impromptu."

"Well, it's nothing to be afraid of. I hope you'll like it here," said the academician hospitably, waving at the wide basalt horizon. "Our underground settlement is a triumph of science. Can you imagine — freedom of thought, freedom from a cumbersome corporeal hull, the chance to live forever, and even to visit the world of the living and nourish yourself on new information and ideas."

"And how about normal food?" Swidersky enquired, "We'll make you comfortable and feed you. We have water here, from underground rivers. We have all kinds of roots, too, including potatoes. And we sometimes get regular food, too, when we have visitors. Today for instance we can offer you butter."

"Potatoes with butter! How Russian!" smiled Ostermann. "Underground potatoes, now that's really something! Where else should you eat potatoes, if not underground?!"

2.

Sofas with dozens of soft cushions appeared from somewhere, along with little empire-style tables, elephants on mantelpieces, tulle curtains, rubber plants and asparagus trees.

You can always find something, even underground!

There was an old gas cooker in the kitchen, a box of matches, soft poufs with round cushions, and a Bukhara carpet with red laurel branches framing a very Asian-looking face of Lenin. And all this swirled in front of them in a circle dance of some unfathomable future or some unforgettable past.

"Seems we've landed up in the fifties," smiled Swidersky.

"I can still remember that communal-communist comfort. Maybe they live beyond time, here?" Ostermann suggested.

"But they can go up onto the surface; they should know what's going on in the world!"

The door opened and the sun-like head of their academician-cum-host peered in.

"This is our local hotel for honoured guests," he said. "Yes, yes, we do occasionally receive visitors. I hope you like the decor."

"Oh yes," Ostermann replied politely.

"You have a view over the square. One of the sylvans is always on duty there, so if you need anything, just ask him."

"Yes, there is a wonderful view of the square," said the writer, taking a look out of the window. "Ah, someone's there. A girl with a skipping rope, running across the square."

"That girl is honourable professor Zbigniew Wojciechowski, a gerontologist," said the academician glancing out of the window. "Yes, yes, don't be surprised. The local inhabitants can choose in which guise they appear to others. Oh, I forgot to say, dinner will be served at seven thirty. You have watches, don't you?"

"Yes, we do. And surprisingly, they are still working. But what sort of time are they showing?"

"Quite an underground one!" laughed the academician. "Each of the local inhabitants can choose the time he wants to exist in. But that doesn't apply to our guests, of course."

"There's even a fireplace with a chimney here. Has someone ever lit a fire in it?" queried Ostermann.

"I don't think so," replied the academician. "Chimneys fulfil a very important function here, but not the one you'd expect. They connect our settlements to each other and some of them open up into the outer world. So in fact they are communication conduits."

"And where do they lead to?"

"Oh, different countries — Germany, Russia, other European states. Listen, the wind of geographical freedom whistles in this fireplace!"

3.

And wind really was whistling in the fireplace. Not some allegorical wind but a very real one. It carried dust and sand into the sitting room, so they had to block it with a reproduction of a still-life of the Dutch school: flowers, a decanter of water, pheasant feathers and glasses left on a table — and that's all; the painter's fantasy had not spread particularly far. The reproduction was framed and that is why it made an ideal screen.

"What are we going to do while we wait for lunch?" Swidersky asked.

"To tell you the truth, I was intending to eat at home," said the professor pensively. "It's really odd how we ended up here. I would have at least liked to have warned my wife that I was out visiting so she wouldn't be worried. I wonder whether we can call home from here."

"I doubt it… What do you make of this place?"

"Well, it's interesting, certainly. I never would have suspected there could be something like this underground. A Russian underground under a German town, and these half-incarnated souls… Maybe we are in paradise?"

"Or in purgatory?"

"I always dreamed of something like this, you know. To be freed of the need to feed yourself, to satisfy your physiological needs, etc. Just imagine how much time they have for mental exercises! Not to mention the fact that souls are deathless. No, this is a real miracle. This is the embodiment of humanity's primeval dream!"

"Well, we'll see how they realise this dream here," smirked the incurable sceptic Swidersky.

"I wonder whether we can meet people from the past here. I would have liked to have a chat with Goethe, let's say, or Leo Tolstoy."

"I doubt such transformations were possible in their day."

"Yes, I'm afraid their souls dwell in some unreachable dimensions…" sighed the professor.

"Look here! They even keep a book on the mantelpiece!"

It turned out to be not a book but a brochure printed on

a rotaprint and hand-bound. It looked like an abstract of a dissertation. Swidersky opened it and began to read:

> *Although the town of Andriania has only a short history*
> *of but several decades, this brief period has witnessed*
> *a great number of events....*

"This is all about the underground settlement we've landed in," the writer informed Ostermann.

"What language is it written in?"

"In Russian, funnily enough."

"Why don't you read it all and then tell me later, and I'll make some tea meanwhile. Would you like some tea?"

Swidersky nodded. He drank tea always and everywhere, several times a day. He drank tea when his work was going well, and when he was sitting gazing dully into an unfinished page. He would always add milk to his tea in the Irish fashion, as was customary in his family, but to the surprise of the Russians, who might at a pinch put milk in coffee, but for whom tea was inviolable, the sacred aroma of mysterious countries — India and Georgia — which sent their unofficial and not plenipotentiary representatives into Russia, on the basis of which one cannot make any kind of judgement about these mysterious, perfumed lands.

4.

As it turned out, the underground town was named after a legendary hairy person called Andrian Yevtikheyev. This natural phenomenon doubtlessly originated in Russia. Legends tell that he was born in the Siberian taiga, lived among wolves and fed on wild berries and hunted small animals, skills which he learnt from his carnivorous neighbours. In reality, he was born into the family of a village smith named Feodor and was christened by the local priest. Rumour had it that Feodor was Greek and his surname didn't contradict this. People more highly educated than his neighbours may remember the sculptor Eutychides, a disciple of the famous Lysippos. They may recall the famous statue of Tyche of Antioch which is supposed to represent the fate of the mountains.

Young Yevtikheyev, who of course knew nothing of these etymological subtleties, used to help his father in the smithy. After the death of his parents he was sent to help in Ekaterinoslav university morgue in St. Andrew's hospital. And so he began living there. News of this unusual freak spread through the town, and a local circus became interested in him. He was put on show for money, and soon became so famous that there was not a circus in Europe he didn't perform in. He was known as Zhu-Zhu, and was also called the Human Dog.

Once when the circus was on tour in Warsaw, a scientist — who strangely enough bore the same surname — became interested in the hairy man. He was Vissarion Yefimovich Yevtikheyev and was born in 1846. He graduated from the Kazan veterinarian institute and taught in Kazan, after which he became a professor in Warsaw, and it was he who wrote about this strange phenomenon of nature in his book "A Therapeutic Companion".

According to his description, the hairy man was reminiscent of a Skye terrier: silky, yellowy hair completely covered his face, and grew in particularly dense tufts on either side of his nose.

The professor was also studying another subject: a no less famous rival of Zhu-Zhu who went by the name of Lionel, or Lion Man. This one was born in Poland and his real name was Stefan Bibrovsky, or according to other sources, Stepan Bobrovsky. Like Yevtikheyev, he was shown in circuses all over Europe. Lion Man and the Human Dog never met but heard a lot about each other.

While he was studying the hairy man Yevtikheyev, the professor Yevtikheyev preserved a frozen sample of his blood. Many years later, the old veterinarian received an unexpected visit from a young professor-medic from St. Petersburg who was called Alfonce Alexandrovich Afonsky. He was descended from an impoverished noble family which had given Russia several generations of cavalier guards. "Triple A", as he was known in the faculty, set out to get himself a brilliant academic career, and indeed, he succeeded. His success was helped along by the fact that his uncle, General Felix Afonsky, held a very responsible position on the general staff and, rumour had it, was a favourite candidate for the post of war minister, especially after the madcap military escapades during the Japanese war, in which he, luckily, was not involved.

Professor Afonsky was one of Russia's first gerontologists. He was studying the process of aging on a cellular level, and as a by-product of his work, he improved the construction of the microscope, for which he received a healthy sum of money before the First World War from a German firm, Karl Zeiss, who made use of his invention. Having heard about the veterinary professor's work with the famous Zhu-Zhu's blood serum, Afonsky sensed there may be something interesting lurking there. He went to Warsaw and convinced the old veterinary to give him the frozen samples. He didn't take them anywhere because the proteins in the serum would have been destroyed in transit. Instead, he began analysing the blood serum right there and then, in the department of pathology.

It turned out that the hairy man's blood was no different from the blood of ordinary people. However, the future academician made a mistake one day when he was mixing the blood serum with various other reagents and mixed two reagents together before adding the serum. The result was unexpected, and more than strange: the blood became invisible.

Afonsky thought long and hard about what this could mean, about which dimension or space invisible objects exist in, and whether everything is visible in completely material human specimens — after all, thoughts are invisible, but maybe not only thoughts? Of course, food can sometimes be invisible, or your salary, but all these things are normal and material. Invisible blood – now that is nothing short of a step into a world where only our apparition remains, but our thoughts, in a quite materialised and visible manner, travel from one convoluted brain wave to another. And where does this world begin? Behind which mountain range or which convolutions of humanity?

5.

A group portrait is where several people are depicted on one canvas. However, you can use the same term — group portrait — to describe something quite different: the portrait of one person as he or she is seen by others.

Such a portrait becomes a mosaic made up of variegated little pictures. And the more the others know about the person depicted in the portrait, the more long-winded and expansive the mosaic becomes. Afonsky, for instance, was known by many, and a great many more thought they knew him.

He not only didn't publish his discovery, he didn't even tell anyone about it. In the quiet of his St. Petersburg lab, he continued his experiments. After the revolution and civil war, the new administration put an even larger laboratory at his disposal. His official goal was the prevention of cellular decay, and everybody knew about this part of his work. His advances in describing how collagen levels decrease in the cells of aging organisms brought him well-earned recognition in academic circles. His portrait was painted by the famous Nesterov. However, nobody knew about his secret experiments with the combination of reagents he had chanced upon in Warsaw.

He was trying out ever new combinations of chemicals on the basis of what became known as his "Solution Number One". There were already Solution Number Three and Solution

Number Six. The academician had a state of the art vivarium at his disposal and he tried ever new combinations of reagents on the monkeys. Solution Number 18 finally gave the result he had been searching for: it removed the lab being's body, which became lifeless, and left them their consciousness, shadow and voice. The shadow took on a real existence, as a kind of transparent bluish casing. Empty, it could be folded several times like an inflatable mattress. But when it was filled with invisible, shadowy human content, it could be seen in all sorts of different forms and appearances depending on the will of its owner.

Invisible monkeys appeared in the vivarium. Some of them escaped from the cages and went wandering around the park, climbing trees and stealing food from the nearby grocery stores. Mysterious sounds could be heard in the park at night, and people began to be afraid to walk there. A rumour spread that the park was haunted, that it was home to the souls of animals killed in the name of science. The townsfolk would make the sign of the cross as they passed the park gates.

At the end of the thirties, the NKVD turned their attention to Afonsky, a son of the gentry. They left him be for the time being, mindful of his European or even world fame. People's Commissars and members of the Communist Party Central Committee all drank "the cocktail of long life" concocted by Afonsky, and this was supposed to slow down aging and degradation, especially the degradation of brain cells. Socialist plebs, who were aging no worse than the party bosses, had no information about this cocktail, let alone access to it, and so were successfully aging and degrading.

In 1940, when the Chekists no longer cared about disintegrating Europe or public opinion and were happily snatching anyone who came their way — or more correctly, those who they themselves wanted to snatch — late one evening they came to arrest Afonsky. The academician had foreseen that something similar would happen, right from the moment when he had been shown a defamatory article about himself in the newspaper Pravda. The article was called "Atavist, or the Pull of the Past." From that day on, the academician never went anywhere without a test tube of Solution Number 18. So now, hearing the thud of boots in the corridor, he downed its contents. Those entering the room got nothing more than the academician's cooling body, and that day became the official day of his death. Pravda — which always preferred the country's great people dead rather than alive — ran a huge article about the death of a the great socialist academician and this in turn was faithfully reprinted or retold by all other soviet newspapers.

The academician's shadow — which was not quite a shadow, though we shall call it such for the sake of simplicity — found itself in the loneliness of a vast emptiness populated only by monkey shadows. He refused to share their ease and inactivity in the haunted park and decided instead to get to work. He set himself a difficult goal: to build a new world, brick by brick. The world of shadows.

6.

*You cannot build a world alone. You can build a limited
little world in which you are like a walrus in an ice-hole —
everything is fine, but it's cramped.*

Afonsky didn't feel cramped in space — he could fly wherever he liked, he could take on any appearance he wanted to. He couldn't deny himself the pleasure of flying to his own funeral. The Secretary of the Party Committee delivered a speech which grated on his teeth like a portion of superb quality cardboard on a dinner plate. Afonsky's lab assistants, on the other hand, were genuinely saddened, as were many research fellows. "Good enough," thought Afonsky. "You have to be a really good man for your subordinates to love you." Having found a lab coat from somewhere, he altered his appearance somewhat and joined the throng. Thus disguised, he made an emotional speech about the difficulties the deceased had encountered in the course of his life.

In the coming weeks, he managed to save several scientists who had been arrested and doomed to perish. They drank Solution Number 18 and joined the shadowy academician, forming a certain cohort of the chosen. First of all they set up a laboratory in the cellar of a former stately home which the authorities hadn't bothered to restore and didn't want to demolish. No-one knew that work was boiling away in the cellar of the seemingly uninhabited building. The goal was to produce a certain quantity of Solution Number 18 to be used at any moment.

In the coming years, the number of shadows increased. The academician felt like Noah, the helmsman of an ark drifting towards a new life. Afonsky was the unofficial head of this strange community. He was also the one to select his future companions. These were scientists for the most part, but musicians, actors, writers and engineers were also accepted. The task was to select inspired people, whatever that term might mean. From this it is clear that the academician had tastes which might seem somewhat snobbish to some. Be that as it may, he kept the proletariat at arm's length.

Years of dwelling in the cellar gave the academician an idea, and he announced that the time had come for this small colony of shadows to find its own place. He heard about karst caves somewhere near Uglich and so the colony moved there. This was their first experience of an underground life completely independent from the outside world. The bodiless beings passed their time with philosophical and scientific discussions, listened to music and read books. At times, they visited the outside world as invisible observers or masquerading figures. Their thoughts were shadows of shadows, and as shadows — the incarnation of primordial creative thoughts — they were invisible or brightly dressed. Their transparent eyes reflected the outer world with its multi-storey buildings, its cars and trains, but this world had no power over them. It didn't even have any influence over them; it was merely one of the reflections of reality in their thoughts, and it must be said that this reflection was quite immaterial, akin to historical memory or a weather forecast.

After some time, the underground colony spread beyond Russia's borders. Caves were found in Poland and successfully colonised. The next stage was the colonisation of caves in eastern Germany. The cave under Münsterstadt in Hessen was the latest discovery and the colony's administration, including academician Afonsky, transferred there. They had their sights on caves in the Alps; the colony needed new spaces in order to house newly-arriving shadows. The world of shadows became the real world, the communicating vessels of the caves now serving as a home for tens of thousands of bodiless inhabitants. Today, there is another reality, a secret reality which exists alongside the manifest, surface reality. No, the co-existence of two realities is not something new, but the bifurcation of a once united world and the dualism of the temporal and the beyond-temporal consciousness is something which has only become apparent in modern times, causing a quite understandable mental crisis in those who meet this phenomenon for the first time.

7.

"Interesting," said Ostermann finishing his quite earthly tea when the writer had finished his short synopsis of the brochure. "I wouldn't be surprised if I saw Andrian Yevtikheyev's book on sale one day: "The real story behind the hairy man"."

"Even if it has never been written," Swidersky chimed in, and they both laughed.

"They could have built paradise here, but they've built a state on the matrix of earthly ones, with administrative departments," the professor went on. "And they are colonising new areas and even constructing houses underground! Even though they don't need houses."

"You don't understand. Houses have deep symbolic significance. Take the House of Culture for example. Somehow culture never took up residence there, but it could have. Culture exists in a parallel world somewhere and feels at home there. It won't come to the House of Culture, but it is important to know that there are other possibilities, too, that it could have come there had things been different."

"What's more, they select their guests," the professor went on in the same vein. "Not any old soul can end up here."

"I think it's quite sensible," Swidersky replied. "They protect themselves from many problems that way. It's easier to live in peace and quiet, even for a bodiless soul."

At that moment, there was a terrible clatter in the chimney and the still-life which blocked it fell over. Some kind of ginger-haired, shaggy creature tumbled out of the fireplace. It was very similar to the monkey which had caused such a stir on the central square earlier and was followed by the intrusion of a whirlwind which scattered yellowy-grey sand across the room. Sitting on the floor, the creature felt its head all over, and having reassured itself that everything was in order, it began scratching its armpits. The whirlwind gradually subsided.

"Have you got any plam?" asked the creature in Polish.

"Sorry?" the professor asked, surprised; he had grown so used to speaking Russian lately that he automatically replied in that language.

"I mean that solution they're all crazy about here," the guest said, in Russian, with a Polish accent. "Otherwise, you can see what the surrogate does to people…"

"Are you human?"

"What do you think? You must have been given lab plam, for sure, and that's why you came out so smooth and slick. If they'd made you drink the surrogate, you wouldn't be able to recognise yourself in the mirror."

"Nobody made us drink anything…" said Swidersky.

"What???!!!" the creature stared at him in utter amazement. "Do you mean you're alive, then?"

"Completely," smirked the professor.

"Jesus Maria… I've never seen anyone alive down here. How did you gents end up in these parts?"

"Let's say we were invited for an excursion," said Swidersky.

"Oh-ho, so they even invite people now, do they?! Well, they hound the likes of us out, that's for sure."

"What do you mean, "the likes of us"?"

"Simple folks, that's who. I worked in the shipyards in Gdańsk for almost forty years."

"But how did you get here?" asked the professor curiously.

"In the normal way — down the chimney."

"Is there a hole in the chimney, then?"

"Of course not! You have to make the hole yourself. I was lucky. I found a crack and chiselled away at it, and then I cracked the plexiglass screen with my heels. Once you get here, you can live as long as you like. Just try and catch someone like me! And you can even look normal again, too, if you drink pure plam. But you have to drink it all the time if you drank the surrogate first time round. Plam is like a currency here…"

"How do they choose who to let in?"

"Oh, they have scouts. They'll invite you themselves if they like the look of you. Didn't anyone contact you about it?"

"Yes, they did," said Swidersky said after a short pause, remembering his mysterious night visitor.

Ostermann looked at him in surprise.

"Well, you're a lucky fellow," said the creature, and smacked its lips. "Really lucky… So, did you come to an agreement?"

"I'm afraid not," grinned the writer. "It's too early for me. I want to live some more."

"It's never too early," said the creature indignantly. "They may not make you a second offer, and anyway, you never know what tomorrow may bring — a brick might fall on your head."

"Yeah, it might, but what's happening here can also hit a person on the head just as hard. I'd like to find out what's going on."

"And so you shall, and you'll settle in soon, and maybe even help me, too. I'm Marek, by the way."

The unexpected guest went out through the door and they blocked the fireplace with the still-life once more, after which they decided they had each earned a cup of tea.

Over tea, they discussed whether they should take an excursion into the intestinal world of the cunningly entwined chimneys through the recently opened hole gaping in the fireplace. It was a tempting idea, but they decided to find out more about the layout of the chimneys and the methods of transporting through them before embarking upon such a risky journey.

There are always more exits than entrances, and that is
why it seems easier to exit than to enter. And it would be
nice to know where you are exiting from
and where you will end up.

When you lose your temper and go beyond what is reasonable, you know where you are exiting from but you don't know where you will arrive, since there is no limit to yourself, as you have gone beyond. But there are many entrances into you — garden gates, and doors and all of them are locked by your own hands, an excuse to block out the outer world. But the locks and prohibitions are no obstacle for the outer world; it knows how to seep in and out, here and there, and who knows where.

The fireplace listened. It listened to their musings and misgivings, and pronounced its full agreement with them. In its own chimney-language, of course: it howled with the wind and naughtily scattered some sand.

8.

*We take handfuls of flour to make bread; we take cubes of
plasticine to make human figures; we assemble people to
make a crowd. And a crowd is nothing else but an aggregate
child. This child grows up and takes a handful of flour, thus
triggering a circumgyration of objects.*

A similar kind of circumgyration was going on inside Swidersky's head, as he couldn't sleep. He only knew how to sleep in a place he was used to; he could never sleep a wink in a place he wasn't accustomed to. And so now he was tossing and turning, tossing and turning on the old-fashioned, creaky bed. The bed was creaking on about some business of its own — maybe about how tired it was of its restive rider. Professor Ostermann was snoring away busily in the next room.

Swidersky decided to get up after all. He went over to the window and saw streetlights wandering along the street. There was something strange about it — either about the streetlights or about himself. He went out in the hopes of clarifying the matter.

A gentleman in a top hat walked by, his stick clopping on the cobbled road. A lighted lantern was running along in front of him on a lead. It was a strange shape, sort of elongated. The writer examined it more closely and was amazed: it turned out to be not a lantern but a shining, luminous cat.

"A little pussycat, sir, a lunar cat," the passer-by answered his mental query.

"I've never seen..." Swidersky stated. "How did it end up here?"

"There's an eclipse here today, you see, and that means that the cats are free and can walk wherever they like. I'll let it off the leash later on, and my colleagues will release their charges, too, and they will all fly together as one up into the firmament, and the moon will shine again."

"Your colleagues?"

"Yes, that's right. Workers at the local zoo. We have a lot of experience in dealing with animals. Take monkeys, for instance! As for cats, our task is to make sure they don't congregate together. They give off so much light! Imagine what it would be like if the moon suddenly shone right here in the middle of the street!"

The man with the luminous cat went on his way. Another followed him, keeping a respectful distance.

Swidersky went back in and admired the procession from above, from the bedroom window. Then he fell asleep. The claw of the crescent moon was scratching at the window in the night. The moon's pancake hissed on the frying pan, a spiral of luminescent sausages was circling round his bed...

In the morning he asked the professor whether he had had any dreams or not.

"Yes," he replied. "Such a beautiful dream! A procession of little solar dogs was trotting down the street!"

9.

In the morning the view from window was quite ordinary, and no strange beasts wandered the streets. Swidersky and the professor had breakfast and then sent themselves off for a walk.

*You send yourself for a walk when there is
no-one else to send.*

It is all very well for parents — they have children. You can send the kids off somewhere and then you are free to engage in your super-important business. But what about childless individuals? Who can they send out, if not themselves? Incidentally, it's important to give the house a break. It has to put up with us round the clock, after all.

Oddly enough, the writer and the professor didn't run into anyone at all during their walk. Their shoes beat out a regular rhythm on the black cobbles but they were not joined by the echo of other shoes. Maybe the citizens lived a night life?

They got back to find a sylvan standing by their door. He immediately handed them an official looking document. They were invited to dinner in the town hall.

The town hall was on the other side of the square. They had already spotted it from their window. It was a two-storey, concrete building with a little pseudo-gothic clock tower, and Dorian columns flanking the main entrance.

"Eclecticism, pure eclecticism!" said the professor. "They could have stuck to one architectural style."

"Who knows, maybe eclecticism is their style," grumbled Swidersky, who was suffering from the morning sullenness which afflicts all writers.

They whiled away the next few hours talking. At last the clock struck seven. They left the house and crossed the square. Two sylvans with identical faces grown over with black hair stood at the entrance to the town hall. Do they mass produce them here, or what? Swidersky wondered. The sylvans bowed their hairy heads and, with a gesture, invited them into the building.

Dinner was in the best traditions of official hospitality, except that no-one at the table ate or drank anything even though there was no shortage of food. They were served by two sylvans dressed in identical black dinner jackets. Palm trees in tubs swung their multi-fingered leaves politely whenever anyone brushed them, which didn't happen very often, by the way, as the sylvans were deft and dextrous.

Academician Afonsky was sitting at the other end of the table. Turning to the writer, he said:

"I expect you would like to see your stepbrother?"

"Is he here?"

"Well, yes and no. He spends most of his time in the lab. We need to produce a certain amount of that Solution Number 18, you see, so that we can attract new members to our not-quite material society of souls."

"Are you talking about plam?" Ostermann chimed in eagerly.

"Aha, you've already learned our jargon I see!" the academician grinned. "Who have you been chatting to?"

They told him about the new-comer who had arrived through the chimney.

"Well, he's not the first and I'm afraid he won't be the last. The idea of immortality, you see, has black market value. That is why they manufacture a surrogate."

"Couldn't they just be supplied with plam?" asked Ostermann.

"Well, it's possible in theory, of course, but quite out of the question from a practical point of view. And we are actually very fussy about who finds their way here. If we weren't, we'd be facing exactly the same problems as those which beset humanity."

"You already have the problems of smuggling and unwanted visitors," said the writer.

"True enough. Actually, we cannot decide what to do with those creatures, whether to send them back to their caves or to intern them here in some barrack or camp. But they are so fleet-footed, so very fleet-footed…"

"Can't you civilise them somehow?" queried the professor.

"We've thought about it. We're working on a reactive chemical… By the way, our lab isn't here. It's in Russia. So you'll have to wait until tomorrow if you don't mind. We've already let your brother know you're here. He'll finish his chemical analysis of the current batch of Solution Number 18 and then come to see you."

After lunch they were invited into the music salon.

"You have the unique opportunity of hearing the new piece by the great Respighi. No-one has heard it yet," the academician told them. "It's called *The Catacombs of Münsterstadt.*"

10.

You sense the forest by the chill which rushes along your spine. You sense spring by the wind in your hair, and you sense cities by your feet. If you want to get to know an unfamiliar city or town, take yourself for a walk round the streets and don't let anyone accompany you.
Just feel, and take it in.

During their philosophical walk at the end of the day, the writer and the professor discovered another square. A huge bronze statue of Voltaire towered at one side. The other side was occupied by a granite pedestal adorned with an antique-looking shoe. The monument offered no explanations. There was nobody around.

"What do you think it could mean?" wondered the professor.

"Maybe it's a monument to the local cobblers?"

"Do you think they have cobblers here?"

"Who knows…"

Just then a voice rustled:

"This is a shoe from a monument to Karl the Twelfth."

Turning around, they saw a pale man in an old-fashioned suit smoking a hooked pipe.

"And where is the monument itself? Where is Karl XII?" the professor asked curiously.

"Someone stole his bronze sword, you see, and so he's working to get himself a new one."

"What do you mean, working?"

"It's quite simple. He walks along the street, shoe in hand, and swats rats with it. In return for this service, the magistrate is putting aside money for a new sword."

"What connection do Voltaire and Karl XII have to this town?"

"None whatsoever, funnily enough. These statues probably fell through some hole or well, because we found them down in the caves, in different ones. We like them. We say one symbolises thought, the other action."

The professor and the writer strolled on. Closer towards evening, the shadowy inhabitants of the town of shadows began flitting by. As they were returning home with night almost upon them, a metallic din rang out. They turned a corner and saw a bronze giant in the guise of the once-glorious King Karl XII. He was banging the bronze heel on the black marble cobbles, evidently doing his best to swat any living thing with his shoe. Forget the rats! The shadowy townsfolk themselves only just managed to run for shelter, scattering in all directions.

"It's tough being a conqueror," the professor whispered as they hid behind the dwarf cypress trees at the porch of some house. "He squandered so many souls while he was alive, and he can't stop even now."

Swidersky hemmed and said:

"If the statue of Voltaire came out into town, I wonder if he would start beating people on the head with his bronze book, or whether he'd be happy just to smile?"

II.

A sylvan came in the morning, smiled hairily, and invited Swidersky into the fern garden. The sun shone green. An artificial breeze was swaying the brushes of the leaves. A little silvery fountain was gurgling about harmony between man and nature, even if nature was an underground one and man only existed as a human casing.

Closed space, thought Swidersky. In the end, it's just another closed territory. A fenced paradise. A Friedhofstadt, a cemetery-city where the deceased lead a very active life. Everyone lives in their own period, reads books and nourishes themselves with the ideas of their epoch. If people from different periods and places gather in one time, then that time is non-being...

"Aha, you've found this most important place! The place where clever thoughts enter your head!" a familiar voice rang out above his ear.

The writer turned around, and it really was his stepbrother! He was wearing a very good quality English tweed suit, and so Swidersky — who was used to seeing his brother in a student sweater — hardly recognised him at first.

Arefiev wasn't alone. He was arm in arm with a very pretty black-haired girl.

"I see you've already managed to meet someone down here!" Swidersky was surprised; he hadn't been aware of his step brother's interest in the opposite sex before.

"I wouldn't say we met down here. In fact, we arrived together. By the way, let me introduce you to Milla. Milla, this is Witold, my stepbrother."

"Yes, I've heard a lot about you," smiled the girl, and her smile was open but somewhat sad.

"Pleased to meet you," said Swidersky, after which his subconsciousness managed to butt in: "It's a shame we didn't meet before, when you were still corporeal."

"Ah, yes, I'd forgotten you're partial to the opposite sex," Arefiev laughed. "Too late, old chap! Now Milla is completely ethereal."

"Are love and courting allowed here?"

"Who can forbid it?" replied Arefiev, somewhat taken aback. "Of course, all feelings here are purely platonic. We would have liked more, but it's out of the question, so I'd use the word "friendship"."

"They say you're working here somewhere?"

"Yes, I am, but not exactly here. We have a large lab in the cave under Uglich. Milla helps me. We once worked together in Moscow, too."

"Are you manufacturing Solution Number 18?"

"Ah, so you already know about it! Well, that's our main product. The production lines are already up and running, and normally there are no surprises. We just check the quality of each batch. Our main task is to look for new reagents."

"Are there only the two of you there, then?"

"No, no, there are lots of people. Part of our population — if of course you can call it a population — works in other laboratories. Incidentally, I'm working with some scientists I used to work with on the surface. Our latest achievement is a reagent which allows an ordinary person to leave his or her body for a short while and don a bodily casing akin to mine. Our coryphaeus — the academician – already offers this service to visitors, a kind of excursion round our world in the body of one its inhabitants."

"That's true, he does offer that," admitted the writer.

"You can try it, by the way. It's completely harmless."

"I wonder if my brother is tricking us, by any chance?" Swidersky said, winking at the girl.

"I believe him," she said simply.

"What happened to you in Moscow?" the writer asked.

And his brother began the tale of his last days before his departure into the world of shadows. The fern fronds listened to his tale, swaying their shadows indifferently, as though reminding everyone that they were in the very heart of a bodiless world where human emotions seem nothing more than quaint. The pearly fountain of human speech purred on. The green sun was trying hard to look like a tender underground star.

"I think I'll give it a go after all," said the professor pensively when Swidersky came back to his little house. "I want to know what it's like to part with your body. As a scientist, I just can't pass up on this chance!"

"I quite understand. All the more so as the process seems to be reversible."

"And what have you decided?"

"I haven't made up my mind yet," said Swidersky.

A heated debate was going on inside him: his writerly entity was pushing him to agree, whereas his cautious self-control was begging him to think of safety.

12.

"A whisper, deathly breathing…"
"Faint breathing," the red pencil corrects
the written paragraph.

Swidersky is dreaming he is in paradise. There are school desks everywhere and souls are learning the art of angelicity. From time to time the students manifest their human nature and then the countenances of the exacting angels take on the likeness of the letter "o".

And then once again: "a whisper, faint breathing, the trills of a nightingale…"

No, let us leave it as it was written: "deathly". After all, the hand knows what it writes…

Mornings were usually a time of reckless moods for the writer, and all the prudence of the night hours dissipated.

Sipping his tea, he said to the professor:

"I've decided to give it a go, too. Maybe I'll be able to describe it. I am a writer, after all…"

Everything was settled in the blink of an eye. They told the sylvan on duty about their decision and were invited into the fern garden again. First of all they were given breakfast. The tea had an unusual tomatoey tang about it, but it was soon masked by the fruit and sandwiches. They quickly fell into a semi-sleepy state.

"When are they finally going to give us the solution?" said Swidersky, throwing himself back in the chair.

"Maybe the tea was the solution," the professor responded, finding it difficult to move his tongue now growing heavy.

That was the last thing the writer heard before falling into a green, fern-like dream.

A red light. Hell appeared with all its attributes: half-naked labourers, red-hot stoves, fire-proof tools and a display reporting on exemplary workers…

A yellow light. Purgatory seeped in. A waiting room for

trains to nowhere, dim lanterns dangling from the ceiling, withered grass between the benches, a little stream trickling from under the door of the male toilet…

A green light. A sign appeared:

"Choose paradise".

He pressed button Number One and found himself in a boxing ring. It smelt of fists and blood. A man in a white suit was persistently setting him against some vague opponent…

He pressed the

Escape

button, then button Number Two. A smell of frankincense and lily-of-the-valley. He found himself in an esoterically ecclesiastical emptiness. "Pray!" the emptiness appealed to him. His ears grew red with shame. He banged his forehead on the table assiduously, and his nose landed right on button Number Three.

A smell of mould and thought. "Such a familiar smell!" he thought happily, and neither thinking nor not thinking, he pressed the button

Enter.

"We have issued you with a permanent library pass," said a female voice.

13.

Inside the library, transparent girls were handing out lives which had been recorded onto a kind of film. They could be worn as shirts. You could don the appearances of others. Guises. You could invent exotic outfits, or you could swim in your own transparency. You could soar above the underworld or fly through the chimneys into the world of men, deceiving them with your bodily manifestations and transformations. You could just simply sit in the library and read the lives of others or listen to music, already composed or not yet composed. You could sleep or not sleep, for human casings have no need of sleep. Actually, sleeping had become all the rage here, particularly day dreaming. Everyone was busy with colourful, four dimensional dreams. They lent them to each other and re-told others what they had seen. The dreams played with each other, throwing each other the balls of planets. They interpreted themselves to others, and others to themselves. Dreams lived here, and people dreamt dreams of themselves and of others. Swidersky dreamt of the professor, and the professor dreamt of Swidersky. They talked to each other via dreams. As for the dreams, they would find human casings for themselves for a while, and then they would call themselves townsfolk.

The town was strange, even stranger than it had seemed at first. It was inhabited by shadows, and those shadows talked about it in a strange way. It transpired that all the barometers in this town always showed "fair", no matter what the weather was – if there was any. All the towns' streets led to the North — even if you went in the opposite direction, you'd still end up in the North.

There were weathercocks in the town, too. Every night they would gather together and creak on about something known only to them, but in the morning they would all amicably face in opposite directions.

The clocks in the town would go forwards for half a day, then backwards for half a day. Twice every twenty-four hours the hands would overlap and the clocks washed their hands. Water dripped onto the cobbles. Evil tongues said that was how the clocks cried, but why should they cry?

There were never any incidents in the town.
In fact, that was its name: Town Without Incidents.

A stony sky hung heavy over the city. But the shadows were always saying that someone had covered the town with a glass cowl. Because it was an entity in its own right, open to view. If the shadows looked at it from above or from the side, it really might have looked as though it were covered by a glass cowl. Perhaps someone from outside even came to take a look at life there from time to time. Someone big. A god or a child.

14.

The town hall clock struck thirty-three. Swidersky understood it was time to go for a walk, and fell out of the window.

Floating along was easy. The corners were turned by themselves. Someone's black cloak was brushing the cobbles in front. "I'll catch him!" thought the writer. But he didn't manage it: the figure in black was floating at the same slow pace as the writer himself.

Suddenly something golden slipped out of a slit in the cloak. The writer slowed his flight and picked up the lost object. It turned out to be a gilded piece of paper with the inscription:

"The Sun".

The cloak stopped, too, and emptiness looked expectantly at Swidersky from under the hood. Swidersky moved ahead but the cloak began floating away at the very same instant. Turning another corner the writer picked up another note, a silvery one. It was inscribed with the words:

"The Moon".

The black cloak stopped again.

The writer shrugged and tried to reach out to the figure in the cloak again, but it floated on.

Round the next corner, the basalteous smoothness was carpeted with fallen leaves. How did they get here? Swidersky wondered, surprised. Without pausing, he picked up a leaf. It was green and felt like cloth. It was inscribed with the words:

"The Stars".

Dropping the leaf, the writer continued following the cloak. They turned a corner — and fell into an abyss.

He flew slowly for a long time. The dawn beaches of the Sun, the quiet nightly village of the Moon, and the green starry gardens flitted by him. His weightlessness prevented him from stopping. He could hear something which sounded like owls hooting, and someone's mocking laughter.

At last the destination became visible — the central square of the underground town he was already familiar with. Swidersky slowly floated into the wide open window of his bedroom and landed right on the desk.

"I am returning to my primeval choice, after all," he smirked. "I want to work, to write books."

But as soon as he said that to himself, he realised that while he was here he wanted nothing and wouldn't write anything.

The town hall clock struck thirty-three.

15.

On the eve of a morningless day; on the dawn of a night that drowns in itself; on the day that breaks after a sleepless night…

Nobody was doing anything. All the masters of the brush and quill, all the creators of sounds who, in life, had held any minute precious, would spend days and years in idleness here. If, of course, the local time could be measured by earthly measures. "Who knows, maybe they lack earthly disharmony or emotions or something else?" pondered the writer. "As for me, what do I lack? What stops me from working? From writing? But what should I write about? Nothing happens here…"

At night, the electrical suns transformed into electrical moons, and the mooniness overflowed onto the roofs of the old-fashioned little houses like streams of double sour cream. Swidersky dreamt he was walking along the firmament of the underground heavens. In waking reality the heavens were cloudless, but in his dream, sweet, foggy candy floss was condensing around him. Sugary. Tasty. He licked his lips.

The candy floss soon finished and he began chewing on more dense clouds. They seemed even tastier and hail crunched between his teeth.

Without noticing it, he went beyond the edge of the electrical moon. The clouds were black there and turned out not to be clouds at all but swampy slime and foam.

Dirt penetrated his very core. There was no-one there in the darkness to be ashamed in front of.

"Press the button and switch the light on!" came a thundery voice. But there were no buttons to be seen.

"Press the button. With yourself!" the voice came again.

He stepped to the left, to the right, in front — and fell into an abyss.

In his dream, years passed. Who knows whether they passed in waking reality or not; waking time had long since seemed but a distant reality. Crashing through the earth's crust, he reached the bottom of the abyss. The depths exploded, firing dawn into the neon dusk of the earth. Being a light switch is a dubious honour, he thought, having woken up. But light is good, of course.

16.

> *The quacking of ducks doesn't produce an echo, and no-one*
> *knows why.*

"It's like that here," Swidersky thought. "Thoughts don't produce any repercussions. Not in your own head nor in anyone else's.

Silhouettes don't produce shadows, and shadows, long since separated from their former owners, have declared their sovereignty and are already in the process of choosing an anthem. Soon they will start issuing passports and visas. Only instead of photos there will be black silhouettes, for this country is called Facelessness…"

"What about my past, wasn't I living my life as a shadow? People like me are like shadows on a sunless day: we exist but we're invisible, we live inside ourselves, and our bodily casings are not transparent. We never notice each other, and no one ever notices us. We crave for sunlight but they only give us twilight, in the everlasting kind…"

"It is time to return. It is time to think about re-unifying with my body. My body is probably missing me. Missing me like a wife misses the husband who has gone off to a resort: it's all very well for him to frolic there, but what about us?"

He went to the town hall. As usual, the sylvan on duty smiled into the beard covering his cheeks and gestured the writer to enter. Swidersky found himself in a long corridor which ended in a fan of doors.

There were no signs on the doors, and what's more, they all turned out to be locked.

He knocked on one. There was no reply. He went on, and reached the end of the corridor. He went up the stairs to the first floor. The building seemed dead — there were no voices nor even the slightest sign of anyone's presence. He walked along the corridor on the first floor. There was a sign on one of the doors:

"SUPERBOOK".

He knocked, but there was no reply, so he gave the door a shove.

And found himself in another corridor. A lot of people in white suits were lined up there, standing with their backs to him.

Are they sylvans? Then he noticed something which turned his blood cold: each of these people was he himself.

Utterly aghast, he said:

"Hello!"

"Your faces greet you," replied the people in chorus.

Why "faces" and not "face"? he thought. Taking a closer look, he realised that they were all different ages and in different moods, as though they were different snapshots of one and the same person: he himself. Or different pages of a book.

"Page One," rustled a whistling whisper.

One of the figures broke rank and offered him its hand. He shook the outstretched hand automatically, after which the figure disappeared as though it had dissolved into him. He began thinking about his childhood and felt like a boy again. But this time he understood everything, even the things which had previously been hidden from him.

The same happened with the next figure, and with the next, and with the next…

Before the last figure disappeared it said:

"End of Volume One."

He realised this was not yet the end. He went out, closed the door behind him and wandered further down the corridor lost in thought, heading off to live on and write Volume Two of the SUPERBOOK.

17.

At the end of the corridor was a door padded with black leather with a spy hole in it. Tucked behind the metal ring of the spy hole was a scrap of newspaper with the words:

"Dichotomy of history".

Swidersky pushed against this door, fully convinced that it, too, would be locked. But the door swung open. He found himself in a large hall with a green and white checked marble floor. Four palms surrounded a mahogany table. Suffused, cloudy light came in through the large Venetian windows. Two people were sitting at the table playing dice.

Having heard his steps, the players looked up.

"Who are you?" they asked.

They were two short-haired young men dressed in crimson jackets. Had they been in Russia, Swidersky would have assumed they were New Russians, but how could New Russians get here? Or are they in fact ubiquitous?

He replied:

"Well, I was just passing…"

"Aha, just passing!" the players smirked. "Then you can stay, we've nothing against that. By the way, do you know what we are playing for?"

"For money?" Swidersky suggested hesitantly.

"No. For future historical events. We're just about to determine who will win the Afghan war."

"I bet on the Northern Alliance," declared the second young man immediately.

"I bet on the Taliban," said the first and immediately threw the dice. "You win."

"Have you been playing this game for long?" asked the writer.

"No, not long. We sat down after the Flood when people were divided into tribes. As the years passed, it became more interesting. You can't compare the quarrels of animal herders with modern battles! By the way, there was a very interesting game not long ago, about the outcome of the Falklands war, and before that we played on the outcome of the latest World War. Hitler got two and his opponents got three."

"Do you only play about wars?"

"No. We had games like "Stalin versus Trotsky", "Bourbon kings versus Napoleon". Incidentally, we had to have a replay of that one as someone forgot the rules of fair play."

And the second player shook his fist at him.

"So do things always turn out the way they do in the game?" the writer asked.

"Yes. After all, people don't object."

"Do you ever both bet on the same side?"

"No," the players laughed. "When one of us chooses one side, the other has whatever's left, then we swap next time."

"Don't you ever get bored of the game?"

"No. It's a nice way to pass the time after lunch. And no-one's called us for dinner yet."

18.

The writer was about to leave but couldn't contain himself and asked one more question:

"Could you tell me why all the doors here are locked?"

"I don't know about the other floors, but on our floor there's an archive of unclaimed letters."

"Does anyone ever show any interest in them?"

"No. But an archive ought to be locked. The most interesting part of ours is the archive of unclaimed wisdom. But no-one shows any interest even in that archive. The letters are still unsorted. Wisdom, you know, is always unclaimed."

"I would have liked to take a look, if possible."

"Yes, of course! No need to ask!"

Here it was,

"The archive of unclaimed wisdom".

The letters on the plasticy rectangular boards were transparent, even spectral.

Groucho Marx to Karl Marx: *I never liked your theories, especially what your followers cooked up out of them, but I admit that behind the lowered iron curtain the play was greeted by a hundred percent hurrah.*

CAMUS TO BAKUNIN: *A rebel is a man who says no. An intellectual is a man who, in a similar situation, says "why?"*

BISMARCK TO BERNARD SHAW: *I completely agree with you. If the police begin playing at anarchism then they will be the champions, and in this game, the most undefeatable police force of them all is the German one.*

MONTESQUIEU TO FREUD: *If the patients of Bedlam begin to draw freedom, it will be depicted in a straight-jacket.*

CHARLES PERRAULT TO HINDENBURG: *Sister Anne, Sister Anne, can't you see what is drawing nigh?*
HINDENBURG TO CHARLES PERRAULT: *Dust, I can see only dust.*

MUSSOLINI TO HITLER: *Everyone is always asking me for something, and now they even want fascism, your Goebbels is writing to me about it. I won't give it to you! Fascism is not an export commodity, it is an absolute necessity and we need it ourselves.*

KHRUSHCHEV TO KENNEDY: *There in the West you like to talk about great-power politics. But you don't really understand what it means. In reality everything is very simple: great-power politics is the politics of other great states.*

CHARLES STEWART PARNELL TO LLOYD GEORGE, CC BREZHNEV: *No man has the right to say to the people: thus far shalt thou go and no further. When you are told to let a nation go, blocking your ears in an attempt to fake deafness is stupidity rather than firm opinion.*

AMBROSE BIERCE TO MARK TWAIN: *Public opinion is the opinion of ill-informed people about things they don't understand.*

ANATOLY KUDRYAVITSKY

STALIN TO MANNERHEIM: *You say God doesn't approve the annexing of territories? But how many divisions has God himself got?*

VOLTAIRE TO MONTESQUIEU: *After years and years of observing the vegetating shoots of human superstition, I would define an atheist as a man who believes he doesn't believe.*

AESOP TO FEUERBACH: *Beware of losing what is invisible when you grasp too firmly at the material.*

TALLEYRAND TO GISCARD D'ESTAING: *Unification is the beginning of division. Association is the beginning of dissociation. The end of the beginning is the beginning of the end.*

TITUS TO THE CONSULS: *Friends, I have two pieces of news, one good, one bad. As for the good news: we have successfully lost the day. As for the bad news: we have inadvertently lost Rome.*

BROTHERS GRIMM TO A FEMALE READER: *Rapunzel, Rapunzel, let down your hair! Let the irrational play!*
ST. MATTHEW TO THE SAME READER: *Even the hairs on your head are counted and recounted.*

SPINOZA TO DARWIN: *Nature cannot bear emptiness, and emptiness cannot bear nature.*

MARCUS AURELIUS TO EMERSON: *Our life is what we think of it.*
EMERSON TO MARCUS AURELIUS:
If the red slayer think he slays,
Or if the slain think he is slain,
They know not well the author's ways
Of solving problems in his brain.

SOCRATES TO TOLSTOY: *Death cannot harm a good man, but it may do a lot of damage to a bad man.*

OSCAR WILDE TO GEORGE MOORE: *A real gentleman, you know, doesn't give anyone cause to suspect he is a gentleman.*

TERTULLIAN TO NAPOLEON: *Look how these Christians love one another! Even to incest and blood spilling!*
NAPOLEON TO TERTULLIAN: *My god! Let them love, no matter how. In my idyllic times all we ever thought of was love. To earn the love of the whole nation, now that was worth something! De Musset alone suspected foul play and wrote to me: you mustn't trifle with love.*

NABOKOV TO SWIFT:
Leafing through "Onegin",
I marked the margin:
How little doth the author know
About his subject!

GEORGE ORWELL TO TOLSTOY, TURGENEV AND DOSTOYEVSKY: *War is peace; fathers are sons; the crime is the punishment.*

ARISTOTLE TO TACITUS: *Poetry is more philosophical and of higher value than history.*
TACITUS TO ARISTOTLE: *Let us compare our royalties.*

SOLZHENITSYN TO BREZHNEV: *You are so busy rooting out dissidents… but don't you know that any classic, no matter which you take, is a dissident of the epoch which precedes him?*

SHOSTAKOVICH TO ROSTROPOVICH: *The symphony is my creative reply to them, and it is in my diary that I hit them where it hurts.*

OPPENHEIMER TO BERTRAND RUSSELL: *Everyone says we live in the age of erudition, and goes bragging about their mental accumulations… but erudition is nothing but a mass of information, which is more often than not forgotten, about things which are more often than not useless.*

DIAGHILEV TO COCTEAU: *Go on, surprise me! Nobody can surprise me.*
COCTEAU TO DIAGHILEV: *Do you know who Hugo was? He was not Hugo at all but a madman who believed he was Hugo.*
DIAGHILEV TO COCTEAU: *Wow!*

SCHILLER TO GOETHE: *In the beginning the gods fought against stupidity without much success, but then stupidity began fighting back.*

CICERO TO ERASMUS OF ROTTERDAM: *There is no nonsense which a wise man has not once said. To seem stupid is not a tactic but a strategy. When I am told a string of nonsense, I double my caution.*

SHERLOCK HOLMES TO DR. WATSON: *If we cut off the impossible, the improbable remains; if we cut off the improbable, the unfathomable remains; if we cut off the unfathomable, the insufficient and untrue remain. And at which stage, pray tell, have we cut off the superfluous?*

19.

A headless cockroach will live for nine days before it dies of starvation. This begs the question: isn't the head superfluous? Of course, "Nine Days in One Year without a Head" is a good title, no worse than "The Headless Horseman" or "Quadroon." It's perfect for a horror story about the fragmentation of the one and only indivisible human essence. By the way, a human being can live without a head for even longer — i.e. all its useless life, and nothing stops the head from wobbling and gibbering on the shoulders.

Having experienced the ambiguity of existing as a soul separated from a body, by the ninth day Swidersky was already morally ready to interrupt the experiment at any cost. But he still didn't know where he should look for his body. Having gone through the whole of the town hall to no avail, he decided to ask the sylvans who were lurking near the entrance as usual.

"It's quite simple," one of them said, grinning and winking like a bandit. "Write an application and we will pass it on."

Swidersky sat down to write, but it was no easy matter as he had not much strength left in his semi-transparent hands. Nevertheless, he set his request out on paper and gave it to the sylvans. They rolled it into a tube and sent it off somewhere by tube transfer system.

"The reply will come to the house where you live."

"And how long will I have to wait?" enquired the writer.

"Well, you have the whole of eternity before you!" winked the sylvan. "Just joking. Decisions are taken swiftly here."

Three days passed, if, of course, time passed as quickly here as it did on earth. There was no news.

Swidersky went to the town hall once again. The sylvans gave him the same warm welcome. He couldn't tell whether it was the same sylvans or different ones.

"Haven't you heard anything? We'll check the outgoing mail at once… yes, you were sent a message yesterday. But you say you didn't receive anything?"

"No."

"We'll call right away," one of the sylvans said, and disappeared inside the building.

Hmm. So they have a phone here! The writer was surprised. I wonder if it's for internal use only, or whether someone from above can call them here.

The sylvan returned, clutching a piece of paper in his hairy paw.

"Here. This has just come for you."

Swidersky unfolded the paper.

With all possible and impossible apologies, it stated that his body had been lost and that the storehouse workers were to blame. The incident would be dealt with according to administrative regulations. He would be kept abreast of events.

Hmm. That doesn't make it any better, thought the writer.

20.

A man falls asleep in seven minutes, a cat in seven seconds. But a cat doesn't sleep; it dreams. Just look how the thirty-seven muscles of its ear are working, how its supposedly closed eyes absorb space, and how lazily its paw claws at the air.

> *Even in a dream a cat is a realist but a human is a surrealist. Because a human is searching for something better, whereas a cat is simply searching for more.*

At night the writer habitually retired for rest, although the bodily casing in which he was dwelling didn't need any rest. For him, night was the continuation of day. He went on existing in the world of illusion and illusion went on existing in him, and they both felt at home there.

> *Our feelings probably feel at home in us, otherwise they would go in search of another owner...*

When he got tired of kidding himself he was asleep, he peered out of the window and saw precisely what he should have seen in that surreal world: not moonlight, but a greenish lamp. Its light drew a lettuce-coloured rectangle on the floor, a rectangle which looked very similar to a table covered by a table cloth.

Some shadows had congregated below the window and were singing:

> *O shiny moon of Saint Hertz,*
> *Light up the depths of our hearts!*

They might have been cats or they might have been other bodily casings, but that night they had chosen to express themselves in a cat-like manner. They are the souls of those who have experienced defeat, after all, so why shouldn't they comfort themselves here? Why should I condemn them? Condemn no-one, but be not like them, oh you who seek to be a man. "There is another Loneliness…"

Someone knocked on the window. Swidersky shuddered, remembering that the window was on the first floor. But then he realised that this would not pose an obstacle for the nimble bodily casings, not to mention the monkey-like creatures. This was a very special visitor, however; Swidersky recognised the familiar features of the pale face pressed against the pane: Nemglan!

"This time I have come to you as an uninvited guest," he said when the writer let him into the room. "I think we need to talk."

"Always a pleasure," the writer said politely.

"I have the feeling you are itching to do something very stupid," said his nightly guest, straightening his cassocky black cloak.

"I think I understand what you are getting at, but I don't think I have another choice."

"Come off it! Those who end up here always have a choice! By the way, I approve of your decision. I didn't think you would get here, especially not without my help. The local inhabitants are the Tuatha Dé Danann, children of the goddess Danu, and they are inspired people. Have you heard about them? Having been defeated in battle, they went underground and ruled the world from there by suggesting solutions to people's problems."

"Yes, there is a glory in defeat," Swidersky admitted. "And only defeats help a person to accumulate wisdom. However, I am not so happy that I ended up here."

"Now that is what I don't understand. What do you miss?"

"Firstly, I miss life, with all its tragedy. I can't work here — there's nothing for me to write about. And the local pastimes aren't my forte."

"So you miss tragedy? That's a strange reason to leave!"

"Oh, I miss so many things here! Smells, the taste of food, the basic feeling of tiredness when I walk. But most of all I miss emotions. Any emotions. I feel like a fish in distilled water here. Tell me, I'm not the only writer here, am I? There are others, too, aren't there? And painters, composers, architects.... what are they doing here?"

"Nothing, believe it or not. They are satisfied with their life."

""Satisfied with life"... That doesn't mean they are happy. Remember what Byron said to Thorvaldsen when the latter set out to sculpt his bust: "Don't make a successful man out of me"."

"Who are you writing for? Aren't you writing for people who are just as idle?"

"To be absolutely honest with you, I am writing for myself. It sounds egoistic and outrageous, I know, but it's because I'm orientated towards my own taste and not towards the taste of the readers. Though of course I certainly don't object if people like what I write. Heaven knows, many of them have difficult lives! Why shouldn't they distract themselves with something?"

"Here it's the scientists who work, like your brother, for example."

"They're lucky. It's easier for them of course. On top of that, they spend their time in the labs, far from this citadel of idleness... OK, so you have science here, but you don't have anything else. There is no philosophy, literature, art or music... Too much is sacrificed."

"Let's say you're right, but do you have an alternative?"

"Of course I do: to return into my body and return my body to where it was."

"You mean, back to that tiny little box room?"

"Yes, for a while. And then I'll leave for Ireland."

"It's very commendable to return to the country of your ancestors, of course. I can understand that. But do you realise that Ireland is just another alien country for you?"

"Ireland is my grandfather's country. It is a land of poetry and music which I have always loved — how can it be alien to me?"

"No matter how much you may love it, it will take several years for you to adjust, and they are all lost years… You will come empty-handed and will have to start from scratch, from where your grandfather left off. Are you sure that is what you want? That you will like it? Are you sure you want to live in that country?"

"Do I want to live in Ireland? I don't know, but I know I would like to die there."

"I think I understand… Well, your English is good, and that will be your salvation. You will probably get an Irish passport. But what will you do there? How will you support yourself? After all, you're not exactly a rich man, are you?"

"No, of course not," the writer smirked. "But I'll manage somehow. As for what I'll do. I'll do what I can't do here: work. Write. Otherwise my life is wasted."

"Which language are you planning to write in?"

"Russian."

"But you're bound to want to be published eventually."

"Hopefully… If I can, I'll write in English."

"Oh, you'll be able to write in English one day, but when? And even then, you'll have to be accepted as one of them before they publish you. After all, everything about you is alien to them — your surname, your accent, even the way you behave."

"Funnily enough, they used to say the same in Russia," Swidersky said passionately. "Our world is not intended for people of mixed origins. It's not meant for hundreds of thousands of refugees and asylum seekers fleeing from nowhere to Erewhon, who flood the immigrant "Heims" in Germany, who climb the barbed wire wall in Ceuta or who crouch in the bushes by the Eurotunnel hoping to sneak onto a coach to London. Maybe these underground halls could accommodate them all, but there is a process of selection here, too, and there are plexiglass barriers instead of barbed wire fences. And what's the result? Mountains of "human garbage" which all our multinationally glistening spades unanimously shovel onto the rubbish dump. But everything could have been different. These people are no worse than others. The only difference is that no-one taught them anything useful. Nobody even taught them the art of being human. And I would like to write about it. It's too early for me to go into well-earned retirement."

"Have you definitely made up your mind?"

"Yes."

"You are a strange man… Well then, we shall invoke all the Celtic gods to your aid. If you run into trouble, remember my heraldic bird."

"I won't forget, thank you. By the way, where should I look for my body?"

"Return by the well-trodden path of inverted evolution, back to the monkeys."

"To the monkeys?"

"Well, to those regarded as monkeys. They'll help you."

21.

The most common name in the world is Mohammed. The hairiest animal is the chimpanzee. A human has the same number of hair follicles; he just doesn't make the most of his potential, that's all.

Unless, of course, he is Andrian Yevtikheyev. What's more, a chimpanzee doesn't shave 20,000 times in its life like a male human does, so it accumulates plenty of time for mental work, such as pulling faces and contemplating its own belly button.

"How can I go to the monkeys if I don't even know who or where they are?" Swidersky thought. "Heading off heaven knows where to get heaven knows what… Well actually, I know what I'm looking for, and I'm very familiar with it; I won't mistake it if I see it."

Taking advantage of his recently-acquired skill in assuming any appearance whatsoever, Swidersky remembered his childhood impressions of a visit to the zoo, and manifest a quite acceptable resemblance of a monkey. Then he lay in wait on the roof of his little empire-style house.

He didn't have to wait long. A shadow flitted by on the next roof. The author who had just transformed himself into a similar shadow began tailing it. The chased shadow obviously felt quite at home in the landscape of pitched roofs, little towers and weather vanes, but even so it couldn't shake the pursuer.

The shadow finally dived into a manhole. Swidersky followed suit, thanks to the fact that in its hurry, the shadow had neglected to close the manhole lid after itself. The manhole sucked Swidersky in like an air pump. He flew somewhere along the chimneys, the wind whistling by. "I seem to be in some aerodynamic tube," he thought. At that very moment the chimney spat him out into an official-looking room with a tiled floor. Had he been in his corporeal appearance, he would probably have broken every bone in his body. But his bodily casing acted like a spring or a ball: he bounced, and landed like a sack on the floor.

"Name, surname and patronymic," asked a voice from somewhere above him.

Swidersky looked up. A humongous monkey in round John Lennon glasses was sitting at a desk, obviously ready to enter the information into a ledger lying in front of it. It tapped the end of its one pence Chinese ballpoint impatiently on the desk.

"I repeat: your name, surname and patronymic?"

Swidersky introduced himself.

"Reason for your visit?"

"Hmm. I'm looking for my body. I don't want to exist as an empty casing."

"Looking for your body?" the monkey asked in amazement. It took its glasses off and gazed amazed at the writer. "I thought you had come to us as a tourist. They fly in on us from time to time, and we send them back… And what do you want to do with your body, if it's no secret?"

"I just want to get back into it."

"Strange… why don't you want to have eternal life?"

"Because this is not life," stated the writer.

"Kkrrrmm," grunted the monkey uncomprehendingly. "I can't see any sense in it, but OK. Regarding bodies, if they disappear somewhere then they are discovered here in our place later. They are objects of barter, so to speak. You have probably heard about a certain chemical compound everyone is crazy about here?"

"Yes, of course I have."

"So you understand why you can find anything here which can be exchanged for that substance."

"Do you think my body might be here with you?"

"It's very probable. We'll look. Here is a piece of paper. Write a statement about the loss of your body, with a detailed description."

For the next fifteen minutes, Swidersky described the characteristics of his forty-something body. The monkey periodically distracted him with questions.

"Tell me, can you procreate hanging upside down?"

"No, I can't," replied the writer frankly.

"And can you think by clubbing together?"

"Yes, I can do that."

"So you are already half a monkey," said the monkey and pulled a cute grimace, after which it looked like Robert Frost resting from extremely strenuous peasant labour. "I shall have to give you the most arduous work. You will sit and draw conclusions. We are not very good at that."

The first conclusion the writer came to was as follows: his relocation to the monkeys was successful. He'd been worried he would be forced to think hanging upside and procreate by clubbing together!

When he had finished his statement, the monkey took the piece of paper and, putting its glassed back on, began to read. Having made it to the end of the document, it gave another snort, produced a cardboard file from the desk and duly filed the statement.

"Well, there we are. All the formalities have been observed. Will you live with us while we are looking for the body?"

"Yes, of course," Swidersky agreed lightly.

"That means you'll have to work. We have a principle, you see: those who don't work don't eat…"

And so saying, the monkey pressed some button and a net fell from the ceiling and engulfed the writer. He began struggling desperately. Two more monkeys appeared from somewhere, grabbed both ends of the net and began carrying the swaddled writer, swaying as though he were in a hammock, along the endless corridors and underground passageways. It obviously wasn't difficult for the monkeys to carry him as they showed no signs of effort.

22.

Nothing happens the way it was promised, and nothing is promised the way it was implied.

Instead of drawing conclusions, he was given a very particular assignment: he was working as a litter bin. In the mornings they would carry him out of the underground onto the surface into some small, provincial Russian town and leave him there on the street until the evening, when he was taken back. People would go up to him and leave everything they didn't need in him: sweetie wrappers, chewing gum chewed to super-stickiness, yesterday's ideas, and youthful misgivings. He was clad in a black polythene bag which was stretched over him like a cloak, and when he took it off in the evenings he had to tie the ends in a knot because it was full. He was still bodiless. He still had to earn his body, and the best thing was that his bodily casing — or to be precise, body-less casing — turned out to be impermeable to dirt; not even chewing gum stuck to it.

In the evenings he would sit in his barrack and, out of old habit, would scribble his thoughts and impressions in a notebook.

"My homeland is vast and broad... it's six am on May the sixth. You are listening to the broadcast "out and about in my dear homeland"..."

A click... silence... Behind the window adults hurry along to work, then kids skip along to school. Somewhere up there trees are readying themselves to become green. Window panes are particular here: you can always see blue sky in them, even though there is no sky.

We go up onto the surface as a brigade and overhear a conversation: "How can we become a happy country? Should we lose the war, or what?" There, on the surface, they think their life is worse than ours!

Today, for a change, they sent me to sweep the forest. There are many fallen leaves left from the winter, and they have to be swept away...

On TV there is a report about an Australian business man Mr. McKidney. He supplies this little Russian town with artificial kidneys because there is a uranium mine here and all the workers' kidneys are depleted. Mr. McKidney is motivated by humanitarian considerations; he doesn't take money from the workers but is content to take portions of the ready product, i.e. radioactive materials.

In fact, everything is free here: bread, pasta, two eggs and an apple. A food ration. You have to queue for it for two hours, sometimes for two and a half. Everyone queues after work, and everyone works. The supervisors are strict and they have hands with built-in electric shocks and an X-ray gaze. In the evenings they show films on the obligatory TV. They show an old-fashioned flat with a telephone — they had a telephone! Someone rings someone, and the answer phone repeats: "Into the loo, into the loo, into the loo."

I go to sleep on the sleep-inducing pillow.

The next day:

"My homeland is vast and broad… it's six am on May the sixth. You are listening to the broadcast "out and about in my dear homeland"…"

A click… silence… Behind the window adults hurry along to work, then kids skip along to school. Somewhere there on the surface the trees are naked but are readying themselves to get green. As usual, the window panes pretend to reflect the sky.

We go up onto the surface as a brigade, passing a group of old men sitting on a mound of earth. Here is the conversation:

"Why did countries where they love music so much lose the last war? Probably because unmusical people came to power there." Old men are worse off than we are, of course, but by how much?

Today we were sweeping the forest and sowing ground-elder and wood-sorrel in the former thicket.

In the evening: TV. Business man McKidney: "In theory, an artificial kidney can be pulled along behind you in a wheel barrow…"

A bedtime film. Someone is sitting on the loo and speaking over the phone (they had a telephone!). The answer machine gives useful advice.

I lie down to sleep on the sleep-inducing pillow. I dream a forbidden dream: books.

The next day.

"My country is vast and broad. There are many forests…"

At the mention of an unswept forest I hurl my pillow at the loudspeaker. As the pillow is flying over to it, the loudspeaker manages to spit out: "It's 6 am on May the sixth…"

Silence. Adults are hurrying along… children… The window panes, sky the colour of good weather, naked trees in waiting on the surface. Someone's conversation: "Who could we lose the war to? Who could conquer us? Nobody needs us…"The eternal search, the one who lives beyond the village fence is better off.

We are sweeping the forest and sowing nettles for communal soups.

Evening: TV. Mr. McKidney: "Look! This man with an artificial kidney has such beautiful urine…"

Afterwards, a film. Answer machines tell each other to go to the loo.

I lie down to sleep on the sleep-inducing pillow.

I dream: the wind whirls the clouds like tea leaves in a glass. I am flying somewhere too, piercing a sheet of paper…

There are many people in the room where I find myself. They are all sitting at a table and dealing out cards for a huge game of patience.

Something is not right here, I can sense it: there are neither windows nor doors in the room.

"Are we prisoners?" I asked aloud.

"No, we are guests," an elderly dame replies, and her diamond gleams pensively.

"Who holds us here?" I asked a second question but received no answer.

There is a telephone on the table. I dial several numbers. The answer machine repeats several times: "double zero — short castle, triple zero — long castle." I try dialling two other numbers but the reply is the same.

"Do they give us food here at least?" I ask.

"No, but we are never hungry," replies an officer in a reddish-gold uniform. "We don't live, you see."

"But does anyone really live?"

"Yes. People live, but they also die. But we are immortal. We are bodily casings."

And they all fold into four or into eight, and then for some reason take up more and more space, and squeeze me out of the room.

I take a run and jump at the wall. The sound of ripping paper, and someone says:

"My homeland is vast and broad... There are many... It's 6 am on May the sixth. You are listening to the broadcast..."

A click... Silence.... Adults hurrying... children... window panes... blue sky... naked trees... Coming to the surface with the brigade... Conversation on the street:

"In spite of everything, we shall become a happy country. We achieved great successes last week, and summer draws closer every day..."

But it was always one and the same day. Maybe it is lying sick somewhere nearby and cannot go anywhere, and it is worse for the day than it is for all of us, but we are no better off than it is...

We are transporting leaves on carts, and we take turns at pulling it.

Evening — TV — Mr. McKidney: "Trollies for artificial kidneys can be transformed into little carts and leaves can be transported out of the forest in them."

A bedtime film. A broken answer machine is lying in the loo, and the loo waters it tenderly.

I lie down to sleep on a sleep-inducing pillow but it turns out to be a sleepless pillow. It is the night of May the sixth. Again and again the LP gets stuck.

The town on the surface hums faintly and in the pauses, eternity can be heard.

23.

*The future emerges from the seeds of the past. From
sprouting seeds. But if a seed clings to the inviolability
of its external image, nothing emerges but wounded
pride, unfulfilled ambitions and conversations about
the unjust turn of events.*

People emerged from monkey-people. Some were quite good people. It took millennia. One monkey had an underdeveloped jaw, and his brain started to develop by way of compensation. The monkey survived, and reared descendants, and all those descendants survived. The jaws and the brain are somehow at odds. If you see a man with a superman jaw, observe the line of his brow; it is most likely to be anything but high.

Millennia passed. From the seeds of the past… Around one million species of living organisms inhabit the earth. And the human with its ample cranial chamber is one of them. And the monkey with its large jaw is another. And all the rest are hostile towards these two. The monkey says to the human: "Let's join forces!" But is there anything sensible to be had from the human?! And so monkeys must live the gyrations of their tree life alone. They let their happy laughter ring out, struggle for their place on the liana and for their rightful coconut, and in general do everything for which man is meant. And nobody objects, and hearts in harmony beat a hundred thousand beats in twenty four hours, and life moves somewhere, even though it doesn't actually move at all.

But sooner or later… And something changed after all, even though no-one knows exactly what. One morning May the seventh came around. Sunday.

Oh, that was a very special day! On some Sundays, monkey-like work-horses were pumped with plam — if their bosses had any plam to spare. And this Sunday the work-horses were blessed with the light breeze of happiness.

The kiosk where happiness was doled out was high up,

right under the roof of the underground. Shaggy monkey-like shadows were standing in line, their heads forming a kind of stairway. The monkey-like Swidersky's casing was present, but his thoughts were roaming elsewhere; to tell the truth, his thoughts were rather second-hand. Well, who can get a bright idea while standing in a queue for happiness or royalties?

Those who had already received happiness came swooping down, having either obtained wings again or tapped into some other source of energy. Some descended along the monkeys' heads, apparently too heavy with happiness to fly.

The queue was moving at snail's pace. Some couldn't bear it and fell down. None bothered to think of their fate.

A whisper rumoured that happiness was blown right into your mouth — quietly and tenderly. "Happiness — an aerosol?" thought the writer.

An abyss of time passed. Swidersky was almost at the kiosk. Another abyss of time passed, and his turn came at last.

"Ah, it's you," groaned the bellows somewhere there in the depths. "How much happiness do you need, then?"

"Enough to experience unearthly bliss on earth."

The groaning stopped. Someone was apparently examining his request carefully.

"Here you are then!"

And a whirlwind slammed through the kiosk window. It not only knocked the writer over but began swirling the whole queue up into the air. The writer was swimming in weightlessness, screaming with delight: This is it! Happiness — to be free, to leave behind earthly vanity!

Someone gingery and monkey-like flew close to him.

"Are you the last in the queue for happiness?"

Swidersky kicked him and hollered:

"That's happiness! Take as much as you like! What other happiness do you need?!"

The monkey-like creature flew off to the others to take his place in the queue.

24.

What are we digesting? What can we digest…?

A crocodile can digest steel nails and rework them into something nourishing. While doing so it is unable to move its tongue even slightly. We can descry some certain selective similarity or affinity of our own to the crocodile — after all, what haven't we digested — revolutions, tyranny, corruption, repression, and all this without particularly moving our tongues either, although the muscles of our tongue are considered to be some of the strongest muscles in our body. This sheds some light on the unknown potential of civilisation's digestive tract, and the capacity of its cesspool. Other stable organs of civilisation such as the brain and the heart have developed their stability over centuries of patience: the brain has born the heart's whims, and the heart has born the mind's rationality. Amidst all this, we still have the ability to find some inspiration somewhere inside ourselves — is that not man's most amazing quality? Admittedly, there are those who draw their inspiration from somewhere external, but never mind, never mind, one is judged by the results and they select the best. The rest are destined for the waste paper basket. So no matter what inspires you, everything is yours. You must know how to play the flute of your organism.

Having inspired himself with plam, the writer decided to embark upon some cross inquiries. That Sunday evening turned out to be a convenient time; the monkey-people, unburdened by mental worries, gathered on their bench in the courtyard to play dominoes, tapping their dominoes on their pine tables in a most corporeal way.

Swidersky decided to talk to the leader of the brigade who, it must be said, looked for all the world like an orang-utan.

"You want your body back?" he said, surprised. "You're not supposed to, you know. You have to earn the right before you can submit a petition."

"How?"

"You have to work for about ten years."

"Hmm. Who knows what will happen to my body in that time…"

"Don't worry. Nothing bad can happen to it. Everything is very orderly here."

"What about the contraband in human bodies? Is that part and parcel of your orderliness?"

The leader of the brigade took offense; the hair on the top of his head stood on end.

"We will punish you!" he said. "We'll cut off your TV!"

The writer pretended to wipe away tears, and this threw the orang-utan brigade leader into a blind rage. "We can force you to work twenty-four hours on the trot."

Swidersky shrugged and turned away.

When the orang-utan was out of earshot, one of the monkeys approached the writer. This specimen looked like a gibbon.

"I heard your conversation," the gibbon rustled into his ear, scratching his heels with his long hands without so much as bending even slightly. "You're too direct, old chap. You can't go about things like that here. We're on the latter stages of evolution, don't you know."

The writer thought to himself that this interpretation of the question of the stages of evolution was debateable, but the gibbon, it seems, clearly wanted to help him.

"It's not so easy with bodies. Forgive my comparison, but we say a cow can be led up the stairway to the first floor, but you just try to force it to come down. It's the same here, but I'll try to help you. I'll talk to someone."

The writer never found out exactly who he spoke to, but the next day the gibbon asked him to stay behind after work.

"Perhaps it's against the rules, but I'll take you to the warehouse. Who knows, maybe your body is there."

They went along the deserted streets, passed stately-looking barracks, and the same sounds floated out of all the windows. They were showing a film on TV, and the TV screens flickered blue in every window.

The warehouse manager was a mangy old monkey who was constantly scratching itself in all decent and indecent places.

"A body? Do you have an order for the body?"

"Hey! Listen up!" the gibbon butted in. "If he finds this body and dons it, we'll come into possession of an almost unworn bodily casing. Do you know how much they cost these days? And what's more, we could "forget" to register it, just take it and sell it."

"You've got a point there… OK then," said the old monkey turning to Swidersky. "We'll show you the bodies and then it's up to you to choose one. We've got all sorts here…"

And there really were a lot of bodies. And they all had a similar yellowishness about them, a certain human nakedness quite unfamiliar in this monkey world.

"What's this body of yours like, then?" the warehouse warden kept repeating. "Are you sure you know which body you want to return to? A body's like a river, you know. You can't enter it twice. Well, you can, of course, but will it be the same body? And another thing: don't you want something better?"

"What kind of choice do you reckon I have?" queried Swidersky.

"Take a close look at each body. The owner of this one is clearly Chinese, and the owner of that one is most likely of Jewish origin. Look at its intimate parts."

"Mmm. You're right. Can you tell the nationality of other bodies?"

"No problem. Even if they don't have tattoos on them. You can always spot the Spanish, and the Polish, too. Here's a body with a silvery Celtic cross on the chest. It's obviously an Irish one, and the hair is ginger, too. You can take it if you like. Will it do?"

The writer was at a loss for words.

"There are other criteria, too, not just nationality. We've got Marxists, Muslims, Rastafarians, Russian patriots, philosophers and even one singer. Think about it. What do you really want? We also have female bodies, so you could change sex without any trouble."

"No thanks. I'd like to find my own body," said he writer after a pause, because his attention was consumed by contemplating this other-worldly nakedness, the last incarnation, or maybe the last revelation, of human existence. "If, of course, it's here… Ah, there it is!"

His body was lying quite peacefully on a plank bed as if its owner had just retired to the dimensions of underground sleep. Well, why not interrupt that sleep?

He slipped out of his bodily casing and donned his familiar body, creaking at the joints. Everything was fine, just a little pain in the back, but as we know, radiculitis is no stranger to writers, and battling with a familiar evil is business as usual.

25.

It is already too late to love oneself. Almost from the very beginning.

We love ourselves in ourselves — young, beautiful and full of fierce energy. But then we forget how he was, this beautifully energetic one, and we don't love anyone anymore. And who, you may ask, will love us if we don't love ourselves? Let us at last proclaim a speech in defence of egotism, in defence of self-love, and even in defence of completely unappealing swaggering, for when all is said and done, the swaggerer knows what he is swaggering about. And having stimulated a healthy curiosity about ourselves, let us crown ourselves with wreaths, dress in white clothes and gaze into the silver mirrors without wincing when we see our own faces. And the world will become not what it is but something quite different, and people won't send each other packing to the underworld, but to this world, and not as a punishment.

"Where are you going to go now?" the gibbon asked the writer.

"I would like to return to Andriania."

"Why? You're much closer to the earth's surface here. We can plant you in some little Russian town."

"No. I'd like to return the same way I came. And anyway, I need to talk to someone."

"OK. But you can only get to Andriania via chimneys and you're not exactly built for flying now."

"But is it possible in theory?"

"Mmm. Yes. We'll have to find you a direct connection, and it would be a good idea to wrap yourself in a blanket from head to toe — who knows what you might bump into. From time to time they erect plexiglass barriers there. If you come across one, just give it a good kick. And whatever you do, don't even think of entering the chimney head first."

Having been instructed on all the minute details, the writer wrapped himself in an old blanket and heroically climbed into the manhole they showed him, feet first.

Evidently it was not exactly a direct connection, for after five minutes of rumbling and whistling in his ears, he found himself absolutely nowhere.

26.

A place called nowhere could easily exist somewhere on earth.

Put cardboard placards along some forgotten lane, and there you have it, a backdrop of prosperity, Potemkin's villages. You can even bring important guests there and show them. From a distance, so they don't suspect foul play. But in reality, nowhere whistles there. Ordinary, run of the mill nowhere. However, if there is such a thing as ordinary nowhere, there should also be such a thing as a perfectly ideal nowhere. A place where "let there be light!" was not heard but "let there be shadow!" Let's be clear: there was such a place, and the shadows came there first and didn't need any light. They were all preceded by a large winged shadow which declared nowhere to be the centre of creation. And it was no worse than any other place which lays claim to the same status, by the way.

And Swidersky seemed to have landed in that very nowhere, either in a dream or in waking reality. If it was a dream, then the place of the action was the centre of creation. It was light in a nightly way.

"You have arrived at the final destination," he was informed by a sexless voice. "You can dismiss the dragon that brought you here."

"Splendid," said the writer, and began observing the dragon which was sweeping aside the stars in its way as it flew off.

"If you want to stay here, you have to pay," the same voice continued dispassionately. "The price is nine lives."

"Whose?"

"Yours, of course. You must narrate them all in the first person right up until the last moment."

The moon smiled, the stars were twinkling clearly, encouraging him to begin his tale and verbal adventures.

From that time up until the last instant of the aforementioned portion of eternity, Swidersky retold the emptiness lives unlived by him. Harpies and poets, clearly at home in these parts, were flying by.

27.

But all things come to an end sooner or later, even daydreams.

For the writer, everything ended when he either fell or was pushed into a manhole, but that is not important. What is important is that once again he felt the familiar whistling in his ears and finally he flew through the chimney right into the sitting room of his empire-style house, landing on the Bukhara carpet, which he knew every inch of.

Having felt his long-suffering body all over, he ascertained he was more or less all right. It was nice to stretch his pins-and-needles legs. He walked around the house and realised that the professor was not at home, just as he had suspected. Where is he? Is he searching for his body, too? "The man in search of his body"… A good title for a book. I should remember it.

He sipped a cup of tea, and it served its usual purpose: simultaneously invigorating him and calming him down. In his head, unworn for so long, clarity began to dawn. He thought he was now quite ready to return to transient reality, and he also thought he would certainly not return there without the professor; he didn't want to leave him here.

The question was: where to look for him? Where was the *treffpunkt*, the place where everyone meets everyone?

He came out of the house and circled the square, looking for somewhere to sit down and wait. But the shadows of the town of Andriania didn't need benches, so there were none. On the other side of the square was a little alley leading off somewhere. There was a stone wall on one side of it and a meadow on the other with something like a manhole in the middle.

"Well, why shouldn't I sit on the lid?" thought the writer. "Let's see who walks — or maybe flies — by."

But there wasn't a lid. The manhole was some sort of black hole, similar to the one he had used to return from the monkeys' underground.

The writer sat on the edge of the manhole and dangled his feet into it. It wasn't exactly comfortable, but as everyone knows, it is better to sit than to stand since all of us have a bit of Antaeus in us.

"Well, my path takes me back into the world where there is no place for me, no place for such as I, but I must find my place. I don't need much, and I won't have to clear it out, but where is it? And who am I? Who is searching for this place? I didn't make it as either a Muscovite or a Jewish immigrant. I was not up to giant Russia or voluminous Germany. Not the right size? But who knows what will happen in the little country of Ireland?

In our time of labels and tags, what shall I choose for myself? Something which people are familiar with? And do I really need to choose? Or at least decide for myself who I am, since I chose this body which is not easily identifiable. How much of me is Polish? Irish? Jewish? European? Russian writer? No, I know who I want to be, and who I will be. I want to be a stranger everywhere I go, and I know that I was, am and ever shall be a stranger, even in Russia, in Moscow, on the street where I was born because I am not of this world, and each person is not of this world, and even the world is not of this world, but they all know how to pretend. But not me. I find it boring.

I was late to emigrate. Twenty-year-olds were leaving, thirty-year-olds were leaving, while my generation was sitting in the kitchen waiting for death because there was no life. But death was in no hurry, either. It was busy with something else, and didn't promise an early visit. My grandfather left for America too late, historically, and when he arrived there, albeit as a youngster, everything had already sorted itself out nicely without him. Both of us are from a generation of laggards. These are the generations which come every other generation, and I don't envy my grandson if I have one…"

And so he sat, thinking and waiting. It wasn't clear what he was waiting for but what he got was a telling off from one of the omnipresent sylvans who happened to be processing by.

"So here you are sitting on the edge but do you know that your feet are in the other world?"

"What do you mean, the other world?" asked the writer, rather shocked.

"In the world you came from. If there's someone nearby, he'll see legs sticking out of a manhole."

Swidersky imagined his legs, which had made their way into the other dimension, and appearing there in the shape of a Latin letter "V", and he hurried to bring them back.

"So this hole is an exit to the outside world?" he asked.

"No. It is an entrance into ours. There are many entrances, you see, but only one exit."

28.

If, of course, there is an exit.

It was worth thinking about the exit. He should let it enter his thoughts and not let it exit. Swidersky was quite sure that if he expressed the desire to leave the confines of this hospitable place they would not cause obstacles for him, but first he had to find the professor.

He decided to ask the sylvan.

"Are you looking for your friend?" said the sylvan. "We have a warehouse for friends here. That's where you should look."

"A warehouse?" the writer was amazed.

"Have you been in the town hall cellars?"

"No, never."

"Let me show you."

Not far from the entrance to the town hall was a door leading to a concealed lift door. Had it not been for the sylvan, Swidersky would have sworn it was a mirror in a metal frame.

The cellar was dark, quiet and smelt of mice. Cupboards lined the walls. Cupboards, cupboards and more cupboards.

"Open them up and take a look. Maybe you'll find what you're looking for," said the sylvan phlegmatically.

Swidersky opened the closest door. There was a man sitting inside, staring out at him. The writer started and closed the cupboard quickly.

"What are they doing there?" he asked.

"It's a kind of game called "choose your friend". The idea is that you cannot choose your friend yourself. The friend should choose you, so people who want to be friends with someone climb into an empty cupboard and wait for someone to choose them. Would you like to try?"

"No way!" said the writer pulling a wry face. "If I were a shadow I might have tried, but not in my human appearance. No way!"

"So you managed to find your body?"

"Yes, but don't ask how."

"I won't ask because I can guess how," said the sylvan smiling like a bandit, which was not so difficult thanks to his black hairy face. "I'll make a note in the log book that your query has been resolved."

Before leaving the cellar, Swidersky acted on some strange impulse and opened the door of the cupboard closest to the exit. There was a girl inside. Magda!

"Choose me!" she said with an infernal voice and a stony smile.

29.

It is amusing to retrieve a person from a cupboard.

Swidersky helped the sylvan to take the girl out. Together they walked into the square. The two greenish artificial suns were shining, faking a quiet, greenish evening.

"What happened? Why are you here?" asked the writer.

"Better not to ask. I fell out of favour."

"So these cupboards are for punishment?"

"Yes, something like that."

"What did you do?"

"I helped the professor find his body."

"Oh, is he flesh and blood again?"

"Almost," said the girl mysteriously. "I would have helped him go back, but he didn't want to leave without you."

"How touching. Are you sure he really wants to go back?"

"Yes. He said he now wants to research the phenomenon of bodily casings because they don't age. He wants to develop a human body which is immune to aging. That will be his new scientific goal."

"But he doesn't want to stay in a casing forever himself!"

"That's what I said, too. But he said it wasn't an obstacle. He said you don't have to be a tiger to study tigers."

"Quite logical!" smirked Swidersky. "That's Ostermann all right."

"You know," Magda began whispering in his ear. "They suspect him of hiding his bodily casing somewhere and of trying to smuggle it out. So he can't leave by the official route now."

"So what shall we do?"

"Who knows…"

"But where is the professor?"

"I'm afraid I can't tell you that for now. I think someone is eavesdropping on us."

"But there's nobody about!"

"Someone bodiless, transparent."

And the bodiless, transparent air began singing with dragonfly wings. Emptiness embraced them in the same bodiless way and accompanied them home, i.e. to the little empire-style house, and then sang them a lullaby:

> *O shiny moon of Saint Hertz,*
> *Light up the depths of our hearts!*

The full moon showed itself, and "full moon" was written on the flip calendar. On the back was a picture of an electric lamp burning in the skies and the caption: "The Moon of St. Hertz". Tomcats in the attic were eating potted mice and washing them down with some sort of white, sour-cream like substance which was light and transparent like the light of the painted moon. In the black rectangle of the attic window, a cat's physiognomy would appear, peer about, and then disappear in the darkness of the underground night. Shadows were playing at cats, or maybe cats were playing at shadows, if, of course, there are any cats underground. However, where there are houses there may be cats, too. There must be.

The little empire-style house opened the doors of its huge jaws in front of them, and smirked to itself. The jaw of the door yawned and the hinge clicked. Someone else goes there, too, and we cannot be sure whether he will ever exit, thought the house melancholically. If, of course, houses can think.

Magda turned her cameo-profile to the writer, moved the still-life still covering the fireplace, and said cheerily:

"Follow me, sir! Feet first, and don't forget to wrap something around your head!"

30.

*In fact, our head will come in handy again. We have
a heady life before us, we simply have to learn to use
the head, and not leave it too late.*

And here, under this glass, there are children. Children, for some reason. Walls with pale tiles — is it a hospital? It is warm here, and light and clear, and instead of a portrait of Hemingway there's a portrait of someone's hairy face. No, the children didn't add a graffiti beard to a picture of Lenin; this beard was clearly printed in the printing house. The face is that of a beast, but all medicine stems from the Evil One, of course, and that is why we should not be surprised by the portraits on the walls but marvel instead at the sight of pale, sleepy children in glass cupboards with rubber tubes sticking out of their mouths, and some liquid bubbling away in flasks. We should marvel at the absence of staff, and at the faraway voices on the other side of the building, and at the absence of windows, and also at the fact that Swidersky's feet are braced against somebody's "below the back", and that back is most decidedly female.

"Here we are," whispered Magda, and took the towel off the writer's head.

"Welcome to our laboratory," said a voice from nowhere which made Swidersky start. "Please make yourself at home."

Magda and Swidersky, still sitting on the floor, began to look around. The voice was evidently coming from loudspeakers hidden somewhere under the ceiling.

"Our staff are busy in other labs just now," continued the invisible loudspeaker. We apologise for any inconvenience. One of our employees will be with you shortly."

"They obviously don't have that many employees here," said the writer quietly.

"Quite right," said a voice behind him. He started and looked around. "Let me introduce myself. I'm Doctor Dr. Mepel," said a middle-aged man in German. With his grey hair, beard and bushy black eyebrows he looked like a medieval alchemist.

Swidersky introduced himself and asked:

"Are you the head of the laboratory?"

"Yes, I am responsible for everything that goes on here. Did you want to ask me something?"

Swidersky hesitated, and Magda replied instead of him:

"We would like to speak to staff scientist Arefiev, if possible."

"Of course it's possible. I give you my full approval," said Mepel importantly. "His office is right at the end of the corridor on the left."

Arefiev's office was crammed with lab instruments and some complicated apparatus. They found the owner holding an automatic pipette in his hands.

"One moment," said Arefiev, sitting with his back towards them and emptying the contents of the pipette into a test tube. He gave it a little shake then poured the potion into a flask. This procedure complete, he placed the flask in a thermostat and finally turned around.

"Oh, it's you!" he said, surprised. "How did you find me?"

"Your colleague Dr. Mepel showed us the way," said Magda.

"Ah, Doctor Doctor Mepel Mepel!" grinned Arefiev.

"What, what?" asked the writer.

"That's his nickname. He's from Germany, you see. He's a Czech of course, or a Slovak, judging by his surname, but educated in Germany. And in Germany, PhD holders are called "doctor", and a doctor of science is also called "doctor". Doctor Mepel is very proud of this and always introduces himself as Doctor Doctor, so our lab assistants decided to double his name as well as his title. It stuck, funnily enough. But of course we only call him that behind his back. He's a sweet man, actually, despite all his quirks."

"Is he the boss here?"

"Yes, something like that. He's the boss of the production laboratory, responsible for the production of Solution Number 18, i.e. plam. But I work independently and I report my academic results directly to academician Afonsky."

"Listen, what on earth is going on here? Who are those children in the glass tanks?" Swidersky asked.

"This is one of the academician's ideas," said Arefiev a bit bashfully. "We sort of saved several terminally ill children by turning them into bodily casings. The idea was to observe how our famous plam affects a child's organism. But actually it turns out that such children are not very strong, so we don't do this anymore, and the children we worked with are kept on life support machines. We hope they will survive somehow."

"But these children aren't your main scientific task, are they?"

"Of course not. I study various factors which affect the bodily casings and seek to make them even more stable and durable."

He looked at his watch, then took another flask from the table and placed it in the thermostat. Turning to Magda he said:

"You, Professor Ostermann, are also quite interested in the problems of bodily casings, I gather."

31.

"All right, all right, you're among friends here," Arefiev smiled seeing his visitors' embarrassment.

Swidersky didn't understand what was going on. He was staring at his brother wide-eyed, and then turned his gaze on the girl. Magda's appearance began to fade somehow, and blur. After a couple of minutes, Professor Ostermann was standing in front of him, dressed as a woman.

"One moment," he said, in a half-male voice, after which his metamorphosis continued, and he finally stood before them dressed in his own clothes.

"Nothing surprises us here," said Arefiev. "It's ridiculously easy to change the outward appearance of a bodily casing, that's why it's like a fancy dress party here — everyone chooses a mask and costume and parades around in that guise."

"How did you know this is the professor?"

"Well, first of all because Magda doesn't exist and never did. Or to be precise, it was me who invented her. I copied her face from a statue above a certain tomb you know. After all, I had to lure the two of you here somehow!"

Swidersky was in a state of shock but having looked at the professor, he realised the professor was no less amazed by the last revelation.

"And secondly, because I was waiting for the professor," Arefiev went on. "He was bound to visit me to get his body — it's stored here with me, after all. As for you, professor, haven't you decided to transfer into a bodily casing forever?"

"I don't know," the professor panted. "Let me come to my senses… So how come Magda spoke to me in German without any accent?"

"Ah, now you've caught me!" Arefiev gave a boyish grin. "I must confess, I took the guise of Magda once, when I led you to us through the tomb. Someone else had been playing that role earlier."

"And that person was of course Doctor Doctor?" Swidersky winked at his brother.

"Ah, you've always understood me too well! Imagine how difficult it was to convince such a respectable scientist to take part in such an adventure. If it weren't for his penchant for dressing up…"

"Well, your respectable scientist certainly knows how to flirt!" said the professor, rather vexed.

"That's true! You should see him in a lady's dress when he goes to town — our town, that is. He only ever shows up in our town in female guise. By the way, the sylvans helped to arouse your interest, too. They have such an unusual appearance!"

"It really is a kind of fancy dress ball!" growled the professor.

"Well, it makes our life more interesting," replied Arefiev diplomatically.

"By the way, talking about the interesting life after life and so on, let's decide who will do what in the future," suggested Swidersky using his practical wisdom. "I'm not asking you, brother, because you are at the forefront of science here and you have found your calling. As for me, I'm going back because I want to write something more."

"Yes, of course," Arefiev smiled at him. "You are at the forefront, too! May you have a happy life in the new place. You'll be sure to send me a copy of your new novel, won't you?"

"Surely they don't deliver post here?"

"No, of course not. But send it to me by email as an attachment."

"By email?" said the writer amazed. "Do you have email here?"

"Well, we have computers here so why can't we have email? I've got some business cards with my email address on the desk right here."

"I always thought there was something other-worldly about emails," the professor spoke up finally. "As far as I understand, you are both waiting for me to make some sort of decision." He fell silent for a while and then continued. "I'll be frank with you. At first I had decided to remain in the bodily casing — eternal life, freedom from your own body, it all sounds very attractive. But then

I thought about how I, this concrete I, can best apply my talents and use my knowledge. It seems to me that in their current state, bodily casings cannot solve all humanity's problems. We are still faced with the same problem which academician Pavlov formulated some time ago: how to extend a person's creative life. The first fifty years of life are the mind's childhood, the next twenty-five are its adolescence, so very few manage to survive to maturity, and even if they do, they are prone to disease, vascular sclerosis, dementia and other nice things. So that is what I want to fight against, and for this, I must return to my university, to my lab."

"I quite respect your decision," said Arefiev. "And I can help you return. I feel as though I'm helping two refugees from Noah's ark to return to the pre-flood shores."

"Do you seriously predict a flood?"

"There have been several, so why shouldn't there be another?"

"Well, if that happens we'll ask to be taken back into the ark again!" smiled the professor.

"You'll always be welcome guests here. By the way, you take a card with my email, too, professor. Let's keep in touch. If you decide to retire and move here, let me know. We can always find space in our lab for one more staff scientist."

"Thank you," said the professor warmly.

"You can even take your bodily casing with you. I'm sure you'll make good use of it. It's against all the rules, of course, but in this case I shall take full responsibility."

32.

And Swidersky woke up in a dream. In his dream he was inside a mountain. For some reason he knew this mountain was in Phoenicia and was called Geba. Not far from it was a town Gebal, or Byblos. The Phoenicians had once begun producing papyrus there. And everyone knows what that led to: libraries, book markets, love stories, crime novels, and poetry anthologies. It is said that the town of Byblos owes its name to the felonious love of a brother and sister, Caunus and Byblida. The citizens did not approve of such a dubious interpretation of brotherly love, and as a result, the brother had to flee and the sister committed suicide. The town was called Byblos in her name, and since they had chosen such a name, they had to make a library there.

So now I have somehow come back to the beginning, thought Swidersky. The library inside the town of Gebal where he found himself was the most amazing library he had ever seen. It was the real proto-mother of all libraries. Obviously, not many people ever visited it because the librarians greeted the visitor not with the polite indifference customary in public libraries, but from the heart. However, the most surprising thing was that there were no books to be seen.

The library was a huge cave with fires burning all around it, although Swidersky felt no heat. Attendants wearing white tunics and sandals wandered around the fires unhurriedly, but not a drop of sweat glistened on the parchment skin of their faces; it seemed completely dry.

"Where are the books?" the writer asked.

By way of response, he was led to a fire. The fires formed a fiery ring. "The books are there," the warden told him pointing to the centre of the ring.

"Does that mean they are inaccessible?"

"That depends."

"But how can you get through the fire?"

"Some manage. You have to test it with your hand first." The warden touched the fiery tongue. It flickered, then withered under his fingers. The fire was cold. "Come on, be brave," he encouraged the visitor.

And Swidersky stepped into the centre of the ring of fire. The warden was already standing next to him.

There were flames here, too, but they were not high, like a mown lawn. Books were burning there but were not consumed. You could find everything here! Papyrus scrolls, clay tablets and parchment codices, not to mention modern books.

"Can I take a book?" asked Swidersky.

"Yes, you can, but whatever you take will remain yours for ever, so make no mistake."

"Don't I have to return it?"

"No, because nobody else will be able to borrow that book."

"So does that mean that the number of books is gradually decreasing?"

"We have a countless number of books. Not even we know what sorts of books we have, because we are not allowed to open a book until someone has chosen it."

"But how can you know which one to chose?"

"Oh, great ones know how to choose! I remember how Milton came here to take *Paradise Lost*. He knew what he was taking even without seeing it... And Shakespeare came here many times. He had a true aim!"

"But who came here first?"

"One wandering preacher, Kohelet. He said he had been a king before, but he didn't come anywhere near here when he was on the throne, and we never saw him again after that one visit."

"Are there only great books here?"

"No," smiled the warden. "That depends on you. It is said that one may even come across books with empty pages. Would you like to take something?"

Swidersky hearkened to his reasoning, kept quiet for a while and then finally said:

"Yes."

"Then take one."

He didn't want to take either a scroll or a palimpsest, so he fixed his gaze on the modern books. The covers were all alike, the colour of flames, and without any inscriptions.

He looked at one book, then a second and a third, and then finally, looking at the next one, he suddenly understood it was his book, and took it out of the fire.

The book was very light, almost weightless.

"I can't tell you whether you have chosen well," the warden smiled with his parchment smile. "Maybe you'll soon find out for yourself, or maybe not. Very well then, take your book, but remember: it will grow heavier and heavier with each step you take. Try to deliver it."

Having bid farewell to the parchment-like wardens, Swidersky came out of the mountain onto the dusty country track which should have led from the country of dreams into the quarters of waking reality. The book was growing heavy as lead under his arm.

33.

Once more the bustling yellow-red-black flags are fluttering in the almost farewell air of our narration. Swidersky is standing on the Münsterstadt station square waiting for a train which will take him to the airport.

"The air is full of poplar fluff and German words, but my wish is to write poems in the tongue of the wind from the Atlantic and jasmine showing up white under the windows," he thinks. "To write about how I saw tumbleweed under a sorrow-coloured sky, and a tree growing inside an empty house. But I was unable to capture this, for too often the sounds turned out to be pre-sounds and the song held its tongue on talkative lips. And that is why I wish to write in the tongue of the invisible snowflake of a future winter, which now, in May, melts so warmly on the palm of my hand."

A PARADE OF MIRRORS AND REFLECTIONS

Translated from the Russian by Siobhán McNamara

If one lifts a mirror above one's head in such a way
that a young moon is reflected in it, then one will be
able to see as many moons as the number of days old
the moon is. One will always see at least two moons
in the mirror, and sometimes as many as seven.

V. I. Dahl

ANATOLY KUDRYAVITSKY

Prologue

When they woke up, the world began. Immediately, all at once, and everywhere. A world of reflections in mirrors. It panted, trying to get through to people, but they knew nothing and lived without sensing that this world, which is broken into parts — torso, shoulders, shins — was somewhere beyond an invisible barrier.

Then at last the existence of the world of reflections was announced, but people had already guessed that the loud panting heralded just another silence. The world of reflections became disillusioned with people and went into the kingdom of animals. There were sounds here: lowing, bleating, chirping… They did not impede the reign of human silence.

The silence was called History. It was born when events, people and voices died. Only songs, drawings and records were left behind. Books were written from the drawings and records, and together with the songs they were brought to future generations. These descendants detected false notes in the songs, but they could never explain how they had appeared, because the system of recording music usually turned out to be lost. In this way, the false notes lived for centuries as a kind of spicy seasoning to the bland dish of History. To a silence set with gelatine.

PART ONE

1.

Most of the time he slept. Sleep kept him in its grip and did not want to release him. And he himself did not want very much to break free — his previous half-awakenings had taught him a lot.

"Where will I be when I wake up?" he asked himself when he was asleep. But he did not answer. He was not alive, he was closer to death than to life, but in this death he could dream. If you can dream when you are dead, then is death not preferable to life? You say it isn't? We wouldn't be so sure…

Before the half-awakenings he dreamt about the Weather Cook. Surrounded by white fog, with a rosy, blinding smile. He placed an order with the Weather Cook — no, he did not order weather, that would make no sense, — but climate. And then was filled with this climate down to the very depths of his lungs. He absorbed it like a sponge. The next logical step for him was to turn the imaginary dial, and he would end up wherever he wanted. But he never ended up anywhere, only back in the arms of sleep.

2.

What a stupid dream, he thought to himself when he woke up. Who was this Weather Cook? A romantic idea, though…

The weather was obviously not the work of a cook, but home-made: too much water had been added and it was trickling down from the heavenly cotton-wool onto his head, shoulders, and onto the bench…

"Where am I?" He began looking around. The city answered with the beating of pigeon wings. The city was the colour of rain, the pigeons were the colour of rain. "Why am I here? Oh of course, I live here… But why, why do I live here?"

So he had remembered something. Even a grey, three-story building with a hairdresser's sign at the bottom. The ground floor belonged to the hairdresser Geranek, the first floor to the artist Osuzhdin, and the second floor to himself… But who was he? What did he do? What interested him, made his heart beat faster? He couldn't remember. His hands were white, with small palms and no calluses. There was nothing in his pockets. No, there was something after all. A case shaped like a book. It opens and there's a mirror inside. What's to be seen in the mirror? A pale face, eyes the colour of a cloudy sky, wet, fair hair, water dripping onto his cheeks and chin, and onto the mirror. It was time to go.

As he was standing up, something fell to the ground. A notebook! It must have been on his lap. He picked it up quickly, before it could get wet, and flicked away the yellow, heart-shaped leaf that had stuck to the artificial black leather cover. That was a stroke of luck! There were so many names here! Now he would remember everything!

Almost dancing, he walked along the wet cobbled path to the exit from the park, let a hurried, beetle-shaped car go past, and went around a corner…

He must have gone the wrong way. It wasn't a street that was around the corner, and not even a lane. Just a small dead-end between buildings. A couple of sweethearts were embracing. The man was wearing a black mackintosh and a beret pulled down over his eyes, the woman was bare-headed, and her head was thrown back in ecstasy so that only a golden stream of hair was flowing…

He felt no stab in his heart, he had no envy of them, and he noted this sadly. But all the same he shrank back instinctively and went back around the corner. Yes, there was love in spite of the rain, the strange place, the approaching autumn — love to the point of self-oblivion. How that girl had thrown back her head!

But something worried him a little. There was something wrong — in the picture he had seen there was one brushstroke that spoiled everything, as one false note can spoil a masterly musical performance. Could the girl have thrown her head back like *that*? Is that even possible?

Almost running, he went back to the corner that he had already walked away from, turned… and the picture was different. Instead of a pair of sweethearts, there was a girl lying on the concrete, on her back, her throat slit. Blood was flowing and mixing with the rain. Just rain and a dead girl. Nothing else.

The picture he saw was not called "Love" but "Murder".

3.

But something was missing from the picture. The murderer was missing. Where could he have gone?

The dead-end was formed by two blank grey walls — the side walls of old, shabby buildings — and the back wall of another, dirty-green building. There was… no, there was no door, but there was a basement window with closed shutters. No, not closed, but ajar. The heavy brown shutters obediently let him in.

A deserted room. With an oak chest opposite the window. On it was a candlestick with no candle and — in the half-dead, lilac light of the overcast day he could see this clearly — a bloodied knife.

So the murderer had been here! Better follow him. He didn't know why he wanted to follow him — to catch him, or just to look at him: after all, isn't it interesting to see what kind of people murderers are, to see what is reflected in the mirrors of their eyes…?

He opened the door and found himself in a half-dark,

half-asleep corridor. Somewhere far away a light bulb was on. He went towards it. The corridor divided into two. There was a smell of lavender, stuffiness, human habitation. One corridor ended in an enormous oak door. He flung it open — and...

And in came the Sun. An unbearable gold light. He just about managed to jump back towards the wall. The Sun went past, the light faded, his eyes stopped hurting, but he was almost blinded.

He felt his way into the room. Nobody there, it seemed.

"Hello," he heard.

4.

He started, and began looking around. A gold patch was floating in the very centre of his field of vision. But there was nobody in the room! Just a table, an armchair, a sideboard full of dusty crockery...

"I'm hiding," said a voice, a child's voice. "I'm behind the chair."

It was a little girl in a red dress, fair-haired and laughing.

"Are you looking for the big man?"

"Yes," he answered.

"Then go that way," the girl said with a sigh. "He wants to play with you. He has this big black thing that they use to play war."

It was only then that he noticed that there were four doors in the room, so the hint was not unnecessary.

"What's your name?"

"I don't know. Maybe I don't have one..." the girl said sadly. "You look like my daddy. But you're not my daddy."

"Are you here on your own?" he asked, though he could have guessed the answer.

"I'm always on my own," the girl replied. "If you want you can take me with you."

He took her by the hand — how small her palm was, and how cold!

Through the door was a corridor full of book cases.

"Do you like reading books?" he asked the girl, thinking that he couldn't remember a single book he'd ever read.

Did he ever read?

The little girl did not answer — perhaps because a black silhouette had appeared at the end of the corridor.

"There he is, the big man," said the girl. "You hide, and he'll shoot."

There was so little time. As quickly as he could, he shielded the little girl with his body and dropped to the floor. A roar of gunshot, and a bullet burned his thigh. Fierce pain.

The man in black waited to make sure his victim couldn't get up, then he ran off. There were no more gunshots.

What about the girl? Where was she? She wasn't there, his body had been shielding emptiness. But perhaps that little girl had saved his life.

5.

He was bleeding, and he was on his own. Just him and the building. Oak panels creaked, blood flowed, and silence muffled his ears.

He tore off his trouser cuffs, knotted the two pieces together, and tied them tightly around his wounded thigh. Not to worry, it would soon heal.

He stood up with difficulty and, leaning against the wall, went forward along the corridor. Yes, forward, not back — the thought that he would have to go past the murdered girl was unbearable… Why had she been treated so brutally? He wanted to pity her, but what was pity? How do you pity someone, what do you do?

The corridor became narrower. Past the next door the walls were not covered with oak, but painted with poisonously green oil paint that was already peeling off in places. There was a damp, vile smell — probably of gone-off casein glue.

The next door — which was made of iron — was also unlocked. He pushed it and found himself in some sort of waiting room. Silent people were sitting on oilcloth-covered chairs: women in downy headscarves, pensioners in ancient heavy overcoats, two young men with tightly-cut hair and black leather jackets. He went in, and all eyes turned towards him. He became flustered, and froze to the spot. But then another door opened, and through it poured in a crowd of mad people. One of them wailed:

"They let him off! They let the murderer off! Good God!"

Another man corrected him sternly:

"They didn't let him off, mister Leszek, they gave him two years suspended sentence."

"Ah, it's the same thing," a woman's voice said inconsolably.

"Well, when you have the right connections…" someone hinted.

He couldn't see anyone who had spoken. Now nobody was looking at him, and he found a way out. There was a corridor, a staircase, and a door out onto the street. Outside, he looked around. Beside the door was a red name-plate with grubby gold letters: "THE PEOPLE'S COURT".

6.

"I must be a strange sight, a limping man with a trouser leg covered in blood and tied with a cuff," he thought to himself and about himself as he weakly lowered himself onto a wet bench in the small green space near the exit.

Where should he go? Where did he live? He remembered what his building looked like, but where should he look for it? All the more so now, when his leg was on fire and he hadn't the strength to stand up, let alone to walk…

He passed out — maybe from pain, maybe from tiredness.

It was definitely pain that woke him up again: somebody was shaking his shoulder, and every movement of his leg echoed in his eyes in the form of blinding lightning.

"Stop it," he managed to say weakly.

"So you're alive," the smell of stale alcohol hit him in the face. "I thought you were dead… What happened to your leg?"

"Who are you?" he heard himself whisper.

"Don't tell me you don't recognise Pincus… Listen, maybe we should get you to a hospital?"

"No," he said. "It'll get better by itself."

"Well, then, I'll give you a lift home. Are you still living in the same place?"

"Uh-huh," he replied. "What's my name?"

"What?" Pincus was astonished. He was carrying the patient on his back, and he had to stop and lean him against a tree on the footpath. "Have you lost your memory or something?"

"Yeah."

"Your name is Felix. Felix Kangar. Surely you remember?"

"It's beginning to come back to me," was the answer, because some sort of answer was needed.

They crawled along some more.

"So what happened to your leg, then?" Pincus asked, as an old Volkswagen, a beige-coloured "Beetle," was dragging them through the city, which was gradually dissolving in the rain.

"I caught it on a nail."

"Really?" Pincus smiled slyly and began comforting him. "Once when I was drunk I fell out a window, and I came out in one piece. It was in Krakow, I buy my stuff there."

"Keep your eyes on the road" Felix said anxiously.

It was only then that he took a proper look at his companion's unshaven, criminal-looking face, his neck which was covered with black hair. A robust fellow. But how could he get behind the wheel in such a state?

The car was swerving a bit, but nonetheless was moving towards its target. That building was in front of them already —

that building which was familiar for some reason, here was the hairdresser's sign. A bald old woman was looking at them from the hairdresser's window.

The robust fellow lifted him up the stairs to the second floor, then put his hand in Felix's pocket and groped around for the keys. The apartment was empty. Why could he remember what the building looked like, but had no idea what was inside?

Pincus put a sheet on the bed, helped the other man to lie down, and promised to send a doctor before long — "a reliable doctor," as he said. Felix was supposed to understand that this meant a doctor who wouldn't inform on them. When Felix wanted to say thanks, the apartment was already empty.

7.

The doctor came and did something painful to Felix's leg.

"Don't take that bandage off, young man," the doctor said. "I'll come again tomorrow."

"Young man…" Am I really young? Felix lay half-conscious, and tried to remember something about himself. A white diamond shape looked at him with sadness and understanding from the rug. It probably didn't know anything about itself or its origins either.

There were no photos on the walls. There weren't any anywhere. Then he began looking at the books — photos of existence, imprints of thoughts. What was here? Spengler's "The Decline of the West," a volume of Zbigniew Herbert in Polish, a statistics reference book from the Minsk University Press, an album called "The State Museum of Art". What did these titles tell him? Who was he, anyway? A Pole, a Belorussian, a Russian? A nobody? His memory couldn't tell him anything, his papers… Did he have papers? He'd need to look in the apartment…

He found a trade union membership card (the union of

medical workers, with "paid" stamps stuck on), but he couldn't find a passport anywhere. The photograph on the union card was small. Yes, it was him. But why was he wearing glasses?

Felix went over to the window. Somewhere in the distance he spotted a banner on a pompous, Stalin-era building and with difficulty he made out the words "ALL GLORY TO OUR PART". How true, he thought, but then he realised that there was another letter hidden behind a chimney. He frowned, trying to guess what that other letter could be, but then he remembered why he had gone over to the window. Well then, his vision was excellent, he could see just as well up close and far away, he didn't need glasses. So why, then, had he worn them before?

8.

On the corner of Wroblewski Street, two men were meeting in a café. One was stout and chubby, with a grey moustache and wearing a light-coloured foreign-made mackintosh. The other was a cocky, sallow-skinned young man of forgettable appearance. They had just ordered a portion of dumplings each, taken a couple of cheese sandwiches each from the counter, and poured themselves glasses of tea from the enormous metal boiler, burning their fingers on the hot spout. The tea was cooling, the dumplings were due to follow.

"Well?" asked the older man and unbuttoned his mackintosh, displaying to the world the Lenin badge on the lapel of his jacket.

"Yes," the young man answered sullenly, looking at his hands for some reason.

"Did anyone see you?"

"Someone saw me, but I think it was a ghost."

"What?!" the old man said loudly and unexpectedly, and a few customers looked over at them.

"Don't shout," the young man had begun to worry and

absentmindedly bent the flimsy grey fork. "I got away from him. Although I did have to shoot him."

"Shoot him?!" this time the old man shouted almost silently. "Who was it?"

"Kangar."

"You must have mistaken him for somebody else," the old man slipped into the superior tone common among Party members. This happened to him only at moments of anxiety, which are not unknown even among Party functionaries.

"I told you, at first I thought it was a ghost. But he nearly caught me."

"Where?"

"You know where."

"Did you kill him?"

"For a second time? No, I don't think so. Anyway, I had no silver bullets. But I think I got him…"

A girl in a white coat came over to them with the dumplings.

"With vinegar, just as you ordered."

"Thank you," the old man said, but the girl was smiling at his companion, clearly wishing to attract his attention.

One of her front teeth was missing.

"Thank you," strained the young man sullenly, looking at the waitress with watery green eyes.

The girl, now less hopeful of striking up a new friendship, smiled straight at the stagnant green of his eyes.

"So he's alive?" said the old man pensively, and the old-man's marks on his drooping cheeks seemed to get darker.

"How can that be?"

They fell silent.

"What are you doing?" the old man asked suddenly.

"I'm eating dumplings."

"You're mad. The amount you earn, and you eat such rubbish…"

"Actually, while we're on the subject of money…" the young man smiled slightly.

It was a mean sort of smile.

"Take the briefcase up off the floor. Ok, now open it and take out the envelope. No, don't open it, I'm not going to trick you, and we're not in the safest of places. You can count it at home…"

He thought for a minute, then said: "Find Kangar for me. Don't do anything to him, just bring him to me. We have to talk. I can't figure out where the papers are that he had that day, who he could have given them to…"

"Whatever you say," his companion saluted him mockingly. "For a separate fee, of course."

"Have I ever let you down?" his already crooked mouth bent even more; dark eyes looked out stubbornly from the hollows between his eyebrows and wrinkled eyelids. "You do what you're asked, and you'll get what you're owed."

"We'll get what we're owed according to the verdict of the judge," the young man grinned.

"Be quiet, you idiot. Why the hell did I arrange to meet you here? People like you should be met in a laneway somewhere."

"It was in a laneway that it all happened. I took out the knife and…"

"No, don't tell me. You did everything right, I believe you."

"Yes, I did everything I needed to. I made friends with her, comforted her… Maybe I should make friends with Kangar?"

"After shooting him?"

"Well, yes. But they say that's no obstacle for cowboys."

"You, Niku, should be less of a cowboy, I'm telling you," the old man began to get angry, and his southern-Ukrainian peddler's accent appeared.

"Don't blow your top, guv," the gangster hissed, and nudged the old man painfully with his elbow.

"For God's sake, the cheek of you!" the old man said in a feeble attempt to make peace, and began mopping up the tea that had spilled onto his trousers from the knocked-over glass.

"Everyone's looking at us, let's get out of here," Niku said quietly.

They got up and moved towards the door. The waitress got in their way on purpose and looked at the young man with a gap-toothed smile.

9.

That night the city slept under a rainy dome. It woke up in the morning with a smile — sunbeams glowed because a cheerful sun was shining through light clouds. Buses looked brighter than usual as they left the park, the fishy faces of "Volga" cars did not show such deep lethargy, and the Mercedes of the local criminal boss looked like a white supernatural apparition.

Having had a good rest the previous day, Felix went out first thing in the morning. The city called him to itself, as if promising to sate his empty soul with something unusual. It was a city of tanners, craftsmen and clerks. A Polish city, with its two castles and its Jesuit church. A European city — who had not lived here, at this crossroads of all ways?! A Belorussian city — as the powers that be wanted it. A Soviet city with its red and gold official banners — it had become this in the course of a few decades.

But the sun was already heralding the decline of Soviet imperialism and at the same time the impending rise of a timid Belorussian statehood. In fact, all the sun was doing was shining. It is people who imagine symbols and then interpret them. And then they see that other people interpret them differently, and they are surprised.

Felix walked along the streets of the town, — Soviet Street, Proletariat Street, Socialist Street — heard Polish, Russian, Belorussian, Lithuanian, Yiddish and God knows what other languages, and drank in the smell of leather, petrol and cheap food. After strolling like this for half an hour, he wandered into a basement café called "Chez Romualdas" on Bielusz Street. It was a Lithuanian café, and at this early hour it was all but deserted.

The owner did not appear straight away from the back room.

"What'll it be? Tea?" he was surprised, and the parenthesis formed by his straw-coloured moustache changed its angle slightly. "What else? Something to eat? You'll have some pie."

"Ok, I'll 'have some pie'," the young man grinned.

Romualdas left, and Felix looked around the establishment. The tables were sturdy and unpainted, though covered with a yellowy varnish; the chairs, which matched them well, were proud, with slight curvature of the spine. Two unhurried craftsmen were drinking beer and talking in Lithuanian at one of the tables, and a thin, tattered old man was asleep at another table, his head lolling on the tabletop. Felix realised that Lithuanians could do whatever they wanted here — it was like a club or even a refuge.

Romualdas sauntered over with a tray, poured water into a large mug with green and yellow oak leaves, and presented a saucer with sugar and a tea bag. The pie turned out to have cabbage in it.

Felix thanked him and began eating. Then the old ragged man woke up, sniffed, blew his nose loudly onto the floor, yawned, and began looking at the people around him. When his glance fell on Felix, he gave a start, rubbed his eyes with the back of his hand, and then looked over in the same direction again. It was clear that he was struggling with the temptation to go over and talk to him. It must have been one of the conditions of his being here that he was not allowed to annoy the customers, or even talk to them at all, and he had probably been scolded and thrown out many times for being too chatty.

When he saw that the owner had once again hidden himself away in the back room, the old man made up his mind and, staggering slightly, made his way over towards Felix.

"Excuse me, but you look so like the engineer..."

Felix looked at him and said nothing.

"Like mister Michał Kangar."

Then Felix said:

"I am Felix Mikhailovich Kangar."

"I knew it," the beggar became more animated. "I knew I'd meet you some day. I remember. I used to work with your father, Lord rest him. He managed to build and restore many houses here. I was once a brick-layer…"

"Managed to — before what?"

"The war of course, young sir, the war. The Russians came in '39, and the Germans were approaching from the other side. They got here in '41, and that was the end of your kind."

He drew the side of his hand across his throat.

"My kind?"

"Well, Jews. But anyway, your father and Madam Rozalia managed to escape, they only came back in '45. He was rebuilding houses at the time, and decided to build extensions onto some. He built a third floor onto his own house, over Geranek the hairdressers… And have you been back for long? There were rumours that something bad happened to you in Minsk…"

Felix shrugged his shoulders.

"Well yes, I can see that you're all right," said the old man, and finally plucked up the courage to ask:

"Could I have a piece of pie, maybe?"

The young man, without speaking, broke his piece in half.

"You're a good young fellow," the beggar broke into a smile. "Your father was good as well. Did he ever mention Adamas Brazas to you? That's me…"

The owner of the café appeared suddenly at the counter and saved Felix from the need to answer. He said quietly but distinctly:

"A-da-mas!"

The ragged man disappeared as if carried off by the wind. He took the unfinished piece of pie away with him. Felix unhurriedly finished his breakfast and settled up with Romualdas – he had found some money yesterday in the inside pocket of his mackintosh.

"Come again," Romualdas said. "There's never much happening here in the mornings."

10.

And indeed there wasn't much happening that morning. He wanted to fill it up with at something, anything at all.

"God," thought Felix, looking at the wooly clouds that had once again muffled up the Sun, "What is God for me? Do I need to seek the advice of someone or of something abstract, to give it a report on my actions and seek its support?"

He waited for the answer to mature in his heart, and his heart only cultivated emptiness. He did not get weighed down by this — on the contrary, he floated lightly along the small narrow streets. Was it a beautiful city? No, more like picturesque. The medieval buried deeply in the Soviet. But also the Soviet, deeply instilled in the medieval. A dream within a dream…

He wandered into a church — it turned out to be the Orthodox Church of the Intercession. Nobody came over to him, and he stood and looked at the iconostasis, the lighted candles and the smoke under the vaults.

"Can I sense anything different here to what I'd sense in any other place? Anything special, which would nourish the soul?"

He couldn't even sense his soul. He turned around and went back outside, once again becoming absorbed in the maze of side-streets.

In one narrow laneway, three people were coming towards him. Two young men and a girl. He was walking past them when suddenly one of the youngsters ran up to him from behind and hit him on the head with something heavy.

He fell flat on his face. He didn't lose consciousness, and he heard the other youngster say:

"Everything's clear, there's nobody around."

And somebody put their hands in his pockets.

The girl shouted out:

"You're animals. You've killed him."

"You be quiet. We didn't kill him, just silenced him."

The hands continued rummaging in his pockets.

"He only has some small change. Let's get out of here."

"I'm not leaving," announced the girl.

"She's so beautiful," he thought, enjoying the sight of her face. "She's defending me so gallantly!"

"Let's go, he'll report you to the police."

"I'm staying," the girl said firmly. She placed her palm under Felix's head, and lifted it up slightly.

Someone was coming towards the laneway on the other side.

"Well, whatever you want," the young men shrugged their shoulders and promptly disappeared.

"How are you?" asked the girl, looking into his eyes.

Felix wanted to say something in reply, but only groaned. Someone walked past them, dragging an empty trolley loudly behind him.

"He didn't even stop," the girl looked hatefully after the man who had passed by. "Will you be able to get up?"

Leaning on her arm, he got up, leaned against the wall, and thought: "A good thing it's dry here." His head ached unbearably. Despite this he made himself smile at the girl.

"That's a bit better," she calmed down slightly and began brushing his clothes clean with her hand. "Did they hit you very hard?"

He was about to nod, but then he realised that it would be even more painful, so he mumbled:

"Not too hard."

"Let's go, I'll bring you as far as a bench."

He leaned on her plump forearm, as if on a crutch, and they limped to a courtyard with a wooden bench, grown dark with age, and a sand-pit. The pain eased slightly, and he was able to say:

"With your high moral qualities you'd be better not to get involved in things like that."

The girl blushed furiously and, hesitating, finally formed the words:

"It was the first time they did that… before they would only take wallets out of pockets, and I would stand guard. We've no money, we're students."

"Students?!" Felix was shocked.

"Yes. We study in the local university. I do languages, they do history."

"They have a wonderful grasp of history," Felix grinned. "So they never mugged anyone in front of you before?"

"I suppose you're right," the girl said despondently. "They did it without me."

I definitely like her, thought Felix. She's a bit chubby, but she's pretty… Especially her green eyes… I guess only I could fall for a girl who tried to mug me…

"Will you be able to get home by yourself?" the girl asked.

It was obvious that her conscience was still tormenting her.

"Probably not. The thing is, I only arrived yesterday, and I don't even know which way to go."

"Ah, I thought you weren't from around here," the girl said. "Where are you from?"

"Moscow," Felix replied.

Of course, he might well have named any other city, but he preferred to answer this way.

"Oh, you're from Moscow," the girl said slowly and dreamily. "I was there once, on a class trip… How do you not know which way to go? Do you have an address, even?"

He knew the address — that morning he had made a note of the name of the street and the house number. Now he showed the piece of paper to the girl.

"Eliza Orzeszkowa Street… That's not too far from here," she said. "We can get the bus, or we can walk. It's only three stops."

"I can walk," he smiled.

And they set off through the city that was already caught up in its daily routine.

"Why aren't you at lectures?" Felix asked.

"I was at a lecture this morning, and then our tutorial was cancelled."

It was difficult to imagine that only a few minutes ago this sweet, fair-skinned red-haired girl had been part of a gang that had tried to rob him.

"What's your name?" he asked.

"Martina," the girl answered. "My mother is Czech."

"I'm Felix Kangar," he introduced himself. "Apart from that, I can't remember anything about myself."

"Is that since they hit you?" the girl asked carefully.

"No … yes … I don't know."

"You're not feeling well," the girl became worried. "You need to lie down. We shouldn't have walked, we should have taken the bus."

That's my house there, after the statue," he said, beginning to recognise his neighbourhood.

The bald head of the old woman once again poked out through the ground-floor window. It seemed to Felix that this time a kind of limp smile passed across the lifeless face.

The girl helped him get up to the second floor, lay him down on the bed, and pressed an ice-cube wrapped in gauze to his cut.

"Stay," he said, and looked into her honest green eyes — the eyes of a student and a thief.

She stayed. "This is what I dreamed about," she thought "Something real at last. At the end of the day it's better to be with just one person, but all the time, than to divide your time between two."

II.

It turned out that in his thirty years he had never done what physiologists call carrying out the reproductive function. In response to the call of sex he fished out something red and embarrassed, which looked like an immature toadstool, but as for what to do then, he didn't know. She had to direct him. This determined their future relationship. The person who dominates in a marriage is not the one who, according to the superstition, first steps on the rug beside the bed, but the one who knows best what to do after that.

Martina was touched by the childlike innocence of her new boyfriend. She realised that this was what she needed: she could shape his character as she wished. But Felix, although he acquired some good habits, all the same remained someone she could not figure out.

He told Martina about the murder he had seen. Yes, she nodded, a few days ago a journalist was murdered; she had been writing about corruption at an engineering plant. It was clearly an assassination.

"I saw the killer," Felix said, with no expression in his voice.

"Oh," the girl became worried. "We'll have to be careful."

Until then they had spent much time strolling around the city, holding hands and kissing in secluded corners.

"I'll buy you dark glasses," she said.

"And I'll become Mr. Nihil," Felix joked.

"We can even sign our names like that — Mr. and Mrs. Nihil."

"Yes, in hotels, if we go to the West."

"Do you want to go to the West?" she asked.

"I don't know, I've never been there. But this city is strange."

"Yes, it belongs to no-one. It's like a field that's exposed to all winds. It's cold here, but it's where I was born."

"Sorry," he said.

"It's fine. You don't always love the place you're born in."

He sighed and said:

"I don't remember my childhood at all."

"Something happened to you. An illness or a trauma or something else. We'll find out."

He looked like a blind person in his dark glasses — and he walked almost as cautiously, as if he wasn't completely used to moving his feet. His injury had healed. The doctor hadn't come back after all — he had most likely seen the bullet wound and decided to have as little to do with this patient as possible. But by then he didn't need a doctor.

Once when Felix and Martina were out walking they came to a bus station.

"What if we were to leave right now?" he joked.

"We can leave," she smiled. "I have my passport ready."

And they bought tickets. They were shown the bus to Minsk, it was leaving in ten minutes' time.

"I'll be back in a minute," she said.

While he waited for her he studied the advertisements on the big bus "Icarus". He looked up…

When she came back, she saw: he was standing with a chalk-white face and looking through the window at one of the passengers. She looked — and almost screamed: this man was an exact copy of Felix! They were even wearing the same clothes. She looked from one to the other, not understanding anything.

The bus left without them; when the doors closed, the man in the window looked at them with a strange, absent, gaze.

They stood, numbly, for a long time more. Eventually she asked:

"Do you have any brothers?"

But he couldn't remember.

12.

There is multitude in unity, there is unity in multitude. Everyone is a brother to their unborn, and sometimes born, brothers, everyone chooses an "I" out of the multitude. They choose at the beginning, and they choose every day, first thing in the morning. But what do the discarded "I"s do then? Maybe they get on a bus and leave? If so, where do they go? To lead another life? In another city? In another country? Under their own name? Under someone else's name? Maybe they sleep inside our chest cavities, like babies in cradles, and wait their turn?

The next morning, Felix was still asleep when Martina left to go to class. He was woken by a knock at the door. There were actually two doors, with a small space between them where a vegetable box had found a home. There was an enormous chain on the outer door.

He put on the chain and looked out through the gap. At the door there stood a fat, elderly man with unkempt grey hair, wearing linen overalls, from his beard poked out only plump lips, a stubborn bulbous nose, and tenacious black eyes. It was the face of an unrestrained and passionate person who denies himself nothing. When he saw him, the visitor smiled and exclaimed:

"Felix!"

It was a charming smile. It would be impossible to suspect this person of evil intentions. Felix unhooked the chain.

They went through to the room.

"Let me have a look at you," the guest said, and led him over to the window. You're different in some way. You look see-through. A "man without qualities." What happened to you? They were saying that you'd had some sort of accident...

"Maybe," replied Felix. "I can't remember anything."

"Do you remember me?" suspicion passed over the eyes of the guest.

Felix cast down his eyes guiltily.

"I live underneath you," the guest said cautiously. "I'm Pyotr Pavlovich. Well, Petropalych. Yes, it's strange..."

"So you're Osuzhdin," Felix said expressionlessly.

"So you remembered!" the visitor beamed. "And do you remember that you suggested a new technique to me? No? Well, it's using pieces of bottles. Those bottles are selling very well. Rich Poles come, there was even one American... I heard someone moving about over my head. I thought it was either because I was drunk, or else Felix had come back... And what about the girl? I saw her this morning, was she leaving here?"

The young man nodded.

"Well, good for you, it's about time. You were all science this, science that, you weren't even here much, always ending up in Moscow. At least I used to be able to talk with Mr. Michał and Madam Rozalia, but they're not here any more, the apartment's empty, quiet as a tomb."

"Tell me, what kind of science did I do?"

"You must be joking?! What happened to you, anyway?"

"I was hit on the head."

"Oh yes, that can happen, once when I was drunk I fell down the stairs and hit the back of my head on a step, and I could hardly remember my name afterwards."

"Why is everyone in this town always falling down drunk?" Felix thought to himself.

"Well ok, you're a biologist," Osuzhdin continued. "You don't remember? You used to examine some sort of cells through a microscope, you tried to explain it all to me. But I don't understand squat about it. You studied in Moscow in a medical institute, then you stuck around there, wrote a thesis. Then recently you came home and you were working in a lab here in the university."

And then Felix decided to ask the question that had been bothering him for a long time.

"But what's this town called?"

The artist opened his foggy eyes wildly, as if he had swallowed one of his own paintings made from bottle shards, but he managed to answer:

"The town is called Grodno... Listen, I can't have this conversation sober. Do you have anything to drink?"

Felix shrugged his shoulders.

"Sure that's not possible. You always had some medicinal alcohol. Let's have a look."

And the artist did indeed find a large brown bottle with a glass stopper in the Kangars' wasteland of a kitchen.

"Here it is. See, it's written in Latin: *spiritus vini rectificati*. You wrote it."

They diluted the alcohol with water, added wedges of lemon, and washed it down with some bread and salami. It got easy and warm. Felix thought that he was beginning to get used to this apartment and to this town.

"Y'see, you've forgotten everything… Yep, you've been unlucky," Osuzhdin slapped him on the shoulder.

"Jewish luck," Felix remembered an expression he'd heard somewhere on the street.

"Well, you're not really a proper Jew," the artist looked at him, somewhat surprised, and thought: who knows, maybe he is one of those who always identify themselves with the weakest link in the chain? "Mr. Michał was of the Karaites, Crimean Jews" he continued, "but Madam Rozalia was Polish, with a little German blood."

"So what's the correct phrase? Soviet luck?" wondered Felix.

"Just don't utter that word in my presence — Soviet."

13.

The guest left, and Felix paced up and down the apartment wondering what to do with himself. Eventually he remembered about the notebook full of phone numbers. There were a lot of numbers; the figures danced before his eyes.

He made himself comfortable in a deep armchair and lifted the receiver.

A lot of the numbers didn't answer; obviously — they were home numbers, and the clock showed that it was still midday. At last someone answered at the other end. "Medical Genetics Lab," and he asked to speak to Boris Georgievich Voslensky.

"Professor Voslensky speaking," said a rather hoarse, impatient voice. It was clear that the scientist had been interrupted.

"This is Felix Kangar," the young man said a little hesitantly.

There was silence for a few moments, followed by:

"Don't joke with us, young man, we are perfectly well aware that Felix Mikhailovich passed away."

This time the silence engulfed the young man too — he tried to say something but he couldn't.

"The impertinence of those students," a woman's voice said practically beside the receiver, and then straight away they hung up.

"Passed away…" the young man went over to the tall, flyblown pier glass and looked at his reflection — pale, but definitely not transparent. "Passed away… But there he is, me. I'm alive. Cogito ergo sum. Maybe I'm not Felix Kangar. But in that case who am I? Mr. Nihil? Herbert's Mr. Cogito?"

He was not distraught, merely quite perplexed. Martina came back, and he told her everything.

"What difference does it make who you are? I love you anyway," she smiled, hugged him with her cold, white, pale arms, and kissed him.

She was still experiencing the romantic period of the affair.

14.

Is it possible to be nobody? Does a person really need a name — in essence, only a few letters — and also the few numbers used to characterise a person: height, weight, age, waist size, hip size, passport number, driver's license number? Does he need self-identification: "I'm a Catholic" or "I'm Ukrainian" or "I'm a miner"? Is it not enough simply to be a person, and thus equal among equals, even if you're an Aborigine in Australia, a Jew in Russia or an Arab in Paris? The answer: this is sufficient for a person, but not for society. Because it needs a hierarchy. Conclusion: a person can be perfect in practice, but society only in theory. And this contradicts the conditions of the task, shouted out by megaphone, according to which man is originally imperfect, and society is a model of perfection. So, the task is unsolvable, the students are leaving the classroom via the window, into oblivion, but in the corridors there are crowds of hopefuls waiting to take their place.

15.

In the evening Martina took him out for a walk around the town. The ground was wet — it had been raining during the day, and the streetlights were casting gold stains onto the concrete. In this light the girl's hair looked bronze.

Autumn — warm, damp, thoughtful. Fog was gathering over the Neman, and the sounds of clattering dishes, singing, and laughter could be heard from bars.

"It doesn't matter," Martina was saying. "We'll definitely find out everything about you. You have, you just must have, a name, a biography, a profession."

"It seems that I don't have anything," the young man replied, detached.

"*Tabula rasa,*" she said; then, noticing that he hadn't understood, explained — "A blank slate… Didn't you ever study Latin?"

"I don't even remember being a student. But I do know something, I just don't understand how I learnt it."

"You're a mystery man," her splendid green eyes beamed. "Like in an old English detective film. Do you like detective films?"

"I don't know."

"No, you're just marvelous!" she exclaimed and kissed him. "Don't say anything, just stay the way you are."

They went into a bar called "Danuta's Gifts". After the dampness outside, they hoped they could warm themselves up here. A feeble violinist was playing, hunched over so much that the neck of his instrument was facing the floor. Sarasate's *Gypsy Airs* sounded somewhat unfamiliar: in some passages the musician would very skillfully leave out half the notes.

"Soon Lithuania will be free, and I'll go back there," a red-headed lad, by all appearances a craftsman, said in Russian at the next table.

"Belarus, on the other hand, Vitautas, will never be free,"

sighed an old man with a light-coloured moustache, the oldest in that group.

"From whom?" his neighbour wondered.

"From the Russians."

"Maybe it will. If it really wants it."

"We don't know how to really want anything," the Belorussian man said. "We know how to put up with things for a very long time."

"And be stubborn."

"Yes, it's an object of our pride, our national particularity. If it wasn't for that, the Germans would be in charge here now."

"To stubbornness," Vitautas raised a mug of pale beer. "It will save us too."

They drank.

"It's funny to hear other people's conversations about politics," smiled the girl.

"I don't understand anything about politics," the young man said without expression.

"Do you want to dance?" Martina suggested.

The violinist, having sawn Sarasate in two, began purring a Boston Waltz with a monstrous glissando.

"I don't know how," the young man mumbled.

"I'll lead."

It was a long time before he managed to move to the beat. But somehow they managed to muddle through. Martina was gentle and compliant.

At a far table sat a dark-haired young man in a neckerchief. He had just come in and now he was observing them with his nasty green eyes. It was the gangster Niku Lotyanu.

16.

The music had stopped. Martina and Felix, not knowing whether he was really Felix, were sitting out the rest of the evening at their table. Suddenly, from behind, someone slapped the young man on the shoulder.

"Felix! Having a good night?"

It was a bandit-like, unshaven physiognomy, with drunk, sad, black eyes which showed ineradicable Judaic fatalism and similarly ineradicable recklessness…

"Pincus!" the young man was glad he could at least recognize someone. "Martina, this is Pincus. Pincus, Martina."

"A serious girl. Red-haired and opinionated. I approve" Pincus said solidly, which did not sit well at all with the sleazy winking of his gloomy eye.

"Martina's at university," the young man announced with satisfaction.

"Ooh, you're a student, miss," Pincus grinned and gallantly bowed over her hand. "You're not a colleague of Felix's, by any chance?"

"I study languages," the girl said with a certain pride.

"Ah yes, and he's a doctor. So you don't have that in common…"

"Listen, Pincus, I've been hearing terrible things about myself" the young man mustered up the courage to say. "It seems something happened to me and I died."

"Well, judging by this girl's glowing appearance, it seems you're alive and kicking," grinned Pincus, showing a couple of gold teeth. "I don't know, I hadn't heard any rumours like that. Maybe someone's spreading them deliberately."

The young man shrugged his shoulders.

"You know what, kids," Pincus turned to the sweethearts, "to make sure nothing does happen to you, I'll give you a lift home. If you want, obviously. I've had a drink and a bite to eat, and now it's time for me to head home — I'm going away tomorrow for a couple of days."

They paid the bill and went out onto the porch. Pincus put his hands around his companions' shoulders. Niku Lotyanu, who had got up to follow them, kicked a rubbish bin in the corridor in disgust with his polished boot and knocked it over.

He thrust a crumpled banknote at the bar owner who was running after him, and came out into the rain just as his quarry were trying to squash themselves into a beige-coloured "Beetle". The red Fiat went off after the Volkswagen. A quarter of an hour later, Pincus was dropping off his passengers. Taking note of which door they went in, Niku began waiting to see in which window a light would come on. A window lit up on the second floor.

"Now I have you, honey," Niku said to himself and went home to bed.

17.

He came back at about ten the next morning. Martina had already gone to class, the young man was asleep, and the doorbell did not wake him up straight away. "Should I open it or not?" he wondered. At the end of the day, he didn't even have a name — for whom could he be dangerous? Who could be dangerous for him? So he decided.

Niku had begun to lose patience and was holding his finger down on the doorbell. Then downstairs the main door slammed. Niku straightened up and looked down the stairwell. Stamping loudly with their boots, two policemen were coming upstairs.

Niku cursed and feverishly began looking for a place to hide. There was nowhere on the landing — all he could do was go further up. But the third floor was the highest; although there was a door to the attic. There. Closed! But if he flattened himself up against it, he probably wouldn't be seen from below. So that's what he did.

Just at that moment Felix opened the door. Nobody! He went out onto the landing and looked around.

"Sir, are you from that apartment?" a voice said.

Two policemen were standing on the landing between the second and third floors, looking straight at the young man.

"Yes," he answered.

"We'd like to have a word with you."

"Please, come in. Was that you ringing the bell?"

Niku didn't hear the answer, as the door had already shut. Not wasting a second, he raced downstairs. If it emerged that it wasn't the policemen who were ringing the bell, but someone else, then that someone else would face an unpleasant encounter.

But the door didn't open — obviously the policemen weren't paying attention to the young man's words.

Fifteen minutes later, Niku was sitting in his car when he observed through dark glasses the victim who had escaped him being led down the road. He set off after them unobtrusively. All the way to the police station.

Then Niku drove to the nearest phone booth and dialed.

"Caught," he said gruffly into the receiver.

"You?!" cried a startled voice.

"If it was me, I wouldn't be calling you now. They caught the client."

"Where is he?"

"The police have him."

"Which station?"

Niku told him which one.

"It's fine — the rest is my business. Consider your mission accomplished. I'll meet you tomorrow in the same place."

Niku thought: it would be great if all missions got accomplished by other people. Especially by the police.

18.

Martina came home earlier than usual — just after twelve. She went up the stairs and froze when she saw a white piece of paper with a seal on the door. The long-suffering inhabitants of the Union of Soviet Imprisoning Republics had known since the 1930s what this kind of paper meant. And when they saw it they didn't ask themselves why because there was usually no reason.

The girl stood like a lost child at the sealed door. Where should she go, how could she help? It didn't even occur to her that she should just leave it all to fate and forget about it. No, she had invested too much in this strange creature who was at the same time a person who remembered so little about himself and trusted her so much. No, Felix had got into trouble, so she must help him! Despite all his doubts, to herself she called him Felix. Blissful. Or, to be more exact, a simple soul.

Somebody was coming up the stairs, a small person in a starched white coat, wearing glasses.

"Please forgive me, miss, I beg you to hear me out. I am very guilty before you."

She looked at him, not understanding; the sun was reflected in his rimless spectacles and she couldn't see his eyes.

"It's all my crazy mother's fault," he explained. "She informed on you."

Martina still didn't understand anything.

"On me?"

"Yes. I'm Václav Geranek, the hairdresser. Well, you've walked past our window… Did you see an old woman there?"

She nodded.

"That's my mother. She's completely crazy. She keeps track of everyone, then calls the police and informs. They laugh at her there, but they use the information. You see, she's an old hand — she used to work for the NKVD, which later became the KGB."

"But what have I got to do with it?" asked Martina.

"Well, you've been living here without a permit…" Geranek said in distress and took off his glasses. They were unhappy eyes, tearful from a long-standing pain, darting here and there. "Forgive me, I have nothing against it. And she snitched on you to the police."

"What happened to Felix?"

"They must have taken him away — do you see the seal? Maybe he had a problem with his papers."

"So they took him away because of me?" The girl sighed, and

suddenly remembered: he had no passport — that was the problem!

She thanked Geranek and ran home as quickly as she could. As she passed the hairdresser's window, she couldn't contain herself and stuck out her tongue at the old woman.

19.

Felix sat in the custody cell minus his belt and shoelaces. He was bored and afraid. On the other side of the cast iron bars, police life was bustling along, placid and uncomplicated. One-layered. Along to someone's whistling, the young man tried to remember what Martina had told him about her family. This is what he remembered.

Martina's father had met her mother in very romantic circumstances. In April 1945 the Soviet troops liberated a village near Olomouc from the Germans. The battle was fierce, many houses had been destroyed, and even some trees had been felled by shrapnel.

One of the houses that had been left standing was being used as the regiment's headquarters, another as a military hospital, and a small house had been taken over by SMERSH, counterespionage troops. Their commander, thirty-year-old Captain Suloy, went to the hospital to get a bandage for his arm which had been cut by shrapnel. SMERSH usually didn't participate in battles, so the injured man would be justified if he thought himself unlucky — he simply found himself close to the battlefield.

The wound was near his elbow — more painful than dangerous. On the way back, Captain Suloy took a wrong turn — it wasn't easy to get your bearings among all the ruins. There were more destroyed houses here; obviously, a lot of shrapnel had fallen on this part of the village.

Suddenly he heard a barely-audible groan. The captain stopped and listened. Everything was quiet.

"Is anyone there?" he shouted, and took out his gun, just in case.

For a long time there was silence. Then another groan. It was coming from a half-destroyed house. A corner of this wooden building had remained standing, but it was covered by a fallen roof. There was no door or window in this part of the house.

Suloy brought his soldiers to the house, but even working together they couldn't do anything.

"We need a bulldozer," one of the troops said.

But of course they didn't have a bulldozer. Disappointed, Suloy went to walk around the village, came to the hospital and saw a truck that had already been unloaded –something had obviously been delivered to the hospital.

Suloy found the driver.

"Do you have a tow-line?" he asked him.

"Do you even have to ask, comrade Captain?" the driver grinned.

They drove the truck to the ruins, attached the tow-line to a corner of the roof, and drove off — and part of the roof fell inward, forming an opening.

"Well, now we've ruined it completely," someone said.

But when they managed to get into the house, Suloy and one of the soldiers, with torches, found a figure in the corner, under the table, bent into an unnatural position. It was a girl of about twelve, and it looked like her leg was broken.

They carried the girl out of the ruins. She was obviously in shock — she was pale and her eyes were shut tight. They brought her to the hospital in the same truck.

A couple of days later the girl was sitting in the garden beside the hospital; there were crutches beside her and her leg was in plaster.

"Thank the officer — it was he who saved you," a nurse said to her in broken Czech when the captain called in to visit the patient.

He held out a bar of chocolate which he had obtained with

difficulty. The girl took the chocolate and kissed the captain's hand. A skinny, red-haired pale little girl, still a child. Her gratefulness touched his heart — he had sent many people to their deaths, and now he was glad to have done something good; maybe in his heart of hearts he wanted something like this — as atonement.

"She doesn't have anyone left — her parents were killed," said the nurse.

"So where's she going to go?"

"Probably to Prague, to an aunt. But I don't know how she'll get on there — the aunt already has two little children…"

Suloy took a "Belomor" cigarette packet and a pencil from his pocket.

"Get her to write the address here, on the packet, and I'll visit her."

And the girl wrote her name: Milena Kohoutkova and the address.

"Where's that?" asked the captain.

"Somewhere in Hradčany, they say."

"Tell her I'll definitely come to visit her."

The girl turned her solemn green eyes to him and looked at him for a long time.

On the following day the troops moved on, followed by SMERSH. They left the hospital behind. Soon the war ended.

Captain Suloy took leave and went to Prague. The cigarette box was in his breast pocket.

The family was poor. Milena's aunt was raising two young children and her husband was an invalid. The captain unpacked a string bag full of groceries onto the table, fell silent, and then said:

"Give me the girl, I'll raise her as a daughter."

The husband could understand a little Russian. He asked:

"Do you have children?"

The captain shook his head.

"A wife?"

"Yes," answered Suloy, and from his pocket he took out a photograph of a fair-haired, smiling young woman.

They passed the photograph around. No-one said anything. Then the woman, the man and the girl spoke amongst themselves in Czech.

"Very well," the man said at last. "She'll be your daughter."

Beggars can't be choosers.

It didn't take her long to gather her things. The girl threw her bundle of things over her shoulder, kissed her aunt and said:

"Já vâs mám rád. I love you."

And then she held out her hand to the captain.

Soon he was demobilised, and the Party sent him to Grodno to rebuild a car factory. For many years he worked there as the head of human resources.

A few years later his wife died — it turned out she had an undetected heart defect. Milena finished school and went to university. She had long ago learnt to speak fluent Russian.

Once she said to him:

"I never looked on you as a father."

And looked at him with her solemn green eyes.

"How, then?" he tried to make a joke of it. "Better or worse?"

She didn't answer, just smiled.

Six months later he was summoned by the Party representative, Brikatushkin.

"Don't you want to legalise your relationship with the girl?" he asked with Party frankness and unrelenting winks.

"I want to," Suloy answered. "But the law won't let me; she's my adopted daughter, after all."

"Well the law won't be an obstacle to you," the Party representative said.

And indeed, after another six months they had a modest wedding. At first people gossiped about it, but then they forgot.

Their first child was stillborn; their second they named Martina.

In 1968 the family almost broke up — Suloy had the insensitivity to express aloud his approval of the Soviet invasion of Czechoslovakia. Saying nothing, Milena began packing her bags. She was held back by her daughter, who was three and a half. With one little hand she gripped her mother's skirt, with the other her father's sleeve, and in this way she kept them both, staring at them with her solemn green eyes. They both knew well the meaning of a look like that.

Obviously the man of the house had from the very beginning taken on himself contact with various Soviet institutions.

Remembering this sentimental, girlish story, Felix wondered: would her austere papa intervene on his behalf?

At that minute a stone flew through the window and landed right at the young man's feet. The stone was wrapped in paper. A note, Felix realised.

"Don't tell them anything," was written in pencil on one side. The other side was a bit of newsprint, an advertisement for the film "Tell them everything".

20.

Half an hour later Martina had run home, and before long her "austere papa" who always saw things from a different angle, was asking her the perfectly reasonable question:

"How can I intervene on behalf of someone I've never even seen?"

However, arguing with a daughter who's in love is probably the most thankless task on earth. His surrender was worded as follows:

"Ok then, I'll just find out what's happening."

So he phoned. Then said to Martina in surprise:

"They're sending him to Moscow today. It must be something serious. They don't know anything here."

As Martina's father was talking to the boss, another man was talking to one of his subordinates. And he was told:

"Yes, we have him. He's in the custody cell… What? You

want to talk to him? No, I can't organise it now. If you want, we can do it this evening, when everyone has gone home. As it happens, I'm on duty tonight."

At that same moment Martina realised that they could only send Felix off on the Moscow train, which left at 14.19. She had to hurry. Before she knew it she was buying a ticket and was waiting on the platform. And with good reason.

21.

It is not true that no one can stand the sight of a basilisk. After all, the basilisk is depicted on our highest value banknotes, and smiles a crooked smile at some people, to their mutual satisfaction.

About three hours later, a respectable-looking man with a grey moustache went into the police station.

"Well?" he asked.

"They sent him to Moscow earlier today," was the answer.

"Why?"

"Our boss called Moscow, and that was the order."

The respectable-looking man with the grey moustache spat on the floor in a completely non-respectable way, turned around, and left.

Late that same evening Niku was driving home down Sportivnaya Street in his red Fiat, along the bank of the river, and stopped at a kiosk to buy some beer. A man came up behind him and began looking at the window in a leisurely way. Niku opened his eyes wide: it was Felix Kangar. "They've let him go!" he thought. So now he would have to do the job he had been given.

Niku bought two bottles of beer and two packets of peanuts, then turned to Kangar:

"Like to join me for a beer?"

Kangar gave him a strange, transparent look and said:

"I won't say no. Thanks."

"He doesn't recognise me," thought Niku. "I've been lucky today. Maybe he really is a ghost?"

They sat on a bench at the very edge of the cliff. Here there was a wonderful view of the river's flood-lands, which were twinkling with golden lights on a background of dark, velvety sky. But Niku was not thinking about beauty; he was figuring out how best to hit his drinking companion so as to knock him out.

Once he finished his beer, Niku grabbed the bottle by the neck, lifted it, and…. his drinking companion, trying to escape the blow, lost his balance, waved his arms and fell down headlong towards the river.

Niku himself almost fell down after him. Anyway, he needed to have a look down there to make sure the victim wasn't hiding or lurking in the bushes.

Half an hour later, having checked through all the puddles and bushes, covered in pine needles, Niku scrambled up with difficulty towards the road. He laid newspaper on the car seat. "My suit's ruined," he thought. "Well, someone's going to have to pay for that."

At home he took a bath, changed his clothes, and gave some food to his two Australian birds of paradise. Then he made a call.

"I drowned him," he relayed the news.

There was a long silence at the other end, followed by a hesitant question:

"W-who?"

"You know who," Niku said in his usual manner, but this elicited a furious response.

"I don't know who!" the voice shrieked. "I know that I asked for Kangar to be brought to me, but instead he was brought to Moscow today under armed guard."

"Wh-what?" Niku was astounded.

"And don't think that you can knock off the first person you meet and then demand money from me."

"Listen, it was Kangar," Niku said firmly. "I talked to him, I even had a beer with him."

Another silence, followed by:

"Maybe they tricked me — at the police station? Maybe they didn't send him anywhere, but actually let him go?… What am I paying them for?"

Niku tutted in sympathy.

"Ok then, I'll see you tomorrow. We'll have some dumplings. I owe you."

"Tomorrow evening I'll go to the tailor," thought Niku as he tried to fall asleep.

That night he dreamt he was walking past the police station, and a smiling Kangar was standing at the roof hurling dumplings straight at his fancy new suit.

22.

Next morning, Chief Didura came to work in a good mood. The disturber of the peace had been dispatched to Moscow, which meant that everything would get back to normal.

"How did the night go? Nothing out of the ordinary?" he asked the duty officers, who had already begun the morning shift.

"Yes, we just had one fella brought in, he's in the cell — he got drunk off his face and they found him rolling around in mud."

The chief set off towards his office, and on the way he threw a glance into the cell. There in the mournful cast-iron square of a cage could be seen an unshaven, dirty, but completely unruffled Kangar.

"What, again?!" Chief Didura whispered with lips that had gone pale.

This time he didn't bother phoning Moscow. He brought his own white Lada nearer to the door, opened the cell, dragged Kangar out by the collar, flung him onto the back seat, and hit the gas so fast that the police station was covered in a cloud of dust.

He drove all the way to Vilnius without stopping. There he threw his silent passenger out in front of the train station, put fifty roubles in his pocket, and said:

"Don't let me see you in our town again."

On the way back he made only one stop — he bought a bottle of vodka, and then, not even stopping at the police station, went home.

23.

The train crossed the whole of Belarus. The guards had the calmest of prisoners: he sat right next to the window of the compartment and it looked like he was absorbing views of the landscape as it rushed towards him.

Martina was in the next compartment: she had had to pay the carriage attendant for this. The girl had seen Felix only once: he must have asked to go out to the toilet. One of the guards went with him; when they were on their way back, Martina "just happened" to appear at the door of her compartment. The young man raised his hand and looked at her. Poor, pale Martina! Without the guard noticing, she put her finger on her lips.

They arrived in Minsk that night, at eleven, and Martina got out of the carriage after Felix and his guards. She saw the guards hand him over in the waiting room — the new guards must have been from Minsk.

Half an hour later the train set off again. She met Felix's eyes again and he smiled at her. Martina's heart lifted a little: it was good that he was so calm. Felix, or the happiness of being simple… Night waves rocked the carriage, rocked the girl…

In the morning, the train slowly pulled in to the Belorussky station. Moscow! Martina walked along the platform almost directly behind Felix and his guards. He was quickly led through the station. At the entrance, a black Volga car with steel antennae like a moustache was waiting for them. Felix was put into it, and the Volga sped off. Martina didn't have time to catch a taxi and go after it. The trail had been broken.

PART TWO

I.

The best exhibit in a museum is a person. Especially if he's asleep and dreaming about people who find him interesting. There are not many people who would find any of us interesting in ourselves, and an exhibit who's awake is not going to be very successful. Sleep changes things. Why aren't portraits done of people when they're asleep? Scientists, builders, writers, leaders... Inspiration comes in sleep and while we're awake. In sleep it is static, which is just what an artist needs. While we're awake, it spills over with gestures and shouts, and with actions that aren't thought through. When an artist sees this he has to restrain himself from swallowing his own brush, and we can understand him completely. Another thing altogether, for example, is a generalissimo's dream. Now here are wide open spaces for creative grotesquery! So let us begin to record the dream, if, of course, it is not "The Dream of Reason".

2.

The sarcophagus of the Maya tribe, where man does not sleep but presses on levers, is not, as some people think, a prototype for some sort of space ship belonging to aliens. There haven't been any aliens lately. There hadn't been hundreds of thousands of years ago, if indeed there ever have been. Neither is this sarcophagus a shelter for the afterlife. How is a dead person supposed to press on levers?

No, the sarcophagus of the Mayan Indians symbolizes a state

which Coleridge called "Life-in-Death". Now it can be characterized more simply: anabiosis. Controlled anabiosis. The sarcophagus is not made of stone, but metal, with controlled temperature and pressure and little dials to show the body's vital signs.

These sarcophagi are kept underground; there are a lot of them – a whole hall full. Over them is the atypical typical Russian village Cherepkovo. It is atypical because it is a village inside Moscow. Here there are crooked, unpainted houses, restless hens wander about, and stooping old women grow carrots and marrows; it is a hilly area, with the hills bent slightly in the direction of the far-off Kremlin, and the houses in the other direction, to the unfathomable Russian countryside. This very countryside begins only a couple of hundred metres away: the ring road is not far off. In winter time, beginners at skiing come here to ski down the hills. When they get a bit better they go to the neighbouring Krylatskoe.

There is no entrance into the underground kingdom from the village of Cherepkovo, even though it is directly above it. You can get there from two places: from "The Hospital of the Fourth Main Department" i.e. from the Kremlin Hospital, and also from the laboratory building of the tiny local hospital just past the ring road. To this very laboratory building nurses in white coats, and blue padded body-warmers in winter, bring test tubes full of blood, jars full of urine, and phlegm from ailing inhabitants of this unremarkable Moscow-region neighbourhood. But there's another entrance to this building, planted with "Kremlin" blue spruce trees. It is always closed, with silence and security guards inside. When they are asked what is there, the hospital staff answer "a research lab". But it's not just any old lab, and all sorts of dreadful rumours circulate about it.

3.

The underground kingdom was constructed by personal order of Brezhnev at the time of "Malaya Zemlya" (the book about the battle, not the battle itself). This was to be another Malaya Zemlya, a fortress of health in an ocean of the elderly's frailties. Brezhnev set a task: to ensure his immortality. Two scientists with whom he had a tête a tête promised immortality only for his embalmed mummy, and a third — probably the most shameless — promised a result within five years on condition that he would have a lab with the most up-to-date equipment at his disposal. It is not known whether he expected to achieve a result within five years; more likely he knew for sure that Brezhnev would not live that long. When he heard the promise which he had already stopped hoping for, Ilyich the Second burst into tears and pressed the scientist to his wide chest. This is how Prof. Nestor Nebus, a balding man with a pear-shaped head and ruddy, babyish cheeks, became Director Nebus. Approximately as much money was given to the lab as would be given to a small African country each year.

By nature Nebus was a risk-taker: seeing as he had taken such a huge chance with this venture, he made many demands – and he was given what he asked for. His small blue eyes were always darting around looking for what else he could acquire or appropriate, his pink cheeks (the bottom of his head was considerably wider than the top, just like his hips were wider than his shoulders) blushed even redder when he managed to acquire or appropriate something; his hedgehog of grey hair lifted itself into something resembling a peacock's tail.

4.

A houseplant called *Promissorium* needs regular watering from a telephone receiver that drips with something tempting. After that, it grows rapidly and may even turn evergreen. Swellings, occasionally appearing on its branches, suggest abundant fruit. However, the fact is that *Promissorium*, although blossoming iridescently, never yields anything but bursting swellings.

Nebus's promises, however, resulted in the appearance of

an underground kingdom constructed in no time at all. As soon as it was ready, Nebus began putting planets into his galaxy. The first person he invited was a man with squinting eyes and a wrinkled face who had the strange surname of Tyryntyn. Nobody knew what his first name was. He was either a Buryat or a Mongol or perhaps belonged to that rather small tribe of Tongor, once described in a novel. Tyryntyn worked on anabiosis and was outstanding in his field. Whenever he met someone he would smilingly suggest freezing them for a while and then defrosting without any damage to their health. In the institute where he used to work everyone avoided him. He froze mice, rabbits, and monkeys. Nobody knew whether he had done any damage to their health; the patients couldn't complain. Once he almost persuaded a lab assistant to let him freeze her. The girl was won over not so much by his shaman-like gestures and plaintive voice as by the possibility of lying in a sarcophagus for a year and then being a year younger than her biological age. But her friends rescued the brave girl from Tyryntyn. He didn't get disillusioned, and continued nabbing everyone he met in the corridors of the Institute and asking "Well, when are we going to freeze you?"

In the new lab Tyryntyn also began experiments on partial awakening from anabiosis, which gave the opportunity to regulate the functions of the body that had been disconnected from reality. So far he was experimenting on rabbits. The animals were kept on the lowest floor of the underground lab. Here there were mice and rats, rabbits and guinea pigs, dogs and rhesus-macaques. All that was missing were animals that looked like humans: apes with chests that would be wide enough to display many medals, if apes were awarded medals; these kinds of apes would have to be found however, as the experiment got nearer to a successful conclusion.

A certain Ignatius Maimaga looked after administration. He could get whatever was necessary from wherever necessary. Maimaga seemed to be a shadow — an empty white coat with a yellow head, or even a yellow face, attached by a thread. You could never find him in his office, but he always answered the phone when called. And his phone wasn't even a mobile, just an ordinary one.

Six months after the work began, Brezhnev summoned Nebus for a chat.

"Are there any results?" was the question.

"Well, you see, already we'd be able to freeze you now, and then after, say, fifty years, defrost you again, and you'd be the same as you are today."

Ilyich II thought for a moment, and then gave a crooked laugh.

"Sure who'd need me in fifty years? They'd have found somebody else… No, you'll have to come up with something else…"

"We'll think of something, Leonid Ilyich," Nebus puffed his chest in a businesslike way.

"If you need anything…"

"We need people for the freezing experiments. You wouldn't find any volunteers for that."

"There'll be people. Take those sentenced to the death penalty — it'll be a reprieve for them, and if you can't defrost them, it's no problem."

"It's no problem for us," Nebus grinned.

Ilyich the Second just laughed.

5.

When there was the possibility of prisoners being in the lab, security was tightened and given a new boss. Chief Mikhail Mordovich Pugan had previously served in an elite branch of the KGB.

He was square-shouldered and bear-like, and his Adam's apple was always moving and his nostrils quivering; it seems he was always aware of nearby enemies. When he arrived, all doors began opening and closing only by means of special plastic cards.

Pugan soon got his first prisoner — a skinny lad with ringworm, a robber and a murderer. He was passed on to Tyryntyn, who joyfully began singing his shamanic song and putting the lad into the sarcophagus. The lad struggled desperately, thinking this was some sort of electric chair.

Tyryntyn said weightily:

"It's for sleep! You're going to sleep!"

Then he began swinging his head and in a couple of minutes the subject was out cold. The freezing, and more importantly the defrosting, were successful. The lad was kept in anabiosis for five days and then safely defrosted.

Six more human anabiosis experiments were carried out successfully. The seventh was catastrophic: the cerebral cortex of an old inveterate rapist didn't work after he was defrosted.

"I wonder if it ever worked" Maimaga said, appearing out of nowhere.

"It's time we began other, more complicated, experiments, and you…" Nebus puffed his cheeks in offence. "Please, develop anabiosis until it can be done automatically — we won't manage without it."

That night, a stretcher with a corpse was carried out of the "research" entrance.

6.

This is how they live: they multiply, divide and swarm in Petri dishes. This is how they die: on a metal hook that has been scorched until it turned red. That's bacteria. Cells, on the other hand, grow slowly, thoughtfully, with attention to their internal structure and external comfort. Somebody once had an idea; if there is one cell, another one just like it can also appear. But not as a result of division. No, it is possible to make two immediately out of one, from one embryo, two, three or four can be made…

From one person — a throng of shadows. By simple stabs of a pipette.

And there was a stab-master — Professor Stanislav Afanasievich (behind his back the lab assistants called him Euthanasievich) Zbronjo, a ruddy-cheeked amateur billiards player. His head was reminiscent of the "Isabella" variety of pink grape, and his hands were autonomous. That is to say, they had a life of their own. The professor could be reading a book, and his hands would be braiding something intricate from the fringe of the table cloth. Billiards fed the future professor well when he was a student, and, evidently, prepared him well for his subsequent professional activity. A pipette is just like a cue, the cells are like balls. What would happen if the balls multiplied?

Zbronjo was also an expert at preparing cultures for the cells. Not just mixing them — any lab assistant can do that. His gift was in creating recipes. There was always an unbelievable stink in the labs where Zbronjo worked. Strangers would run away from there, but the cells thought it was cosy: they are not easily frightened.

Zbronjo had soon taken up a good half of the underground kingdom. He mixed agar-agar, chose ingredients, and grew cell cultures. A very powerful ventilation system cleaned the air. It was so powerful that it once almost swallowed up Ignatius Maimaga. The poor thing's face was sticking out of the pipe and was the colour of peptone-meat broth. Zbronjo raced over, found the damper on the pipe, and cut off the flow of air. Maimaga fell to the floor like a soft white coat. What colour was Zbronjo's face at that moment? The colour of blood agar.

7.

First they cloned a mouse, and from one embryonic cell they got five mice. They showed Nebus. He looked and said:

"Hmm, what about a rabbit?"

They cloned a rabbit. Once again, they got five rabbits from one. While they were looking for Nebus, the rabbits multiplied.

"Aha, quantitatively we're winning," Nebus purred in satisfaction, looking at the dozen identical rabbits. "What about a monkey?"

They cloned a rhesus-macaque. Even Nebus got flustered when ten identical monkey-eyes fastened themselves on him, and then all five macaques began "teasing him by puffing their cheeks" (this is how it was recorded in the lab log book).

"What's next?" Zbronjo was asked.

He tried to imitate King Kong and struck his sunken, professor-ish chest with his fist. And indeed, soon a human-like ape was brought in.

The experiment was successful. Soon the lab was hiding five gorilla embryos under its bushel.

"And now…" said Nebus, who had come in to congratulate his colleagues, and repeated Zbronjo's now legendary gesture — he struck his chest with his fist.

Nebus's watch-chain jangled like a medal, and everyone laughed.

"Are you sure you'll be able to get a fully-functional embryonic cell from an old man?"

Nebus blushed — he hadn't been sure of anything from the very beginning.

"Maybe Ignatius Loyolovich will get the embryonic cells for us?" the director cautiously expressed his wish.

"They're not lying around in the store-room," Zbronjo jeered. "You won't even get much from under Maimaga's white coat."

"Even though I know who you might get them from," Maimaga flickered in the air, having just materialised there.

"Who?"

Maimaga trickled out of the room, and then returned, leading by the hand an embarrassed young man in a white coat.

"But that's my assistant, Felix Kangar," Zbronjo was worried, and his fingers fluttered over the edge of the chair.

"A completely sexually-mature person," Maimaga announced curtly and disappeared.

The sexually-mature person shifted from foot to foot under the rapacious gaze of the professors.

"Yes," said Nebus.

"Hm — yes," Zbronjo pronounced.

"Tyryn-tyn," Tyryntyn began singing a song, and the lines on his face started to resemble sunbeams.

Soon the human embryos were sleeping identically in the silence of the night.

8.

"It is with deepest regret…" the bass tones of the loudspeaker rang out all over the underground kingdom. "It is with disdain and dread…" the country heard.

"He didn't live to see immortality," Nebus stated in satisfaction. "The death of the patron in a remarkable way normalises the situation in the lab."

And indeed, it was as if everyone forgot about their overall task, which was the five-year immortality plan. The embryos grew, work went on, and nobody wore mourning clothes.

However, when you expect to benefit from someone's death, you rarely get what you expect. Professor Nebus was summoned by Andropov.

"I know. I know everything about what's going on in your lab" the new General Secretary said, with an unpleasant smile. "There's huge scientific potential in the lab, and we have to use it rationally."

"You mean, work out how to make you immortal?" Nebus asked cautiously.

"You're not going to fool me with fairy tales about immortality. But your experiments on cloning are interesting. I'd like to take part in them."

So to the "F. Kangar" embryos were added some more,

labeled all over as "A. N. Drop". Zbronjo stood in the middle of the enormous hall and looked at the twelve sarcophagi. A parade of mirrors and reflections! No, no matter what people said, it was pleasant to be the mirror yourself and decide who or what would become the reflection. Who would be brought to life as a reflection.

"Who informed on me about the cloning experiments?" Nebus was thinking at the same time, sitting in his nice office; there are offices like that everywhere, even underground. "Who's in cahoots with the KGB?"

The question did not go unanswered. It turned out literally everyone was in cahoots. Even Nebus. He would just not admit it to himself.

9.

The Tsar-Cannon shoots tsars at us. This began a long time ago, when Ilya Muromets, whose evil enemies covered him with the Tsar-Bell, hacked his way into the Russian folk epic. In 1917 the muzzle of the Tsar-Cannon was plugged with the Decree on Land and Liberty, but very soon both land and liberty were shaken out, and the cannon spat out the next couple of Russian autocrats.

Nobody knows how to stop the cannon. Just now, actually, a lean figure in a mousy-grey overcoat and a militia-man's peaked cap has flashed like an aeroplane over the cell where these humble lines are being written.

10.

The Epoch is a prudent boarder, dwelling in a house behind a rank of oaks. Her spectacles, left upstairs on the windowsill, catch sight of some mysterious flashes in the distance, but her eyes and brain, drowsing within the blind walls of the garret, ignore weak signals from outside. Yet, everything seems to be all right, not counting mosquitoes that hatch out in the swampy cellar and cause a disagreeable summer surprise, even in the wintertime.

Andropov did not ask for immortality. And he did not get it. Death befell him.

Soon Nebus was summoned by Chernenko.

"I have a wheeze," he wheezed. "My personal doctor says so. It's so people don't think I'm too healthy. So everyone's going to be waiting for me to kick the bucket, but I'm going to live and live… By the way, you should research old people — you're a geriatrician, aren't you? Our nation should be the wisest — and the eldest. I want everyone to know that we respect and care for the elderly… by the way, you're doing cloning, heh heh. Ok then, clone a couple of old men — make the clones so they turn out old."

"And this one knows everything," thought Nebus, and puffed his chest huffily.

"What's important," wheezed the General Secretary, "is that you destroy all those little embryos of Andropov's. You know, by accident — a short circuit or something like that."

When he got back to the underground kingdom, Nebus summoned Professor Zbronjo and told him everything.

"Let's have a look at them one more time," he finished his almost mournful speech.

But there was nothing to look at. Half of the sarcophagi were gaping, their insides empty. The A.N. Drop embryos had disappeared mysteriously. Along with them had vanished Ignatius Loyolovich Maimaga. This time for good. On the floor was an eerie yellow mask with a Chinese smile.

"Should we report this?" the professors looked at each other.

II.

An atom is made of emptiness. That is why atomic energy is incredibly destructive. Like youth, which is also made of emptiness. From fierce emptiness.

In old age, the emptiness is filled in by habits, illnesses, prejudices, tiredness with life and with oneself. Energy untwists itself along its internal orbit and evaporates. All that's left is to crawl quietly towards self-destruction.

So this embryonic emptiness had to be filled in. The babies had to be turned into mature people, and not over the course of years, but literally in months.

Nebus began an experiment in hypnopaedia. Information that people absorb over years was given to the embryos in a concentrated form. Zbronjo developed a miracle-culture in which the embryos very quickly developed into normal-looking children.

Kangar had by now got into the habit of paying frequent visits to what were in a certain way his offspring. As a joke, Nebus increased his salary to that of a father with many children. And it was a bit awkward now to impose the childlessness tax on him.

12.

Hamlet's father's shadow... It's not frightening, it's funny. What's frightening is a father's shadow (your own father), and Hamlet's shadow (cast by you). "Hamlet's father's shadow." Two genitives in a row... yes, that's funny. Nearly as funny as living in a country whose name is Shadow-on-the-map.

Now Felix Kangar had Kangars' sons' shadows, or perhaps brothers' shadows. In reality, he was not married and he had no brothers. A few years ago he left the walls of medical school, and even before he graduated he had completely devoted himself not even to science as such, but to cultivating cells. He had enormous ability in this area, and for this reason was given a job in the secret laboratory. His father had said to him when he let him go off to study, "You'll always be an outsider: as a Jew among Poles, as a Pole and a Jew among Russians." His father knew what he was talking about. And here he was now, Felix Kangar, who had in his time just about managed to fit into the quota on Jews who got into university, here he was now at the very heart of the Soviet empire, in a citadel of intrigues. He, not even a member of the Party, and with a dodgy background. The Great Soviet Dream had become reality!

And now there were… many… of him. There were six more future Kangars! Each was in a sarcophagus and each looked about five years old. The experiment in accelerated maturation was going well. Information was filling up the gaps. Condensed information, viscous like condensed milk. Black and white milk. A jumble. But rejuvenation was possibly only in fantasy novels. Kangar did not like fantasy novels — his own childhood had been too like a fantasy novel.

13.

"Well, how are those little embryos of Andropov's?" Chernenko whistled and wheezed the question.

"Goodness, Konstantin Ustinovich, if I didn't know you were putting it on…" Nebus tried to avoid answering.

"I'm not putting it on any more," Chernenko wheezed. "I got so used to wheezing that now it just happens by itself…Anyway, how are those embryos?"

"You probably already know," Nebus began cautiously.

"I know they got stolen from under some gawks' noses…" the General Secretary squinted. "Because there are CIA agents there in your lab."

"The CIA, too?" spluttered the professor.

Chernenko looked at him in disgust.

"We'll catch Maimaga. The son of a bitch ran off to France bringing the embryos in a Chinese thermos. Who knows, maybe the French are going to produce a live Andropov in a couple of months. Or even six Andropovs…"

"Six would make no sense," said Nebus, having thought for a moment.

"Exactly. One is enough."

14.

The "F. Kangar" babies grew to school age. They were in an anabiotic state, but they were taken partially out of it during the hypnopaedia sessions. Their "matrix", Kangar, would spend a long time looking at one or other of them through the window in the sarcophagus. But the strange thing was that the "F. Kangars" did not look like him. That thin-lipped mouth, that stubborn chin… "Where have I seen that before?" Felix asked himself. He would have to find an old family photograph album, if, of course, it hadn't been left in Grodno. "Marian Kivatitsky's photographs." Which of the well-dressed people from the last century would the "F. Kangars" be like?

The answer was provided a month later. Felix found a copy of *Pravda* in his desk drawer with a picture of Andropov in a black rim; he was about to throw it out when he glanced at the portrait. Those lips, that chin…

Ten minutes later, when he was completely sure of the fateful similarity, the young man, his face distorted, burst into Zbronjo's office.

"Those clones of ours… I've just realised…"

Zbronjo put an agar-scented hand over his mouth, and cocked his head at the wall expressively.

"Let's go for a stroll in the forest," the professor said merrily. "We can talk about the experiment there."

15.

"So you know?" Felix cried out when they had gone far enough away.

The suburban Moscow forest was dry and composed of pine trees. There was a hazel grove below and now, at the end of May, last year's pine needles and last year's hazelnuts were lying on the forest path.

"I know a lot" the professor smiled, and the crown of greyish leaves over his pink, grape-like head fluttered accordingly.

"About how the embryos were switched…"

"And who do you think switched them?"

Kangar stopped and looked in horror at his supervisor.

"I wanted to save our experiment," the latter said. "I couldn't just let part of the material be destroyed."

"And you wanted my embryos to be destroyed?"

"No," Zbronjo grinned. "I didn't want that. I knew they would be abducted. I even knew who would do it."

"And you didn't stop them?"

"No, because as a result all the material remained whole. Maimaga will continue the experiment in the Pasteur Institute in Paris."

"You mean, where *my* embryos have ended up?" Kangar asked a little more calmly.

"They're not embryos any more. I think that by now their biological age is the equivalent of fifteen years — if, of course, they use the same methods abroad as we do here."

"What's going to happen to them?" the young man asked in confusion.

"Maimaga's soon going to realise what he's dealing with. He'll have to work with this material. It's true that it's not so much of a sensation any more, but it's a unique experiment. He'll bring them to your age…"

"And then?"

"Then… if I were him, I'd set the clones free. I'd look at how they behaved. In your home town, Grodno, for example."

"When could that happen?"

"Very soon. Are you curious?"

"Obviously!"

"Would you like to go there? To do some work, maybe? There's a certain Professor Voslensky there, a former colleague of mine, he's a geneticist and a microbiologist. You can help him in his work with cell cultures, as a sort of consultant. At the same time you can collect all your clones and bring them here. You can consider that your mission."

16.

June. Blooming nature hurls itself at the train, throwing incautious flies and bugs at its glum face. The train drones unhappily and moves towards the West. Smolensk, Minsk… In Minsk, a young golden-haired woman with a light traveling bag sat down beside him. She took out a book and began reading. She was a beautiful girl! How did one do that — get talking to women? What did one say in these situations? It would be easier to deliver a lecture…

The carriage shook and his cup of tea wobbled, aiming yellow liquid right at the pages. Felix grabbed it in time and stopped it from falling over.

"This book is about that exact thing," the girl said somewhat unexpectedly.

"About what, exactly?"

The girl showed him the cover. Green writing on a poisonous yellow background. "Negative Emotions and How to Overcome Them".

They both laughed. It turned out you didn't have to say anything special.

It transpired that the young woman was called Ima (probably short for Seraphima), was a journalist for *The Grodno Pravda*, and was reading the book about emotions with the aim of self-perfection. But everyone knows that women are not perfected by books, but by nappies, by standing in queues, and by the kitchen. And the result is the perfect Soviet "woman without qualities", in whom there is very little of woman but much from the kitchen and queues. The golden-haired journalist Ima had been assigned her "qualities" generously; it was as if she had paid for them with the inexhaustible gold of her hair. The young man felt that he had also been bought — there had been enough gold for him, too.

17.

And henceforth the gold began flowing on him like a river, rewarding him for all those years he had wasted in libraries and labs. There was plenty of gold — June gold, then July gold. And it was nice to swim with the current in the Upper Neman, and it turned out that it was pleasant to swim according to the will of the waves — not moving your arms and legs but relying only on the power of thought.

Apart from gold, there was also dirt. On the side of the road, in drinking water, in the air, in accountants' books, in the pockets and hearts of some people. "I want to wash the city clean of dirty deals," Ima would say. "And fill it with your gold," Felix would say. "There's too much dirt here," Ima would say. "But there's gold, too," Felix would say. He could only see the gold, she could only see the dirt. She shoveled this dirt aside and bathed in it. He bathed in his dreamed-of gold; the dirt was, for him, *her* enemy, *her* windmills. Because he was as much a Don Quixote as she, the raids on these same windmills were carried out by the two of them. In reality, he shielded her with himself — so a second Don Quixote instead of Sancho Panza.

During these raids she only looked straight ahead. She had a sweet face, but it always looked worried. He, on the other hand, kept glancing all around — would his double appear anywhere? But so far he hadn't come across any clones in the city.

18.

If someone seeks dirt, he'll always find it. "There's no dirt," a little boy is told in a cartoon in Punch magazine as he puts his galoshes on. "But I'll find some," he answers completely reasonably. Adults find it more quickly. There's house-dirt, newspaper-dirt, people-dirt. With an aesthetic pince-nez or the black curls of a poet. No matter what your reason was for going into the dirt-house, no matter how coincidentally you opened a dirt-newspaper or spoke to a dirt-person — perhaps only to ask directions — the result is always the same: you'll need to take a bath, and your clothes will need to be dry-cleaned. Because it won't be removed by washing powder or soap — like after rotten fruit or a stinking bug.

Ima found a dirt-factory, nominally an engineering plant, met some dirt-people there, breathed some dirt-air, and was given some dirt-incriminating dirt-documents by someone — not a dirt-someone. These very dirt-documents needed to be brought to Minsk with good intentions. With the intention of cleaning the air, the moral situation, and in general the city of Grodno.

"Is it dangerous?" Felix asked.

"Not at all," Ima shook her golden hair, perfectly aware that she was lying.

"Then I'll bring them," he said, perfectly aware that she was lying.

And it was he who brought them. She didn't even go to see him off, not wanting to draw attention to him.

The station was thronged full of people in the daytime. Felix just about made it to the train. Beside him in his compartment sat a young, green-eyed, brown-haired man in a neckerchief. He held in his hand, and presumably intended to read, the unusual book: "Australian Songbirds".

19.

"So what did you do to him?"

"I took the knife and…"

"And the second time?"

"Drowned him in the river."

"So why did I see him again today?"

"Where?!"

"I'm afraid he was coming out of *The Grodno Pravda* offices. In any case he was just walking away from that building."

Niku felt the hairs on the back of his neck stand up.

"But that's impossible…"

"What are you doing?"

"I'm eating dumplings."

"Again?"

"Well, I have to do something. You told me about such things…"

"Have a drink from this flask. You're a bit pale."

"What is it?" Niku asked suspiciously.

"Brandy. Drink up."

And Niku took a swig.

"Crappy brandy. How do you say it: with the amount you earn… By the way, where's the money you owe me?"

The man in the pale mackintosh with the grey moustache cleared his throat apologetically:

"There was a bit of a mix-up. Tomorrow…"

Niku grabbed him by the collar.

"Give me the money, you old bastard."

The man in the pale mackintosh felt something sharp pointing at his stomach.

"Listen, I really don't have any money on me," he squealed. "Tomorrow, tomorrow…"

But Niku didn't understand anything. He swayed, looked at the man with the grey moustache with unseeing eyes and began falling straight at him.

"What… did you give me to drink?" the man with the grey moustache heard, and the knife plunged into him above his naval, punctured the peritoneal aorta and pinned him to the floor, and on him lay the heavy body of the other man.

"H-ha," the man with the grey moustache wheezed and went into convulsions.

The cashier got out from the behind the till, put her hands on her substantial hips and began spitting out the words:

"What are you doing lying there, you drunkards? I'm going to call the police!"

And she did have to call the police, because of the blood, because of the knife, and because of the two bodies — one of which wasn't moving, and the other was still shuddering slightly. And then the silence was broken by the crazed wail of the waitress who had just come in. She was wearing a white coat, one tooth was missing, and in the unmoving body she had recognised the object of her wretched, miserable dreams.

20.

Pincus was partaking of some of "Danuta's Gifts".

"Tell us, Pincus, did they fire the director?" beery people wondered.

"They did, they did."

"Was there an investigation?"

"Party Committee inspectors came from Minsk."

"Why did they fire the director?" a sober person shot into the conversation.

"For being sober," muttered Adamas Brazas, appearing from no-one knows where.

Everyone laughed.

"But why, really?" the questioner was not deterred.

Pincus took out a blood-red handkerchief, wiped his brow calmly, took in with a glance the miserable luxury of the establishment — the chipped parquet, the gilt heraldic lions on the wall — then said:

"How could they not fire the director, if his second-in-command was consorting with gangsters?"

"We all consort with gangsters," Brazas' tired voice rang out unexpectedly loudly in the pause that had settled.

The thought occurred to Pincus that maybe the remark was directed at him, but then decided that a filibustering businessman was not quite a gangster, and calmed down. He even bought a beer for the old Lithuanian.

"Thanks mate," Brazas nodded. "Tell me, did the party inspectors touch the regional committee?"

"No," Pincus replied.

"So that means that the new director will steal too, and the gangsters will protect him…?"

Then the door opened and in walked a pale specimen with a blank look in his eyes. Wrapped up in a threadbare coat, he stopped in the doorway.

"Felix!" Pincus exclaimed. "Where did you disappear to? I heard you'd been taken away?"

"Sorry, but I don't think we've met," the newcomer said quietly.

"What do you mean, never met?" Pincus was upset. "Where's Martina?"

"I don't know who you're talking about."

"He must've gone off his head," Pincus announced to his companions. "Or else he's drunk. Ok so, do you want me to give you a lift home?"

"I have a home?" the young man said in some surprise.

"Ok, let's go. You might be more with it when you've slept it off."

"You're a good man, Pincus," Brazas said sadly. "Even if you're a nincompoop."

And the pale young man was brought to Orzeszkowa St.

"Oh, the door has been sealed," Pincus whistled. "No bother, we'll break it…"

The seal was broken and the young man installed in the apartment. As Pincus left the building, every inch of his body was being scrutinised by the old woman's eyes.

21.

The police got the call late at night. The duty officers went in the jeep — the autumn night was dank and the dampness had seeped into the offices through the window frames, and even through the walls.

The seal had indeed been broken. They rang the bell and knocked on the door until the sleepy young man appeared. Soon he was sitting, or rather lying, behind bars in the custody cell and watching the rest of his people-less dream.

Next morning, Chief Didura was on his way to his office as usual when he glanced into the semi-darkness of the custody cell as he walked past. In this semi-darkness the major got such a shock that he shuddered and began groping for the light switch. Yes, it was true; Kangar, sleepy and unperturbed, was once again sitting in the custody cell.

The boss turned green with fury and started shaking the bars.

"Why ... have you ... come back here?" he croaked, using more indecent words than acceptable ones.

The young man stared at this enraged person in some surprise.

"I mean, to our city. Why did you come back to our city?! I brought you all the way to Vilnius ..."

The young man looked at him for a long time, then said:

"I've never been to Vilnius. And I've never seen you before."

It was obvious that he wasn't joking and he wasn't trying to pool the wool over Didura's eyes. The chief's eyes were practised at this sort of thing.

Didura turned around abruptly, stormed out of the building, got into his white Lada and drove to his home village. On the way he called into a post office and sent a resignation letter to the police headquarters. There was now one more bee-keeper in Belarus and one less police chief.

PART THREE

I.

Which is better — having the opportunity to choose, or making the right choice? Making the right choice. Which is better — having a variety of questionable options or a single failsafe one? A single failsafe one. Which is better — writing several rough drafts of your fate or living — and dying — without any corrections or erasures? We can't hear the answer!

In New York, you can buy watches right there on the street for a dollar. They work for a month, then you can throw them out: there's no need for repairs. You can also buy more expensive watches — for twelve dollars. They work for exactly a year. In short, there's something for everyone.

There were six versions of Kangar. Excluding the seventh — the original. The original had indeed been excluded — the gangster Niku had earned his gangster fee. The copies remained, and there was nobody to keep an eye on them, nobody to help. The silver chain had snapped, and the transparent beads in the form of male figurines had flown off in all directions.

"Nobody?" — certain of the state organism's pudendal organs asked indignantly. "But what are we hanging here for?" Professor Zbronjo got as red as a grape and unwillingly squeezed out a description of his vanished assistant's distinctive features, which consisted of the absence of distinctive features. His photograph was copied from the staff photograph, enlarged and distributed to all those who follow and observe — by all accounts the police had yet another person on their wanted list. "A political" — thought the followers and observers, looking at the clearly non-criminal physiognomy of the wanted man. But then 1986 came along, and people deeply rooted in the past began talking about a new way of thinking, about reconstruction, about openness… They still searched for the clones but didn't do it openly.

And they found them. Two in Grodno, one in Vilnius, one in Minsk, one in Lida and one for some reason in Yoshkar-Ola. It seems he found his way onto a freight train, got locked in and had to wait there until he was let out.

They were all brought to Moscow — first to the Lubyanka, and then to the underground laboratory.

2.

How were they welcomed by Professor Zbronjo? He didn't welcome them at all. By this time the Professor was already soaking in the Colorado sun from the roof of the Pentagon's secret laboratory. He had not simply escaped; he had ensured a comfortable old age for himself by bringing six identical people with him, all with crooked smiles and watery eyes framed by accountants' glasses. The passports were made out in the surnames Einsdrop, Zweidrop, Dreidrop, Vierdrop, Fünfdrop, and Sechsdrop. In the airport they had all gone up to different immigration officers. After their shift the immigration officers drank cheap coffee, chewed on bread rolls reminiscent of marzipan and discussed the day they had had. They came to the conclusion that the day had passed under the sign of suspicious-looking foreigners with Jewish surnames. "No good can come of that," the shift supervisor said.

All the former A.N. Drops were kept under lock and key and under observation for many years just outside Denver. At the beginning of the nineties their regime was loosened somewhat and they would be let out for walks — accompanied by staff from the CIA. One of them liked to stroll around Denver, another would go climbing in the Rocky Mountains. Yet another one — the former Fünfdrop — once found himself at a fair and took part in a look-alike competition, where he came third in the Frank Sinatra category.

3.

In this world there are healers and there are doctors. It's a pity that these people are not always one and the same.

"What am I supposed to do with them?" Professor Nebus wrinkled his pear-like cheeks as he looked at the six Kangar clones. "I've been landed with them… I'll probably be told to destroy them. That's easier said than done. "Destroy"… they're living people, after all. Let the powers that be do the destroying…"

Meanwhile all six were put in controlled anabiosis chambers. That is, into the sarcophagi which had for the past while stood empty. Of course, these clones had to be studied, but nobody knew how this was to be done. And there were no orders from above. It was easier just to keep them in anabiosis — at least they weren't going to run away. Just in case, Nebus reported the return of the clones to his bosses by telephone. The overall boss, who at this time was Gorbachev, announced that the clones were to be left alone and that experiments on the rejuvenation of the body should be carried out. Nebus understood "left alone" to mean left in anabiosis.

Winter was at its height. Martina was staying with her aunt in Moscow; she hadn't heard anything from Felix, she cried a lot, sent an application for time off to her university, and she got the time off, not without the help of her father, who called his old military buddy who was now the party representative in the department. To take her mind off things, Martina would go skiing. Her favourite place was the hills near the village of Cherepkovo.

4.

All this time, Felix — her Felix — was asleep, and he was having dreams. It was Felix who appeared in the dreams, wandering day after day and night after night through a cold stony wilderness. The wilderness came to an abrupt end by a large mountain, and beside it was a well with water made from melted snow, covered by a stone. "Where am I?" Felix whispers, and the mountain answers "Far, far away in the East." It is difficult to move the stone – it could take days, years…

But as the day drew to a close, the well opened. At the bottom was a black shine, the playing coin of the Moon, somebody's face – Felix's face. "I look like that?" he said to himself in surprise. It was not easy to accept it, as the face was featureless, as if it had been drawn by an abstract artist. Felix took a pebble and threw it into the water. The image disintegrated, and there were many of him, of Felix, but then the ripples washed everything away. Then once again there was only one face left. How easy it is to disintegrate and lose oneself, to disappear into ripples.

And does this well have a spirit? "Spi-irit!" calls Felix. A man with unkempt grey hair, wearing grey linen robes, appeared in readiness from somewhere in the wall of the well-shaft.

"But you're…" Felix whispered in amazement.

"Yes, you knew me by another name. Although that was not entirely me."

"But how, you're the artist Osuzhdin, Petropalych…"

"You can call me that if you like. Demons take on an appearance that's familiar to the person they're appearing to."

"So you look different?"

"Yes, I'm a large black dragon."

"I don't believe you."

"You see!"

"And what's your real name?"

"Asmodeus."

"Are you the same one who lifts roofs?"

"For heaven's sake, a person does one unusual thing once, and it's all he's remembered for… I was just showing someone how people live. So he would understand what a human being is. I could have shown him the same thing in another way — in this well, for example."

"Show me."

"With pleasure. First take a look at who you are."

And the circle of the well changed from black to grey, and a table appeared, with some equipment on it, and a person studying something under a microscope, something abominably tiny that is swarming in a Petri dish. And it's growing and growing…

"That's your birth. And this is how others are born."

A bed, a woman in agony is ejecting a red lump of flesh.

"And so people are begotten by suffering. You were begotten by curiosity."

"Is it a good thing that people are begotten by suffering?"

"Everything good begins with suffering. Maybe that's bad, but that's how it is. Suffering is a reminder of previous generations. Here's your childhood."

The sarcophagus — steel and glass. Inside is a sleeping child.

"And here's other children."

A sandpit, and a little boy building sandcastles. A schoolyard. The children are fighting. Someone breaks it up and scolds them.

"Games and forbidding, forbidding and games. That's how people learn to be people."

"Is it possible without forbidding anything?"

A silent yard. Two boys mug a third, empty his pockets, then one of them plunges a knife into the victim's stomach and both run away in fear.

"Man is cruel, a beast lives inside him."

"But only a few people are really cruel."

"But there are enough of them for evil to happen."

A compartment in a train. Two men. One of them is threatening the other with a knife, and this other man is the spitting image of Felix.

"You see how easy it is?"

"People call that a sin."

"It's not a sin. It's worse — it's stupidity."

A prison. Prisoners in striped overalls walk around in circles.

"Punishment."

"And my youth wasn't a punishment?"

The sarcophagus. A sleeping youth with wires around his head; some wires connected to speakers.

"What were you deprived of there, inside?"

"Contact with others."

A bar. Students sip beer from pint glasses. Red faces, inane eyes, incoherent words.

"No, it can be different. I know."

"Here's how it can be different."

War, the infantry attacks, into the line of fire.

"But there's also friendly contact, isn't there?"

"There is. You didn't have any kind."

A park. Young lovers are sitting on a bench, kissing.

"You were also deprived of that."

"Until a certain moment."

"Yes, from that moment everything went wrong. Well, what is it you want?"

"To become a person."

"A passionless person, who's indifferent to everything?"

"Am I really like that?"

"All six of you are like that."

A room with twelve sarcophagi. Blue light. The duty nurse sits at the monitors.

"At the moment you are in one of the sarcophagi. You're dreaming. You can even choose what you want to see."

"I want to see a certain little girl."

"Ah, I know. She never lived on earth. She died in her mother's womb. You saw that."

A cul-de-sac in Grodno. A couple embracing. A young woman lying on the ground. A little girl in a corridor. Golden light. No, silver, like the moon. It's blinding. Then — whiteness…

"Ah, you wanted to save her. You've had something human in

you from the very start. It's no wonder you found yourself that girl later on."

"Martina. How is she?"

Martina's on her way home on the metro from skiing, her face flushed but gloomy.

"She loves you. That can remain a splinter in a person's heart for a long time. Could that happen to you too?"

"I think so."

"You are the worst possible: half a person."

"Well it wasn't so long ago that I wasn't a person at all."

"Hm, yes, the progress is remarkable. If you are let out of the place you are in now, even more might happen. Your other 'I's were luckier."

"Luckier?"

"They can't feel anything. They can't suffer. Is it worth it for them to become people?"

"I don't know."

"Ah, you don't know!?" the well filled up with devilish cackles. "And is it worth it to throw stones in the well, do you know that much?"

And instead of Felix's face in the well, Hitler's face appeared. A splash — and there are many Hitlers, and the ripples wash away the tin eyes and the brush-like moustache. Then the ripples settle down, and instead of Hitler there appear a crooked smile, glasses, colourless eyes that had burst their eyelash banks. Splash! — and there are several of these faces. Andropovs. The ripples smooth out, but all of the faces remain.

"Is it worth throwing stones in wells at all?" the voice thundered. "Why did they do what they did? Are people so good that several of each should be made?" The demon grew so big that he looked like a small mountain. "A person passes through life with a bare face, and there is a lot written on this face. Mirrors play tricks on us, but faces are open. Read!"

And in the well faces flew by like a kaleidoscope.

"Do you see what's written on each?"

"Despair and fervent hope."

"And also — what's done to a person by despair. And you can fight it only by killing off the fervent hope you have. So then, do you want to make yourself into a person?"

"I want to go to Martina," he thought. "It was good being with her, and it's bad here. It's bad in the sarcophagus; it's bad by the well…" And he said in a low voice but resolutely: "Yes!"

"Then take action yourself. A person always knows what they have to do."

And a blinding gold light trickled out of the well and liquefied everyone and everything. Then there was blackness.

5.

No, it's not blackness, it's light. Fluorescent bulbs. And not below, but above. So I'm lying on my back, he realised. I'm looking through glass. I'm in the sarcophagus. I'm not alive, the sarcophagus is living for me. But it's very comfortable to lie down. If I just don't think about what's happening around me, about how Martina is… There are some sort of red lights on the wall. They're pulsing…

This was a signal that the sarcophagus-dweller had woken up. Soon a somewhat surprised female face appeared at the window, then some clicks could be heard — and the lid was raised.

"You're not asleep?" the nurse asked.

"No," he smiled.

"The others are all asleep. Why did you wake up?"

"I had a bad dream," he joked.

But not even a hint of a smile crossed the nurse's face — she was so worried. This was the first time anything like this had happened.

"My instructions are to call the laboratory manager. But it's nighttime…"

"But I'm not troublesome. You can call him in the morning."

"But what should I do with you now?"

"Do you have any normal beds around here?"

"Only upstairs."

"Do you not even have any cots?"

"Why, do you want to sleep? Have you not had enough sleep?"

"Yes, of course, I've had enough sleep. But I'm very weak, I want to have a lie down."

"I understand. There's a cot in the on-call room."

"Are there doctors there?"

"No, there's nobody there. I can make up a bed for you there."

So she settled him in the on-call room. He lay down, covered himself with a blanket, and almost felt like a person.

The nurse left. He waited about five minutes, then groped for the phone and lifted the receiver.

6.

First he pressed the number 8. No dial tone. Surely the phone couldn't not be connected to the inter-city service? He tried again. No dial tone!

Then he figured it out: it must be just a local phone, and he hung up quick smart. Was there another phone? Ah yes, here it is! This time when he pressed the eight he heard a resonant dial tone. Hurrah! He dialed the Grodno code and then a familiar number.

For a long time nobody answered. They must all be asleep! Then at last someone answered. A woman's voice he didn't recognise. He asked to speak to Martina, then he heard:

"She's gone."

"Where?"

"To Moscow."

So he could trust the picture he had been shown in the well.

"Could you give me her number?"

"Who are you?"

And he told her who he was.

Seven digits, he must remember seven digits. He repeated them once, twice, then dialled…

The telephone rang for a long time. Then he heard Martina's voice. As if she had been expecting his call.

7.

"Where are you? Where are you?" she asked frantically.

"I don't know. In some sort of underground lab."

"I'll find you."

She was in tears. He told her what had happened to him, about the childhood-less childhood, about the youth-less youth, about a dream without visions, the person without a personality — he told her everything he knew. Then he asked:

"Get me out of here, please."

8.

Martina went to the Ministry of Health. All around her were people, each with their own unhappiness, their own unful-filled hope. Hours of waiting — a civil servant — and a cold answer:

"We don't have any underground laboratories. It's all fairytales."

Martina went to the KGB. Hours of waiting — a civil servant — and a cold answer. The same one. And questions:

"Who told you that? And who exactly are you looking for?"

She didn't tell them.

"Do you have identification? … Ah, from Grodno…. We can't help you."

And then, almost in despair, she phoned Professor Voslensky in Grodno.

"I simply have to ask for your help." she said. "You are the only one who can help me."

"I'll do my very best," the voice in the receiver said gallantly.

"Do you remember the phone call you got from someone calling himself Felix Kangar?"

"Yes, I remember. Somebody's bad joke."

"It wasn't a joke. It was Kangar himself who called you."

"So he's alive?!"

"Not quite. It was him, but at the same time not him."

"Are you joking with me now?" the professor was losing his temper.

"Have you ever heard anything about cloning?"

"They mess about with it in the West. ... Why did you mention it?"

"It's not only in the West that they mess about with it. Kangar was subjected to cloning. Six exact copies of him exist. It was the original who died."

"Have you seen these copies?"

"Only two of them. You see, one of these Kangars is my fiancé."

"You know, Miss..."

"No, it's true."

"And how do you tell him apart from the others?"

"It's not funny, professor," she squinted her green eyes wrathfully as if she wanted to exert influence on the telephone receiver. "At the moment he is locked into an underground laboratory and he can't get out. Tell me, when Kangar went to Grodno to work in your lab, who was it who sent him there? Which institution?"

"Well, I don't think I'd be doing anything illegal by telling you. As for the institution, I don't know, but I can tell you which person. It was my old friend Stasik Zbronjo."

"Stasik?"

"Well, Stas. Stanislav."

"Is he a doctor?"

"He's a professor of microbiology, very well-known."

"Where does he work?"

"As far as I know, in the Kremlin hospital."

"Thank you professor, you've been a great help."

"You're welcome. You've surprised me with this talk of cloning. I'd give a lot to have a look at your… ahem, fiancé."

9.

Some see the law of the jungle as a human law. A tiger's fur looks to them like a scarf. A mirror that chooses what to reflect lives an easy life. But such mirrors are queuing along the road to the garbage dump of history.

Whenever the words "Kremlin", "Party", or simply "call the right person" were pronounced, Martina used her father as a magic wand. His mirror always chose what to reflect but he was the kind of person who was always there for his family. Now the time had come to ask him to open this final door. Martina told her father everything she had managed to find out.

Two days later the old party member called from Grodno, discouraged.

"It seems there's nothing we can do. Do you know what they told me? He's not a person, he's the object of an experiment. How do you like that?! The object of an experiment!"

"But where is he, did you find out? Where's Professor Zbronjo's lab?"

"It turns out this Zbronjo defected to the West. That's why they advised us to keep mum."

"Ah, so that's the way it is?!"

10.

After another two days a short article appeared in *Frankfurter Allgemeine* that read as follows: "Cloning of people has been achieved in the Soviet Union. Professor Stasik Zbronjo subjected a young doctor by the name of Felix Kangar to cloning. Soon afterwards the original was tragically killed, and six exact copies of him are now being kept in a frozen condition in an underground laboratory in the Kremlin hospital. Soon after the experiment Professor Zbronjo disappeared without trace."

Most of all Martina remembered how the cheerful freckled young journalist by the name of Thomas Seidlhofer had hopped around the office with one boot on — he was just getting ready to leave — and repeated ecstatically:

"Stasik! Stasik! That one name alone is going to make me famous!"

We don't know yet whether he was really made famous, but his report caused a sensation and was reprinted in many publications in the West. Until then, the story of the F. Kangars and the A.N. Drops was only known to the American special services, but now part of the secret had been revealed.

Human rights organisations were outraged: living people were being kept in a frozen condition! Protests were held — members of Greenpeace blocked the entrance to the Soviet embassy in Brussels with old refrigerators. The newspaper *Pravda* published a refutation: "No experiments in cloning have ever been carried out in the USSR."

Martina had done her part, and now she had to wait.

II.

Professor Nebus walked sadly around the room with the sarcophagi and looked in their windows. There, inside, everything was peaceful; a reign of sleep had installed itself. There was no such reign in the professor's thoughts, however: there were anarchy and disturbance. His priorities and reference points had been washed away by the turbulent sequence of events. "What to do now?" thought the professor, as he walked around in circles and gradually realised: they would not let him leave everything the way it was.

On his twentieth circuit he began to feel that he was not alone in the room. It was late, and he had let the nurse go for a break. The professor heard a rustle behind him, turned around sharply – and froze. A yellow mask that he already knew too well, and an empty white coat…

"Ignatius Loy…" the professor whispered.

"Shh," a whisper interrupted him. "No names."

"But aren't you in Paris?"

"And no place names. I didn't go where you thought I went. In order to save the material, I brought it to Minsk and there I realised that Zbronjo had switched the embryos, so that means he must have wanted to bring them to the West. I called Moscow, but it was too late. Then I came back, and while you were on holidays I brought the Kangars to their true age. Then they were brought to Grodno and released in the city. Everything was just as I thought: they are not adaptable at all."

"So what should we do with them now?"

"Anything we like, as long as they don't end up in the West. Otherwise there'll be all sorts of trouble!"

"But nothing's being said about the A.N. Drops."

"Well, the CIA is not allowing any leaks. And how are you getting on with the rejuvenation?"

Nebus shivered: how did *he* know about Nebus' secret talks with… The yellow mask looked at him without blinking. He noticed: it's a different mask! On the forehead there's … No, a little higher — what is it, something drawn on? Or like spilled paint — a pigment stain? *A stain!*

"Mikhail Serge…" losing his reason, the professor was just about to start babbling, but he was interrupted again.

"I already said no names. As far as I understand, you don't need the Kangars for your rejuvenation experiments?"

"I don't need them at all."

"Wonderful. Send them to various towns, and I'll see to it that they're given accommodation and a pension. We have to make sure that they're never let go abroad. You, I hope, will keep silent."

"Obviously," Nebus filled up with important air.

"Excellent," he barely heard the answer, because the stained mask and the empty white coat were already trickling out of the room.

"And where was his funny accent today?" thought the professor. "It seems he can speak perfectly normally when he wants to. Maybe he puts it on, like his predecessor did?"

12.

"And all the birds exulted and began to sing…"

Martina's telephone rang.

"Come at seven tomorrow evening to the laboratory building of such-and-such village hospital," an officious voice said. "Come alone, no journalists."

"I'll be there," she answered, still not believing that victory had been secured.

At seven in the evening it was dark and very cold. There were no signs of life from the hospital, not counting the warm yellow windows in the far-off wooden huts. The laboratory building seemed completely deserted.

Suddenly the light came on in the empty glassed-in hallway. Martina saw two men in white coats get out of a lift. They were leading a third man by the elbow. Then they unlocked the entrance door, the man stepped onto the porch, and began going down the steps hesitantly.

"Felix!" she cried and ran to him.

The two men in white coats looked indifferently at the embracing couple.

13.

"Following this blue arrow, barely visible in the quivering air of this grey morning, we'll change our position in time and space and enter the hall where both the floor and ceiling are transparent, filling it with the sound of our steps," our inner self suggests. "We've already been in that hall," our memory might prompt us. However trust, which is the highest degree of transparency, should be deserved and we must find something that gets us through the night and into the morning; as for the blue arrow, now we see it, now we don't.

"We'll leave tomorrow," Martina said in the freezing bus.

"Yes, it's too cold here. But where can we go?"

"We'll go back to Grodno."

"Oh, I'm scared of that town…"

"It can be a very nice place. Like a snuff box with the devil taken out."

"Are you sure they've taken him out?"

"I'm sure. I called home. So we can go back to the snuff box, even if it's old and creaky."

"Now what's in store for us is a borrowed life — we have to live instead of those other two."

"No, we have our own life, we are different. Although I'm very sorry for them. They didn't even manage to get married."

"But we can," he smiled. "They gave me a passport."

And he took out a little blue book and opened it. *Felix Mikhailovich Kangar* was written there in copy-book handwriting.

"I hope you'll be a good husband," she thought out loud, inspecting him with her green eyes.

"I'll do my best."

"Don't forget that now there are five other candidates for your place," she said jokingly.

"All exactly the same as me," he answered seriously.

14.

And they went back to Grodno and lived happily and hungrily ever after — just like Belarus itself.

And then the mirror of the empire shattered, and Belarus became one of its shards, one of the shards from the USSR, of its reflections in the mirror.

Professor Nebus, who had stayed in Moscow, was now vegetating practically without any colleagues and was carrying out experiments on how to rejuvenate members of the government. When he began feeling absolutely miserable, out of grief and notwithstanding all the prohibitions, Nebus cloned Chief Pugan in the form of one hundred and twenty bear-like copies, brought them to a sexually mature age within a few years, and then handed them over to the police academy. "The policemen in Moscow all look so alike!" Muscovites are often heard to say. "They all look sort of strange and laid-back!"

But that is another story altogether. In our story, the world of reflections in mirrors did not prevail, the mirror was broken and forgotten, and its shards — all except one — were shoved into cupboards. Into tiny rooms for invalids in communal apartments. And every night, the Weather Cook appears to all of these shards in their dreams. Swathed in white mist, with a rosy, sunny smile, he comes up to the heads of the beds and looks at the faces with understanding and empathy.

Glagoslav Publications Catalogue

- *The Time of Women* by Elena Chizhova

- *Sin* by Zakhar Prilepin

- *Hardly Ever Otherwise* by Maria Matios

- *The Lost Button* by Irene Rozdobudko

- *Khatyn* by Ales Adamovich

- *Christened with Crosses* by Eduard Kochergin

- *The Vital Needs of the Dead* by Igor Sakhnovsky

- *METRO 2033* (Dutch Edition) by Dmitry Glukhovsky

- *METRO 2034* (Dutch Edition) by Dmitry Glukhovsky

- *A Poet and Bin Laden* by Hamid Ismailov

- *Asystole* by Oleg Pavlov

- *Kobzar* by Taras Shevchenko

- *White Shanghai* by Elvira Baryakina

- *The Stone Bridge* by Alexander Terekhov

- *King Stakh's Wild Hunt* by Uladzimir Karatkevich

- *Depeche Mode* by Serhii Zhadan

- *Saraband Sarah's Band* by Larysa Denysenko

- *Herstories*, An Anthology of New Ukrainian Women Prose Writers

- *Watching The Russians* (Dutch Edition) by Maria Konyukova

- *The Hawks of Peace* by Dmitry Rogozin

- *The Grand Slam and Other Stories* (Dutch Edition) by Leonid Andreev

More coming soon...